UNDEAD
AS A
DOORNAIL

Phoenix Bones: International Monster Hunter Book 1

WILLIAM F. AICHER

www.williamfaicher.com

CHAPTER ONE

I was already dead by the time I was born, and I've died a lot of times since then. But somehow, someway, I came back. I always come back.

The night of that freak winter storm thirty-six years ago? Dead. Stillborn is what they call it. Didn't take though. At least not for long. While my momma stared at me, her vacant eyes dead with shock, and my daddy sat in the corner bawling his eyes out, I was reborn.

And no, the doctors weren't wrong. There was no mistake. I was born a corpse.

But like I said, I came back. My name is Phoenix Bones and I always come back.

Thing is though, I'm not sure I'm coming back from this one.

You're probably wondering how I got here. I'll tell you. Promise. First, though, I have to find a way out of this mess.

First, I have to pry this goddamn bloodsucker off my neck and slam a stake through his heart to send him where he belongs.

The one thing most of the movies don't tell you about vampires is how damned horrendous their breath is. Not that this should come as any surprise. Dead for decades. Centuries. Millenia. Not eating anything but whatever they find rotting around. Maybe some human blood once in a while, but that delicacy is on the menu less often than you'd expect.

Honest-to-goodness *bloodsucking*? Reserved for special occasions only. Like vampire treats—crimson champagne splurged on only once every so often. Makes sense, though, when you think about it. With so many vampires roaming the world they'd be doing a pretty piss poor job of keeping to the shadows if every night they had to suck a human dry. People would start to notice all the other missing people.

So yeah, they're smelly bastards. And when they move in close like this guy right here, snapping his jaws as he tries his best to sink those pearly whites into the juicy flesh of my neck, you're gifted if you can stop from gagging. Stink probably even works as a tool on their side sometimes. Take the victim by surprise, and while they're choking on the rancid exhale they're distracted, and the vamp can chomp on down.

I've tried garlic, and I've tried crucifixes. Way back when I first got my feet wet in this world. Thought it'd work just like in the movies, but it's a bunch of bullshit. Hell, half the vampires I've come across are atheists. Any religion they had gone out the window when they realized no self-respecting god would condemn a man to never-ending life. The only thing from the storybooks that does work is the good old wooden stake through the heart. Can't be a bullet, can't be a sword. Has to be wood. Damned if I know why.

Problem is, I don't have any stakes on me. Momma always told me to be prepared for the unexpected, and I see now I should have listened better to her. But coming into this I wasn't expecting vampires. A graveyard in the dead of a late summer night in rural Bulgaria? Wasn't expecting vampires. But probably should have.

He snaps at me again, the putrid stink enveloping my head like a toxic cloud. I hold my breath and clutch my car keys. One out between the fingers like a stabby little brass knuckle. I take a swing, and next thing you know old vampie's stumbling and screaming. All the while, my dangling keys play jingle bells as they hang from the hole they punched in his throat.

One of those little headstones—the ankle-high kind people who don't have fortunes to spare buy for their loved ones when they pass—one of those headstones trips him up, and he's down on the ground. Still squealing like a stuck pig as his hand scrabbles at the keys to my rental. He tears them free, and in the distance, my panic alarm starts to shout in the night. Yellow and orange lights flicker in the distance. I tear a branch from the nearest tree, lunge at him while he's distracted, and my stick finds home.

Wham. Boom. Straight to the heart, and I'm to blame.

He doesn't bleed—vamp hearts don't pump blood. Not like the rest of us. Instead his body just kind of swells up, like a worn-out blow-up doll that's seen a little too much fun. As his eyes bulge from his head he gives me one of those "now what'd you have to go and do that for?" looks. Then he pops. A big old mess coats the graveyard … and me as well.

I grab my keys from the ground, turn off my alarm, and head back to the car. Blood drips from the tree behind me with the soft pitter-patter of a rain shower.

My name's Phoenix Bones. I hunt monsters.

THEN

CHAPTER TWO

Three weeks ago. That's when this whole mess got started. Or, at least, when I first got sucked into it all. The disappearances themselves started much earlier. I just didn't hear about them at first. Police tend to keep a low profile on these kinds of things. Which is kind of surprising given how quickly they usually issue alerts. A missing kid's no joke. But when the kids go missing from a locked house with no signs of forced entry? When there aren't any leads or clues or anything to help make the cops look like they have a damned clue as to what they're doing? Those are the ones they try to keep secret.

After all, these kids weren't really kids. They were teenagers. Even worse, teenagers from the wrong part of town. The part of town where cops didn't give a shit what happened. The part of town where kids run off all the time—which was probably what these kids did. Or, at least, so their parents hoped. Thing is, these kids usually tend to come back. Might take a day or a week, but they're back soon enough. Life on the street is hard. Harder than any of them might think. And even if they've spent days out there, nothing prepares them for the nights. Some push through. Make it a few days. But usually they give up when they realize as shitty as life might be back home, things aren't as bad as they could be … now they've caught a glimpse of the alternatives.

But for some kids, when it comes to life on the street vs. life in a home filled with hate (or worse, indifference), the street wins.

So no, they didn't register the disappearances. At least not until they started to spread out of the poor places and into the well-lighted streets of suburbia. Not until 17-year-old Nancy Langenkamp went missing from the second story bedroom in her parents' five-bedroom, 4300 square-foot house on the corner of North Genesee and Elm.

That was the first one I heard about. The call came through on the scanner while I was out on my rounds. Amber alert. No details of where she might be or who she might be with. Just a pretty white girl with blonde hair and a big pearly-toothed smile gone missing and the community should be on alert. Check your phones. Check the news. Check social media. Her photo's already everywhere.

I didn't bother to check anything. I already knew they wouldn't find her. When a girl goes missing from a locked house in the middle of the night, all the windows are still closed tight, and nothing's missing, it's never a kidnapper. And it's never a runaway. It's one of *them*.

Trust me. I speak from experience.

Which kind of them? Who the hell knows. But they're the ones who get you. The ones who sneak around at night, scurrying from shadow to shadow. Monsters. Boogeymen.

Spooks, specters, and ghosts. Figments of our imagination. They're the ones that got Nancy. I was sure of it.

Problem was, I couldn't do much to help her. At least not until I got rid of the raccoon.

The call came in around eleven. Something in the attic making a hell of a racket. Usually, when these things happen, people tend to call the cops first. Either that or the wife sends her husband up the ladder with a baseball bat to investigate. Then the husband has to make a choice: put on his big-boy pants and head up those steps and retain his masculinity or call the police himself since he's seen enough horror movies in his day to know you never go climbing around a dusty old attic in the middle of the night.

Once in a while though you encounter someone who's been around the block a few times. They've heard the scratching and the scuttling before, and they recognize that racket as some damned creature making itself comfortable somewhere in the house. And that's when they call me: Mr. Animal Control Specialist.

Truth is though, even when they call, the cops get sucked in somewhere down the line. They call the cops, cops check out the "disturbance" and see a pair of beady little eyes in the corner, then bug out and give me a ring. Back in the old days, they just shot the things and called it a day. But now everyone's all soft and goo-goo-eyed like "Look at the fluffy little raccoon. He must miss his mommy." So, they call me. And I slip on my heavy-duty leather gloves, hop in the truck and head on over to rectify the situation.

Like that night. The night of the raccoon … and the night all this shit started. I was up watching one of those late-night talk-shows that come on after the news, and I heard the call come in over the police scanner — something banging around in an attic down at 401 East 2nd Street. Units were on their way to investigate the disturbance. Could've been a burglar. Could've … but wasn't. I'd been out to Eleanor Jackson's house enough times now to recognize the address. And I'd told her time and time again to call a professional out there to fix the busted vent on her roof. But did she listen? Of course not. So, I was already halfway to her house by the time my cell rang, and they officially called me in.

Now here I am, up in Old Lady Jackson's attic with a pissed off raccoon hissing at me from the corner. She looks familiar. Big fatty, like the one I pulled from here a few weeks ago. Left her out in the woods miles from here, but still, I wouldn't be surprised if she came back. Then again, it could just be another that looks like her. I'm not that good with raccoon faces.

They're are an infestation, you know. People think raccoons are these cute little bandits living a sweet, innocuous life out in the country and come through occasionally to knock over a trashcan, but that's what PETA wants you to think. Truth is, they're everywhere in the country and worse in the city. Bigger nuisance than rats, some might say—since at least those vermin tend to stick to the sewers. Raccoons have gotten fat and stupid around people, and when the sun goes down, the little bastards come out in swarms. If they weren't so smart, they wouldn't be so much of a problem, but raccoons are just as clever as they are curious. If a raccoon sets its sights on getting in somewhere and exploring (or heaven-forbid, building a nest), that nasty furball is going to find a way.

And for some reason, Jackson's damn attic was like a goddamn halfway house for wayward raccoons.

There we were, the raccoon and I, staring each other down. Like a pair of gunslingers set for a duel at noon. I'm waving my Ketch-All trying to find an angle where I can loop her, and she's growling something fierce, looking for a way to scoot past me and into the maze of dusty boxes on the other side of the room. I know if she gets in there, I won't be getting her out and will have to set a trap. But traps are the worst. Sure, they're clean and *fairly* effective, but they also mean I have to come back later and pick up the damn thing once they've done their job and snagged the beast. Most people don't have the patience for them either because once you've got an animal trapped, it can start to make a holy racket. People don't like rackets. Not when they're trying to sleep or enjoy their morning coffee while some animal's upstairs screaming and jumping and shitting all over itself.

I moved in slow, tried to distract her with my voice while I brought my loop down, and she made a break for freedom. Quicker than you can say "Gideon's Bible" I snagged her—and that's when I heard the call come through on my portable scanner.

"All patrols be advised, Amber alert. Seventeen-year-old female, last seen wearing blue and white plaid pajama pants with a navy shirt with a polar bear print at 1428 North Genesee Avenue at 9:00 p.m. No vehicle or suspect information. No signs of forced entry."

Now call me paranoid, but when people up and go missing, I always fear the worst, especially the times there are no suspects or any immediate leads. 99 times out of 100 some leads do turn up. Sometimes they're the bad kinds of leads, where your gut's been screaming, even before you the *bad news* call comes in. Other times it's the kids running off on their own or with a boyfriend or girlfriend. The times when I hear a call with no information is when my heart pauses ... sometimes so long I wonder if it will ever start back up again. And that's what happened when I heard this call. The constant thud of my blood pumper ceased, and I knew this was one of those one-in-a-hundred calls where the cops couldn't do shit.

But I could.

So, I shoved old mask-face into my sack, all the while she was nipping and clawing and making a racket like no other. The woman of the house knocked on the door once or twice, probably wondering what I'd been up to and hoping none of her storage boxes got knocked over. Not that it'd matter though. I didn't have the heart to tell her, but half them boxes were soaking up raccoon piss and would have to be tossed in the dumpster sooner or later.

Bag waggling in my arms, screams still bellowing through the canvas, I pushed down the attic door and ladder and lowered myself back into the living quarters, while Old Lady Jackson stood at the foot of the steps, arms crossed, wearing nothing but her nightgown and a scowl. I gave her a tip of my cap and slung the sack over my shoulder like a hillbilly Santa Claus and moseyed on out. Told her the county'd send her the bill in the mail.

Of course, the county doesn't send any bill for animal removal like this. Special county courtesy. But she didn't need to know. Worst thing that happens is people take my services for granted, and they start relying on me to come on over for free forever, never taking care of their own place or plugging up the holes where the critters sneak in. I'm a lot cheaper than a handyman.

I threw old ringtail into the bed of my Silverado and headed out of town into the country, back toward home. A few miles south of Wilkin's farm, I pulled to the side of the road and emptied the sack. She gave me a few hisses and as nasty a scowl as a raccoon can and scampered off into the woods. I was sure I'd see her again someday. And she probably knew the same.

The old Silverado sputtered down the lane on the chokes of its last gasps of gas until the truck finally died about a quarter-mile from the house. Normally I wouldn't let the tank run so low, but in my rush to hurry home and see if I could still save Nancy, I did the best I could to ignore the yellow light telling me to spring for a fill-up. I rushed down the lane on foot, past the hemlocks and firs and onto the dirt path marking the entrance to Chateau Bones. More a shack than a house. It'd been here for decades. Supposedly an old hunting cabin of my father's, though I'd never known him to hunt. Even so, he still came out here from time to time when I was growing up. Weekends with his pals, but he never came back with any kills. I don't think he liked hurting animals.

But that was years ago. As he got on in age and the cancer got him, he stopped coming out here. And from how beat up the place was by the time I moved in, so did his pals. Because when

I first stepped foot here after mom passed and I lost the family house, there hadn't been a single sign of anyone being here for years. Just an old Playboy with a publish date 23 years earlier water damaged and caked to the stone floor, covered in mouse droppings and mold.

Now my father's old "hunting shack" was the place I called home. And though it wasn't much to look at, the dump still gave me comfort. A place of my own, away from everyone else. A place where I could focus and work on what my, what Mom called my "special purpose." The reason I'd been put here in the first place.

The screen slammed against the clapboard walls and swung shut as I barged through the door. Ripley observed from her lumpy sweatshirt bed on the floor, gave a huff, and dropped back to the wonderous kitty dreamland of slow squirrels and squeaky little mice.

I checked my watch. Almost two hours now since the amber came through. Took longer to drive home than I wanted, and if what was happening was what I thought was happening, the trail would be as cold as a catfish and Nancy'd be lost to God-knows-where. But you can't rush these things. Even now I was here, and ready to do my thing, I couldn't rush. Had to take my time, pace myself, measure, and dose properly. Yes, I'd always come back before, but that didn't mean my resurrection would always be inevitable—and that was a risk I didn't want to take.

I considered waking Ripley. Bringing her up here to my bedroom so she could keep watch while I traveled, but nothing had followed me back since that banshee back in February. Probably nicer to just to let her sleep.

Besides, what the hell was a cat going to do? Call the cops? She'd probably yawn and let the damn thing eat me.

A rusty cutlass, a vintage single-action Colt .45, and a silver flask — that's all I had left stored in the old suitcase beneath my bed. It'd have to do. Chances were by now there'd be nothing to worry about, but still better to be safe than sorry. I slipped my makeshift PKE meter into my front pocket and pulled the night vision goggles down over my face. A green haggard ghost dressed in a pair of tan overalls marked with "Lafayette County Public Services" patch stared back at me from the mirror. I straightened up, puffed out my chest, and mentally prepared to go to work.

Normally I left the closet door shut, just in case—an act of precaution. I sighed as I realized I hadn't gone traveling in weeks. Hadn't had to, thankfully. But that also meant I'd let a pile of dirty clothes pile up in front and now the door wouldn't open. After snatching the stinky rags from the floor and tossing them into a festering heap on my worn-out twin-sized, I checked the door—smooth swing. No barriers. Shouldn't close behind me, and if it did, I should be able to swing the old creaker open no problem.

Now you might be wondering why I don't just take the doors off the hinges completely. And the simple answer is *darkness*. The less the light gets in, the stronger the connection.

So, I took up the length of rope I left sitting on the nightstand and stepped into the cramped, empty space of the closet. The dusty floorboards creaked under my weight, and a knock from my forehead sent the lone incandescent bulb swinging. My shadow danced across the closet, just like you'd see in a haunted house, and I pulled the door closed. With one end of the rope tied to the doorknob, I cinched the other around my waist and pulled it snug, letting out a tiny gasp of breath as the knot tightened.

Better to keep the knot strong and my lifeline firmly intact than to risk the rope slipping off again like it did last October.

Now, for this next part, you might think I have some sort of meditation, mantra, or magic spell I chant to open a portal, but that's not quite how Eitherspace works. At least not for me. For me, I go about things a little differently, and as far as I know, I'm the only one my patent-pending method works for.

I reached down into my pocket, pulled out my Altoids tin, and opened it up. A whiff of peppermint caught in my nostrils, but the mints themselves had long ago been consumed. Now, just a few waxy balls rolled around the tin. I took one, put it in my mouth, and pulled the chain to plunge the space into darkness. Stepping slowly ahead, I moved until the mildewed plaster of the walls met my fingertips and leaned forward. My eyes closed and forehead resting against the wall, I bit down on the little capsule and waited.

But I didn't have to wait for long. Even though I'd started to build up a bit of a tolerance to the stuff, potassium cyanide still works. And within a few seconds, my body started to seize up, my mind went as black as the space around me, and I fell forward—forward through the wall and into the darkness of Eitherspace.

It's a place only the dead—or undead—can enter. At least that's what I've assumed. Never had official training or anything, and kind of discovered it by mistake. But Eitherspace is a place I've been plenty of times before. The point with reality on one side and the ethereal plane on the other where you're stuck between living and dead. On your way from one existence to the other. A kind of limbo no-man's-land where, if you know how to travel it, you can take a trip anywhere you want.

Problem is, you gotta die to start the journey. And the fact that I found myself there now, in this empty void of blackness and space, meant the suicide capsule did its job like usual, and I was dead. Still, even though I'd been here before, the dizziness and confusion settled in just the same. When you're in Eitherspace, up is down and left is right, and nothing quite makes sense. Eventually, you can get some gauge and sense of direction, but you won't find any ground to walk on, and there's nothing everywhere you look. You just kind of step and swim and the air is denser than air in everyday reality, but not as thick as water. You can feel it around you like you're moving through a fluffy cloud of black gelatin, and everything is deathly silent. Like your ears are stuffed with cotton balls, you're trapped in an anechoic chamber, and decide to slide on a pair of noise-canceling headphones for good measure.

Traveling here also doesn't really make much sense. Not in the normal sense of travel. There's no beginning, and there's no end. Once you're in, you're in. And finding your way back out can be impossible. That's what the rope was for. It was my lifeline—literally. My foolproof method to find my way back home.

But I wasn't going home. I was going to Nancy's place. That big old house down on North Genesee Avenue, and getting there wasn't as simple as putting in a GPS coordinate and asking Google to give you directions. Nothing here follows the geographic layout of reality. It's everywhere and nowhere, and you can get where you want to go, or you might end up lost forever. Each of these possibilities seems equally likely, and the first time I found myself here all those years ago, what felt like seconds had been much, much longer.

To travel where I need, I've found the best thing to do is kind of "will it" to happen. Eitherspace exists as much in the mind as in another space, and to be honest, I am pretty sure it's the same place we go when we dream. Or if not the same, at least something very similar.

Over the past few decades, I've learned to control my dreams through a process called lucid dreaming. I've learned to will myself to sleep, and to build triggers into my dreams to let me know I'm dreaming. My most common trigger is a pink softball—and so I've taught myself to implant pink softballs in my dreams by concentrating on them as I go to sleep and pass from the waking world to the dreaming. Eitherspace isn't quite the same, as I know I'm there every time I visit—and rather than be filled with fantastical sights and experiences like our dreams, I'm surrounded by an empty space crowded with nothing. But the same general concepts apply, and like a dream, if you know you're there, you can control reality to your liking.

And that's how you travel in Eitherspace. Or at least how I travel. In the blackness, I imagine the place I need to be, and reality shifts around me like a blacked-out version of *Inception*.

Locations move, and doorways appear and disappear until finally, everything stops, and you're left with a new doorway in front of you. Then, leaving as simple as stepping through a doorway.

There, in the void of Eitherspace, I floated. The emptiness spun around me as my hair and clothes floated in the dense liquid black, and I concentrated. I thought of Nancy, and I thought of her address. I pictured the room in my mind the best I could envision it, knowing that even if my imagination were incorrect, it was the willing of reality that made the travel possible. If I believed that was Nancy's place, and I could see it in my mind, my vision was as good as real, and space would adjust to my will.

Eventually, a door began to materialize before me, the inky black taking form amid the rest of the nothing until it solidified and shimmered against the empty backdrop. I reached out, twisted the handle, and fell through the door, alive and well in Nancy Langenkamp's bedroom.

CHAPTER THREE

When you come back from the dead, it takes a little while to find your bearings. All that back and forth of heart pumping, not pumping, oxygen to your brain, etc.? It gets to you. And that's without factoring in any of the side effects of traveling to Eitherspace, which has its own complications. Lying on the floor of Nancy's bedroom, it took a few minutes for the feeling to return in my fingers and toes and the whole process stung like a billion pins and needles all stabbing me at once. Imagine the worst sleeping foot or other limbs you've ever had, and then apply it to your entire body.

When I came through, my biggest concern was whether the room would still be occupied. Police tend to spend some time in a crime scene once they've started an investigation, and more often than not you run the risk of barging in on a grieving parent or other loved one still in the room. And even though when I come back to life after a trip through Eitherspace, I come back fully clothed and healed of any wound that took me there, I can't begin to count how many times I've been lucky to escape from a herd of questioning detectives wondering how in the hell I wandered into their crime scene.

As I lay there, half-paralyzed on the carpet of Nancy Langenkamp's bedroom, I thanked God the room was empty. With the lights out and only the glow of the full moon through the east window as my guide, I searched the space and breathed a sigh of relief when my eyes fell onto the closed door to the hallway. Probably taped up with crime scene tape on the other side, to make sure no one came in or out without the police knowing.

Still, the house was far from lifeless. The sound of stomping feet and hurried conversation filtered through the vents and floorboards up from the first level. I'd risked a lot coming here this soon, and the chances were high that police were still on the scene. And if even if they'd left, the parents wouldn't be able to sleep. I could imagine Mrs. Langenkamp sitting downstairs on the couch, a cup of coffee in her hand, shivering with a blanket over her shoulders while her husband rubbed her shoulders and the police asked for any information or a recent photo that might be useful. Did she have a boyfriend? Any enemies? Was she happy at home? Had she been talking to any strangers online they were aware of? Problems with drugs?

Or maybe the police were already gone, left the parents to deal with the grief and uncertainty that comes from the disappearance of a child (and to a parent, even a teenager is a child), and she was at the window, pacing back and forth waiting for her baby to come home.

I flexed my fingers and toes as the needles vanished, and mobility returned. After a few more seconds, I pulled myself to my feet, and the first thing I did was step across the room to the window. Squad car still in the driveway, lights off now so as to not cause any more disturbance in the neighborhood than had already happened. Along the street, lamps glowed in several windows, signaling the few who had been awoken by the flashing lights and sirens when things first went down. Silhouettes against some of them indicated not everyone had given up on the show, and still hoped to see some action tonight from the nightmare on North Genesee.

Nothing seemed amiss in the bedroom—just the normal room you'd expect from a teenage girl. Some stuffed animals laying on the floor, likely leftovers from a childhood she still held onto as the last vestiges of innocence slipped away. Makeup on the dresser. A spray of faux-polaroid prints on the wall—a lot of them selfies, but with a variety of friends, all doing normal teenagerly things. A shared ice cream. A view from what appeared to be Mansford Park with the Mississippi River in the background.

Still, the room felt in disarray. And not from the messed up sheets or the scattering of books that seemed like they'd been pushed off the bedside table. No, this was something different. More a feeling than something you could see. A chill in the air. The hint of foul odor in the nose. An earthy taste upon the tongue.

I slid my night vision goggles over my head and flicked the "on" switch, plunging the space into an unearthly green. Even with the increased vision, nothing seemed out of the ordinary. I caught a glimpse of myself in the mirror and jumped at the sight. Not that I was frightening, or looked out of sorts, but I still tend to get spooked. It's unnerving, hunting monsters. You never know where one will come from, and most of the time they pop out from the places you'd least expect.

But other than my reflection, nothing else in the room moved. Whatever happened here when Nancy disappeared seemed to be over, and I was starting to question whether my gut had been right on this one or it had been another case of a bad burrito from El Taco Loco. I gave the room another scan with the PKE meter, checking for any disturbances. This didn't seem like a haunting, though you never know. Better to be safe than sorry—but usually, a ghost can't take someone. You need to be something physical to interact with another physical item as big as a human.

I plopped down on the edge of the bed and took the night vision goggles from my head. The noises downstairs were starting to peter out, and the creak of my butt on the bed could have been audible from down there. Damned spring mattresses. When are people going to give in and spring for the memory foam? It's a hell of a lot more comfortable, and a lot quieter. But then again, when you have a teenage girl at home, sometimes having a noisy mattress is the best deterrent for any unwanted extracurricular activities should a boy come over to "study."

Hearing no disturbances downstairs, aside from the occasional wail of who I assume must have been Nancy's mother, I laid back on the bed and groaned as my back stretched across the cotton duvet. How long had it been since I slept? Sunrise couldn't be far off, and all this time awake was catching up with me. I lit a cigarette and took a puff while I stared at the ceiling, listening for any other sounds in the room and generally contemplating my life and why the hell I had decided it would be a smart idea to hunt monsters.

These things weren't my problem. At least, not usually. The occasional run-in here and there, like when you're walking down the street, and a black cat crosses your path. Most people only see the cat. I see the spirit usually latched on to it. And once in a while, the spirits know I see them, and that pisses them off. Still, fighting off a possessed cat here and there is a small price to pay for immortality.

I took another drag from the cigarette and puffed the smoke out in the air above me. For fun, I slipped my goggles to thermal view and watched as the cloud erupted into a brilliant display of color that slowly faded out as the cancer cloud dissipated into the room. Whoever thought smoking was a nasty habit never watched it from this point of view.

As I rose from the bed, a rush of blood pummeled me in the head along with the nicotine, and the room spun. I snuffed out my cigarette in a pink coffee mug decorated with some distorted horses with abnormally large doe-eyes and the words "Friendship is magic!" printed on the side and got back to work.

Little pockets of heat emanated from the doorway to the closet, like wiggly stars in a night sky. Upon closer inspection, they revealed themselves to be something much less magical, however. A stream of maggots and worms and centipedes had burrowed into the carpeting, a few of them mushed by my footsteps faded out slowly out of view as they cooled to room temperature. I dropped to the floor and sniffed the polyester. Definitely where the stench of decay had been coming from.

Something had been here, and it brought along a trail of death and rot.

My eyes followed the trail across the carpet from the closet, where it stopped dead at the side of Nancy's bed. But there, another foot or two away from the trail's end, from what appeared to be the space underneath the bed, a huge heat signature blossomed. Swelling and pulsing, the technicolor blob changed shape before my eyes, occasionally splitting into several separate parts, then back again into one.

I ventured closer, crawling across the carpet while the bugs crunched beneath my knees. Something was under there, alright. Hiding in the dark. But when I tried to search beneath the bed, I couldn't bring my eyes low enough to the ground with the headset on. So, I took the goggles off and placed them beside me, while I searched the room for something good for poking. Problem is, high-school girls don't tend to have a lot of poking sticks. Since she didn't appear to be on the hockey team or golf team, there wasn't anything like that to poke with either. Just some pencils in a cup on her desk, and they weren't going to help much.

I nudged myself closer to the bed, put my cheek to the floor, cocked my ear toward the bed, and listened. A kind of scurrying, crunching sound crackled out from the darkness, along with what sounded like a bunch of whispered high-pitched voices, almost like a faint song caught on the gust of wind. I sniffed the air and caught a noseful of stench. Whatever was under there wasn't going to be pleasant. But I reached my hand under anyway.

My fingertips lit upon a slick powdery surface that quivered beneath my touch, then was pulled away in an instant. A sharp pain erupted from my index finger, and I yanked my hand back, away from whatever was underneath. As my hand came back into view, a flutter of wings unfurled, and a flock of parasitic fairies flew out from the cavernous dark beneath Nancy's bed. Nasty little fuckers, they didn't look anything like a fairy in a storybook but instead were more like a cross between a bat and an overgrown flukeworm—misshapen, winged, and fanged. The pain in my finger flared up again as I used my other hand to brush the parafairies out of my face, and once things cleared up, I saw one had firmly attached its jaw to the length of my finger.

I flicked my hand around, choking down the urge to scream and alert everyone to my presence, but the fairy held strong. Three others swooped in at me, snatching at my hair and clawing at my face while I frantically stumbled about the room trying to shake the other one loose. Finally, I yanked open Nancy's dresser, shoved the bastard in and slammed the drawer shut as I pulled my hand free. A loud crack rang out as the drawer closed on my fingers, and the fairy's head crushed beneath the blow. A black mess of tarry blood sprayed the room, my face, and my clothes. And when I took my hand from the drawer, the crooked way my finger bent told me in no uncertain terms it had been broken.

The violent end to that parafairy's life sure as hell pissed off the others, and they came swooping in toward me again. As they dove-bomb, I took the flask from my coat pocket, popped the cap, and took a swig. Then I shook the rest of the whiskey out into the air, dousing those little shits until they were dripping.

They sputtered in the air, and one crashed to the floor at my feet. I flicked the lighter, took it to the downed pilot, and lit him up.

By now, my plan of keeping quiet had gone completely to shit, and the room roared up in a blaze of fire. A stampede of feet came trampling up the stairs outside, and I knew I had to get the hell out. Flaming fairies dancing in the air, and Nancy's bed ablaze, I made a beeline for the closet. As I tore open the closet, the bedroom door broke from its frame, followed by a big black boot attached to a pissed off cop. As I dove into the closet, I unsheathed my old cutlass from its scabbard, collapsed onto the blade, seppuku-style, and disappeared back into Eitherspace.

According to the news, Nancy's house burned down to the ground that night. I still feel pretty bad about that. But at least no one was hurt.

Well, no one but me.

CHAPTER FOUR

Believe it or not, plunging an old, rusty sword into your chest *hurts*. Especially if you don't angle the thing right and have to shatter a few ribs on the way to your heart, which is what I had to do. So, when I came to in the inky void of Eitherspace, my chest hurt like a motherfucker. A few broken bones and a hole in the heart, with a big old glob of blood floating there in front of me. I winced as I pulled the sword out, screamed … and hoped nothing heard me.

Even though Eitherspace seems empty, it really is anything but. All kinds of beasts and beings travel through there and inhabit the darkness all around you. The issue is most of the time you can't see them since all the levels of reality are folded onto one another, and for a clear view of any specific reality you have to visit it. And I still hadn't figured out any way to flip through realities, or timelines, for that matter.

So anyway, just because I don't ever really die … or at least, stay dead once I do … it doesn't mean dying doesn't *hurt*. And this one hurt. But it was either that or get caught by the fuzz, and I wasn't about to get pinned for a teenage girl's disappearance. I had no reason to be in that house, and to begin to explain how I got into her *room* would have been a nightmare. But that's the life of an international monster hunter. No one takes you seriously. And you sure as hell can't show up at the front door of someone's house asking to be let in so you can start your investigation. No, they want to see your "badge" or "identification." And even then, if you had something meaningful to show, they're not going to believe you anyway. All people know are those stupid ghost-hunter shows on TV starring a bunch of charlatans out to make a quick buck through some ham-fisted entertainment ... or they saw that godawful Van Helsing movie and think I'm some kind of half-ass Hugh Jackman cosplayer.

Most of the time, though, they either end up slamming the door in my face or calling the police. Neither of those is very helpful in the thick of a hunt.

That's why I travel through Eitherspace. Every dark place is connected to it, and there's generally nothing as dark and as prevalent in homes and businesses as closets. When you ask a kid where the monsters are hiding, the answer is almost always in the closet (or under the bed). And the reason is that's how they come and go. When Daddy opens the door and sees nothing inside it's because there really isn't anything inside. But there was. The creepy crawly just traveled back into the Eitherspace from its own secret doorway in that shadowy cavern and isn't there anymore.

One of the biggest benefits of Eitherspace travel is speed. Much faster than driving or flying. Cheaper too. Especially when it comes down to plane tickets. I always wondered how Indiana Jones and Lara Croft managed to galivant all over the planet. I mean, I know Indiana had the funds of the University of Chicago behind him. And then some of the work was government-funded. But still. There have to be some limits. And regardless, I don't have any of that. Just a petty salary from my work at the county. Not the best government job. Though at least it does have decent benefits. Problem is, health insurance isn't all that useful when you have "abilities" like me.

Actually, that's not exactly true. I'm not a superhero: not a Deadpool or a Superman for sure. I catch colds and diseases and get hangovers. It's just that once I die, I tend to come back in much better shape than I was from the injury that killed me. Still, I can't help but think all those deaths are pretty hard on my system. I'm no expert, and I haven't seen a doctor *specifically* about the issue, but there do seem to be some lasting effects from all of this back and forth between corpse and regular old person. Like this cutlass in my chest? Rusted as hell, and I know I should have taken the time somewhere along the way to clean it up some … but I frankly wasn't all that concerned for cleanliness when it came to how I planned to chop some zombie's head off. Shame on me. Even though it'd heal up, it didn't mean none of that rust wasn't going to get caught in the wound. Thank God I stay current on my tetanus shots.

As I regained my composure and slowly came back to that state of undead that allows you to actually move around in Eitherspace, I took the opportunity to take in my surroundings. Other than the floating glob of blood and the massive stain on my overalls, nothing seemed different from when I first came through. But now that I knew something *had* come through before me … the worms and bugs were enough to give that away, not to mention those damn parafairies. Something had come through, and it was something nasty. Had to be if those were the kind of things it was dropping as it moved.

Speaking of fairies, they're far more common than you'd think. Pretty much everywhere, if you know how to spot them. They're the ones that cause the twinkles in the corners of your eyes. Half the time when you see a butterfly flapping around what you're really seeing is just a fairy in disguise. And for the most part, they're sweet little things. Spreading joy and happiness as they pop around from dimension to dimension.

But parasite fairies? They're nasty fuckers. Think of a cross between Dobby the House Elf, a mutated mosquito and a flukeworm. All slobbery and drippy as they flap around, they don't spend much time in the air at all. Not like their cousins (though if you ask me, I personally doubt if they're really related at all), they're mostly hopping from one foul thing to another, latching on with their suction-cup mouths and burrowing their little tongue straws down into whoever or whatever they decide to feed on.

And since they don't travel much on their own—at least not for spaces of more than a few dozen feet, the chances of finding a nest of them in Nancy's second-story bedroom were pretty unlikely. Sure, Nancy could have been up to no good herself, spending time in graveyards or summoning demons for teenage kicks. But she didn't seem the type. I haven't met many goth kids who were into My Little Pony, and they sure as hell didn't take selfies and hang them all over their bedroom walls.

So, as I scanned the emptiness, instead of focusing on a destination, I focused on my surroundings. This wasn't about figuring out where to go next. It was figuring out what I might be tracking. With parafairies, you've got a variety of possibilities, from werewolves to zombies to mummies and vampires. And that's just the paranormal-type monsters. They'll latch on to people often enough as well and are pretty common in crack-houses and homeless tent cities. Kind of like bedbugs, they gather where they can survive and tend to stick around until someone—or something—comes in and eradicates them—all the while spreading out to new areas as they find a host and get dragged off someplace altogether different.

Here in Eitherspace though, I couldn't find anything. It's usually the case since the darkness eats everything, and eventually either disappears from existence over time or flips through a tripdoor into another dimension as it hits its decay plateau. So, I went to plan B and put on my goggles and flipped on my thermal vision. Night vision wouldn't be of much help here since there's nothing to focus on. Everything kind of fades out unless you're following a path, and I had no path. What I needed was to find one. Shit, find *anything.*

As my eyes adjusted to the view, a faint trail of light appeared before me, heading from the closet door I'd dropped through and winding off into the distance. Kind of like a neon vapor trail, or like one of those photographs people take of a sparkler moving fast in the dark. Even as I stood there, the trail ahead of me faded, and I pulled myself together and started to follow.

The further I went, the brighter the trail became, snaking up and down, side to side—every which way possible. Soon I was out of the view of the door I'd left behind and enveloped again by total darkness with only my neon trail to guide me. When it comes to travel in Eitherspace, you can't really run, since there's nothing to run on. You're kind of gliding, like an astronaut lost in space. Part swimming, part tumbling, you're at the mercy of the vacuum to get where you're going.

But space isn't the same here, as you've likely learned. And distances can be traveled quickly if you know where you're going. I only prayed whoever I was following had a destination of his own in mind, and whatever path I followed wouldn't be a twisted maze to nowhere.

The light of the trail continued to bloom until eventually, it became too bright for my goggles. Before I burned my retinas, I took the headset off and picked up the trail with my bare eyes.

When you're coming in from reality to Eitherspace, you're dragging reality with you. What's stuck on you comes along, and it leaves a stream of existence in its wake—like wet footprints after you step out of the pool. But like how those footprints eventually fade away from the sun, reality trail fades from time decay.

This trail had blossomed into something strong and bright, meaning I was on the right path, and I was likely gaining on who or whatever left it. But it also threatened to fade soon. Again, though I had no real sense of how far I'd traveled, I also have come across enough of these echoes to know reality doesn't stick around for long. If I didn't find where I was going soon, I'd lose the trail completely—and even a set of night vision goggles can't pick up something that isn't there.

Just as I was certain the trail was about to fade, a crack of light appeared in the distant emptiness. Kind of like a floating crease of light in space, the crack shivered and pulsed, as if alive. And with each tiny pulse, it seemed to shrink, as if closing itself up. If I didn't act quickly, I'd lose it. And if I lost it, there would be little chance of ever finding this exit again.

Whatever had come through here had departed at this point of spacetime. At least that's what the trail was telling me. I had no choice but to go through. Holding my breath, I gripped the edges of the split and pried the crack open, and stepped through into the light, all the while praying I wouldn't reenter reality someplace underwater or, worse, outer space.

As I came through, I was blinded by the rush of light as I reentered reality but was quickly plunged back into darkness as my feet touched down on the cold, hard ground. A musty odor surrounded me, and the air had taken on a deep, moist chill. I had to be underground.

The night vision goggles didn't do much good here. The place was completely absent of light so had nothing to key off or amplify. So, I did what any respectable adventurer does, and flipped out my phone and tapped on the flashlight app.

The room took on a harsh glow from the bright white of the phone's flash. All around me was stone and textured walls. Rough and bumpy. A breeze flowed past me, stinking of rot and death.

I stumbled to the wall and set myself down with my back to the textured stone, feeling the bumps behind my head as I sat. The gash in my chest was healing, but my energy lagged. Even taking those few steps nearly took me down to the ground. I had to rest. Give myself a little time to recover.

But no sooner had I taken a seat than the clack of scurrying claws erupted from the silence. I turned my light in the sound's direction, and a rat the size of a Studebaker stared at me with a pair of beady little eyes, gave a hiss, and ran off. As I watched him disappear into the dark, my eyes slowly became accustomed to the glow of my phone, and the room took on a greater definition. Everything seemed to be carved out of the same type of stone, like a tunnel dug straight out of the bedrock. But the walls, they seemed different. Pocked with black holes and divots. I dropped my left hand and reached behind me, feeling the wall I leaned against. My fingertips felt grooves and pockets, matching what I saw across the room. I slowly turned and leaped back to my feet when I realized the walls weren't made of stone at all, but instead a ghastly display of stacked skulls. Ancient ones. Hundreds, maybe thousands of years old. Floor to ceiling, running left to right as far as the light traveled.

Another breeze blew through, and the smell returned. But the death stink didn't rise from the skulls. They'd been here far too long to have anything left on them to rot. Whatever the smell was, it came from a fresh kill. Or, at least something fresh enough to still have some flesh to feed the rats and bacteria and fungus and God-knows-what-else that enjoys gobbling the soft bits from bone.

I could have left then. I could have gone back into Eitherspace and followed my rope back home. But I'd come this far, and I was on the trail of something. What kind of something, I had no idea. But whatever that something was I was gaining on it.

The problem with rope, though, is it has an end. And at only about twenty feet of length, I was at the end of mine. I cut my lifeline, dropped my guide home to the floor, and followed my nose deeper into the tunnels.

The space I'd emerged in turned out to be a larger room branching into narrower tunnels, and as I left the chamber, I also left behind the skull walls. In these narrow caverns, little shelves were carved from the stone, most of them holding partial skeletons. Whatever this place was, it was a place for the dead. With no way to know how far in from the entrance I'd popped in and no way of knowing how much deeper it all went, the number of remains could have been into the thousands. Maybe hundreds of thousands. The dead were everywhere.

As I followed the smell, the tunnels kept branching off into more and more tunnels, some of which had completely caved in. I soon recognized this confusing hive was some sort of catacombs, and I started to regret having cut my line. Popping back into Eitherspace from a place like this, there was no telling where I'd end up. But I'd worry about getting out later. For now, I had to keep going.

The tunnels snaked on and on, and with every twist and turn the smell strengthened until I eventually had to do something about it. Having left my gas mask at home, I did the next best thing and tore a strip of cloth from my undershirt and wrapped the material over my face like a scarf. My crappy little air filter didn't help much, but at least it stopped me from throwing up.

Eventually, my journey led to a dead-end tunnel. Or so I thought. Here, at the end of my path, the smell threatened to eat through my makeshift gas mask. As I searched the space for the source of the stench, bile rose in my throat. I tore the cloth from my face just in time and ralphed all over the catacomb's stone floor. The viscous fluid, spattered with chunks of chicken nuggets and French fries I'd eaten earlier, spattered the ground and I tried to look away so I wouldn't reflexively cause myself to barf again. Then I saw the slippery wet bits of the mess begin to disappear before my eyes.

Down a slight slope in the floor, my half-digested lunch flowed, like a stream of yellow acid, until vanishing into a small hole at the base of the back wall. I ventured closer, careful not to step my goo, and upon closer inspection discovered the wall had been built of stacked stone and boulders. Someone or something had blocked this area off, and from the looks of it, quite some time ago. I ran my fingers along the stone, searching for a loose rock like a game of ancient Jenga. Mixed in with the stone were a variety of aged bones: femurs, skulls, bits of rib. All human and all gold with age.

The only way through this barricade was to break it down. But with stones the size of suitcases, there was no way I could shove the barrier over myself. A stick of dynamite might have helped, but an explosion would risk a cave-in. And although I can bring myself back from the dead, if I died buried under a pile of rock and for some reason couldn't get into Eitherspace, I'd come back to life under the same rock. Then starve to death, die, be reborn, starve, die, and be reborn, pretty much for infinity. Not a very fun option. And besides, I left my dynamite at home.

Back down on the floor, the slimy part of my puke had pretty much disappeared under the stone, leaving only the chunkier bits behind in a nasty little snail trail of vomit. I dropped to my knees to find a better view at where my French fries had slipped through the stone and was welcomed with a fortunate, though disgusting surprise. At the base of the makeshift wall, a small crevice opened in the stones and, shining my flashlight through the opening, was clearly where my little river had gone. A three-foot-wide puddle of barf and water glistened back at me from the divot in the floor, with a six-inch opening between its surface and the stone above. Probably not enough space to squeeze through but that depended on how deep the puddle went.

Pulling back my sleeve and holding my breath, I reached out to the sick pool and swallowed back another torrent of puke as my fingers slithered beneath the oily surface. Down went my hand, then my wrist, and forearm. Nearly two feet of stone-free space greeted me until I finally hit bottom.

I slipped my phone into a Ziploc bag, closed it up, and slid in headfirst.

When I surfaced, the odor hit me like a swing from Harley Quinn's mallet. Whatever had been stinking up the joint had been doing it from in here, and the smell burned my nostrils like a ghost pepper in a vaporizer. That any of it managed to seep its way through the walls and out into the larger cave system no longer surprised me, and I thanked my lucky stars I'd already tossed my cookies and didn't have anything more to spit up.

In the air of the room, a faint glow permeated the atmosphere, and I didn't have to turn on my flashlight. A good thing too, since I didn't want to announce my presence to anyone who might be lurking off in the shadows. The yellow glow of flickering flame against the tunnel walls gave off barely enough

light to indicate something lay ahead, just beyond the corner …
and if I was going to find out what that something was, I'd have
to keep moving.

Along the stone floor, I crept, careful not to let the whet
schlop of every footstep announce my arrival. My hand over my
face, I blocked out as much of the smell as I could … and
somehow, by the time I reached the spot where the tunnel turned
a corner, I'd grown accustomed enough to the stench to mostly
ignore it.

What I found around the corner stopped me dead in my
tracks. A pile of bodies stacked at least four-feet-high lay
slumped together in disarray on the floor. Half-rotted, they'd
moved well past the early phases of decay, and the bottom layer
had already entered the stage of putrefaction. As the stack grew,
the freshness improved, until the top layer, where a few naked
corpses stared at me, their hollow eyes lifeless in their sockets.
Flames of candlelight danced around the room, casting wicked
shadows against the walls. Not seeing anyone or anything living
in the space, I crept closer to investigate.

There was something different about these bodies. And the
closer I examined the mess the more obvious that difference
became. Most of the bodies had been drained of blood.
Exsanguinated is the science-y word. All that remained was a
pile of flesh, bone, meat, and organs—piled up in a fleshy
mountain and wasting away like leftovers.

The scrape of metal against stone broke the silence and my
breath quickened. Searching the room, I found nothing … and
was about to leave the explanation to my overactive imagination
when the sound rang out again, followed by a woman's

whispered moan. Barely audible over the crackling of the candles, the voice called out in weak and desperate pain.

I rose from the pile of bodies, tore a dripping femur from the sloppy mess at the bottom, and ripped a chunk of clothing from one of the ones higher up. Wrapping the fabric around the bone, I created a makeshift torch and dipped it in the waxy goo the decomposing dead leaked onto the floor, then touched the mess to a candle. A ball of flame engulfed the end, and the room lit up in a burst of light.

In that instant, I saw her. The woman chained to the wall.

But I didn't see the other one. The one behind me.

CHAPTER FIVE

By the time I came to, I'd already been hogtied, gagged and blindfolded. There was no telling how long I'd been out since we were still down in those tunnels, but it had been long enough for whoever'd clunked me to shove a gag in my mouth and wrap a few lengths of rope around me. I don't really know where the rope came from, but the gag, on the other hand, was obviously a chunk of shirt torn off one of the dead bodies. The taste alone gave it away, and I did everything I could not to choke to death on the rancid stank.

Unable to see or move, I listened, attempting to gain any sort of knowledge as to who'd snuck up behind me and put me into this predicament. From my left, a clank of chains echoed again against the stone walls, followed by a loud metallic crash. Then another, and another. I scraped my face against the stone floor, desperately trying to push my blindfold loose, but it was tied too tight. A woman yelled, screaming what sounded like it should be an obscenity, but in a language I couldn't understand.

Then silence. I craned my neck back and forth, hoping to catch a clearer earful of whatever was behind me. I stopped at the sound of shoes on stone, clacking louder and louder as whoever it was approached me from behind.

"Qui es-tu ?" a woman's voice demanded. "Qui es-tu ? Où est ma sœur ?" she repeated. This was followed by a swift kick in my gut.

"Hey lady, I can't understand you," I grunted through my gag. But it came out something a little more like "Hgg. Gggag, ga gag gggrng gug." Based on the follow-up kick, I was pretty sure it didn't translate.

A heel to my forehead held my head in place, and I grunted again … but didn't struggle. Whatever this woman was up to, I had a feeling she wasn't about to kill me. No cold gun barrel pressed against my temple and no more inane shouting. Besides, if she did want to kill me, she could have done it long ago. Much easier to whack a guy when he's out cold than when he's able to struggle—even if he's tied up and helpless.

Then a new thought hit me. What if she was one of those crazy broads who likes to tie a guy up then torture him. Blame him for all the wrongs she and rest of womankind had suffered and take it out on him, one piece at a time. I quickly shoved that idea away when the taste of the rotten gag reminded me of the pile of bodies stacked in the room. Unless this lady was one of the worst serial killers in history, it was highly unlikely she'd been behind that mess.

The heel pressed down further, and I moaned as my jaw strained between the pressure of her foot and the unmoving floor beneath. "Ne bouge pas !" she said, and her fingers took hold of the gag and pulled it free.

"Listen, lady, I have no idea who you are or what you're doing, but you've got to untie me," I stammered. "You don't know what you've gotten yourself into here. Hell, *I* don't know what you've gotten yourself into. But whatever it is, trust me when I tell you your world is about ready to turn to shit."

"American…" she muttered and removed the blindfold.

I was still in the room where she'd knocked me out. The stack of bodies melting on the floor about twenty feet away, still stinking the place up. In the time since that conk on the head, I'd been moved to about five feet away from the chained-up girl, sitting with my back against the wall. She'd since stopped moving and looked like she was on the verge of death. But the subtle rise and fall of her chest indicated life. If barely.

Directly in front of me, another woman stood. About six feet tall, wearing jeans, a stained white t-shirt, and a leather jacket. Something had been printed on the shirt at one time or another, but due to a combination of fading and the mess of blood and guts smashed into it, I couldn't really make it out. On her feet, she wore a pair of dirty blue converse high-tops, one of which swung back and quickly reversed course like a pendulum until it landed with a thud in my stomach.

"Who are you? Where is my sister?" she shouted. "Give her to me or I will kill you."

Of course, I had no idea who her sister was … much less where we were. But from her feral expression, I didn't doubt her willingness to follow through on the killing me part. Maybe she didn't *dress* like a killer, but I'd seen that face before. The one where you're desperate and angry and ready to do things you normally wouldn't do. The face she wore looked like her old one had been cut off with a steak knife, and this new one slapped on, stapled and superglued in its place.

"Listen, I don't know who you are or who your sister is," I replied, careful to keep my voice slow and calm. This was much more difficult than it might sound since that last kick had probably cracked a rib. I coughed, spit out a mouthful of blood, and continued. "But you're in a heap of trouble here. And I don't mean from me. I assume whoever that is," I motioned to the woman on my left, "she's not your sister … and you probably aren't the one who brought her here."

My attacker took a step back and crouched, bringing her face level to mine. "You took this woman. You killed all these people." She clutched my lower jaw and twisted my face to meet hers. "Now you will tell me. Where is my sister?"

I thought for a bit, trying to come up with some sort of argument or explanation of why I was here. Down in this mess of caves, catacombs and dead bodies. Something to make any bit of sense to a stranger. But nothing I could conjure would make much sense. Of course, there was the option of telling her the truth. That I'd been back home in Mississippi, killed myself, gone through a magic portal in my closet, gotten attacked by parasitic fairies, escaped back into my portal, gotten lost, followed some random trail, and ended up here. But I had a sneaking suspicion she wouldn't buy it.

She let go of my jaw, and my face slammed against the floor. My teeth clacked shut on my tongue, and I tasted more blood. Just as she was about to haul off and give me a third kick, she stopped. Her ears perked, and she held her finger to her lips. Then I heard it too. The sound of metal on stone. Faint at first, but slowly rising as it came nearer. Soon a grumbling voice singing a dirge in what sounded like Russian began to emerge. Someone was coming.

"You've got to let me go," I urged. "Whoever, or whatever, is coming I'm pretty damn sure it's who you're searching for." I nodded my head in the direction of the body pile and continued, "And I'm pretty sure it's what did that."

The woman thought about this, but only momentarily. As the scraping of metal continued to intensify, the desperate fear in her eyes made it clear: she was about to make a run for it.

At this point, I knew she wasn't going to help me. And I had a hunch whoever was coming our way wasn't going to either. Instead, I'd probably end up on the top of his pile. Though, depending on the circumstances, that was probably something my nature could handle one way or another. But I didn't want to end up on his pile. And I didn't want to let this girl go. She needed help. But she also knew something. Something I didn't. And one way or another we were going to need each other.

So, I went ahead and did something drastic. Something I *hate* doing because it wears me the fuck down. But … desperate times.

My eyes closed, I focused my energy inward, identifying each and every flow of power through my body. I meditated, redirecting my energy into one big ball in my solar plexus. Then I pushed it outward. It hurt. It always hurt. But it also worked. As the energy moved outward, it transformed from power to heat until, reaching the outer confines of my physical body, it transformed to fire. My hair burst into flame, followed by my clothes, and finally, the ropes binding me.

The woman gaped in horror, as one would expect someone would when they see someone spontaneously combust right before their eyes. Then she tore off her jacket, threw it over my flaming body, and smothered the blaze. A few seconds later, I stood up from the pile of ash, brushed the layer of crust from my naked body, and picked up my red-hot cutlass. Then, I grabbed her by the arm … and we ran.

Down the corridor we bolted, opposite the sound of the oncoming stranger. Then, once we made it past the corner and out of the light cast by the torches, we stopped. The shrill, dragging sound of metal echoed louder and louder, and the Russian song finally became clearly audible—though I still had no idea what the words were. Completely foreign and in a tongue I can't even begin to try to mimic on my own.

Hidden in the dark, the two of us stopped. The woman began to speak, but I quickly shushed her with an ash-covered hand over her mouth. Her emerald green eyes bulged at me like she was an animal about to bite. But she held still and kept quiet, eventually sidling up next to me to sneak a peek at whatever was coming out of the darkness, yet careful not to bring herself too close to my naked body.

From the shadow, a figure emerged. Dressed in a pair of ragged combat fatigues and an oily overcoat, he stomped forward one boot clomp after another. In his hand, he held a string of jute, tied to what looked like an old metal milk maid's pail. With each step the pail dragged along behind, screeching and clanking against the stone. As he entered the room, another sound started up. A quiet, high-pitched wail.

The girl. She'd awoken.

Scuttling closer, and still singing his song, the man crouched and reached out to her face. He appeared to be reaching for something. A lock of hair perhaps, or just a sickening stroke against her cheek. But as his finger crept forward, she slunk back against the wall, cowering to avoid his touch. Still, there was nowhere for the girl to go. And even if she hadn't been too weak to run off on her own, the shackles holding her arms to the stone weren't going to let her go.

He hesitated at her movement, eyed her cautiously, and his hand darted into the dirty nest of her hair. When he pulled it back, a two-inch-long millipede wiggled between his pointer finger and thumb. He popped it into his mouth, bit down with a soft crunch, chewed and swallowed.

The woman shaking before him made another attempt to speak, but as the first frantic words began to escape her lips, he hauled back a fist and punched her in the side of the face. Her jaw went slack, and she slumped over, unconscious. My new friend and I continued to watch, careful not to give away our hiding space—though my hand cupping her mouth stifled more than one scream.

I glanced from the stranger and his prisoner in back to this woman who'd knocked me out and held me captive. I should've knocked her out then and there, left her to suffer whatever fate the stranger had in store for his captives. But I couldn't bring myself to do it. The stink of fear sweated in thick beads from her pores. Whatever she'd been doing down here, I'd somehow gotten into the middle of it. Or perhaps she'd gotten into the middle of whatever I was doing here. Either way, we were in this together … for now.

The man in the other room dragged his bucket across the floor, placed it upright at the unconscious woman's feet, and loosened the rope from the handle. Looping it around the woman's feet, he tied her ankles together and swung the other end of the cord up over a hook set high in the wall. One strenuous grunt at a time, he hoisted her up, until her limp body hung upside down against the worn stone wall. The slack end of the rope went through the chains shackling her wrists and into a tight knot and there the woman hung, head down, feet toward the ceiling, unconscious. Her dress draped down over her body like a death shawl, exposing her milky legs against the yellow rock of the cavern.

The woman at my side made another move to help. To lunge forward and do whatever kind of heroics her fit of enraged madness might allow. But still, I held her back. In any other instance, I would have expected her to fight me. To do whatever she could to escape this charcoal-covered naked man holding her hostage in the shadows of some god-forsaken cave of horrors. "Hold still," I whispered, and she listened, slackening in my arms as the man once again dug into his satchel.

Quicker than a jackrabbit escapes a braying hound dog, he drew his hand from the bag. A bit of silver clutched in his hands glinted the reflection of torchlight. With one swift, seamless motion his hand moved upwards and to the left, across the young woman's throat. A torrent of blood streamed out, first in a wild spray, coating the man's face and body. He reacted quickly, reaching out and adjusting the woman's body, coaxing the blood to follow his guidance from her throat and into the bucket below. Once he had her situated to his liking, and the blood changed from a fountain to a waterfall, he moved to wipe his hands on his pants, paused, and licked them clean instead.

It all happened so fast; I didn't have time to react. And by the time I realized what was happening, my hand had dropped automatically to my side to reach for my missing gun (which was still probably buried in the pile of ashes where my clothes had been), and my new friend let out a blood-curdling, wake-the-dead (and if-they're-already-awake-make-them-come-running) scream.

I sighed and rushed forward, wild-eyed and screaming, naked as a newborn but for my layer of soot, with my rusty sword held high, waving it like a madman.

As I attacked, I let out what I thought was a war cry. Something blood-curdling and rage-filled, sure to send this executioner into pallid shock. But the only sound to emerge out was a squeaking "HYEAAAAA" that got his attention, sure enough … but didn't set him quaking in his boots. Instead, he turned his blood-soaked face in my direction, held his blade out ahead of him, and smiled. The whites of his eyes stared out from his crimson mask like two golf balls while his pupils got bigger. His mouth turned up into a smile of cracked yellow teeth like he held a miniature corncob between two dripping ketchup-stained lips.

The woman thankfully stayed behind. Or, at least I thought she had, as I rushed forward ready to take this monster out. Though I closed the gap between us in mere seconds, the stranger before me still had plenty of time to react. In retrospect, I'm surprised I didn't come as more of a shock to him. A crazy naked dude with a sword screaming like a kid playing Indians. But he kept his cool, readied himself, and smiled as the woman who'd knocked me out earlier caught up to me, her left shoe in her right hand ready to club the guy to death.

Now, I'm not the kind of guy who doesn't think a woman can handle her own. We're all equal in my book. But I also don't think most women have dealt with any of the honest-to-God monster sort of people. Maybe an abusive boyfriend here, a mugger there … or, God-forbid, a rapist. But the kind who piles up scores of dead bodies, chains people to walls, hangs them like cattle and bleeds them out into buckets? Not normal. Though, truth-be-told, this one was also a first for me. Still, I wasn't about to let her go at this psycho while armed with nothing but a shoe and a pissed-off attitude. So, I went ahead and did what any other chivalrous gentleman would do in this situation: I stuck out my leg and tripped her.

The screech of pain as she hit the ground worked out in my favor, too, as it doubled as a distraction from my poorly-orchestrated attack. As her face cracked against the ground with an audible crunch, the blood-soaked man's attention was momentarily diverted. He licked the blood from his lips and made a move to attack her while she was down. But my chivalry mode was still on the upswing, and the second I sensed the new danger I pedaled forward as hard as I could, my muscles burning under the strain. Yes, for a moment I worried I'd spring a Charlie horse and plummet to the ground myself since, if we're being completely honest, I was pretty out of shape. But luck was on my side, and I closed the gap between us in mere seconds.

Down came my cutlass, in a heroic arc aimed perfectly to slice the man's head clear from his shoulders. And it would have worked, if I hadn't forgotten about the rope holding the now-exsanguinated corpse upside down on the wall. My sword came down, caught against the rope, and lost its intended target. The dead woman crashed to the floor, her head landing in the bucket of blood with a goopy splash ... and the killer thrust his blade straight into my gut.

Time stopped for a moment as I realized what had happened. The blade hit low, not anywhere near my heart where I'd seppuku'd myself not so long ago. So, it didn't kill me, at least not right away. But it hurt like hell and all I could focus on was the pain. My sword clattered to the ground like a kitchen pan tossed by a toddler who'd grown tired of banging it. I fell forward into the stranger's arms as he plunged the knife deeper, all the way to hilt. I didn't scream, but someone behind me did, and as the scream reverberated through the cavernous space, an earsplitting crack followed. The man's limp body took us both down as he collapsed on top of me.

Although by no means a large man, his full weight was considerably more than I had expected. Mostly because he was dead. Just after his body gave a few final death spasms, each one shoving the knife harder and deeper into my gut from pressure, I tried to push him off but couldn't gain the leverage. I would have rolled over and slid out from underneath, but with the knife jammed into my lower abdomen and his full weight on top of it, any attempt to move sent shrieks of pain through me.

As the echo of the gunshot faded, the only sound to remain was the steady drip-drip-drip of blood—no longer from the captive woman, but now from the recently produced cavern in dead man's head. Most of what had previously been his brains had blown out against the wall when the shot hit, but still, some remained, and found its exit from the place where the man's left eye had been. It fell onto my face … and there was nothing I could do to stop it aside from squeeze my mouth and eyes shut and hope it didn't start running up my nose.

I struggled again to push the man off, wincing in pain as my abdominal muscles clenched at the effort. About to give up and accept my fate, trapped for eternity in some sort of god-forsaken catacombs of horrors stuck under the stinking corpse of a blood-stained serial killer, I took a final breath and pushed.

The body lifted from me easily, as if I'd suddenly added superhuman strength to my list of remarkable abilities. But when the body fell to the side with a thud and I opened my eyes, I saw it hadn't been me, but rather the woman from earlier. I made to raise my arm so she could grab it and lift me from the floor but dropped it just as suddenly when she lopped one leg over my prone body and straddled me. The shoe she'd taken up as a weapon earlier was nowhere to be found, and instead both hands wrapped around the charred grip of my .45 like she was strangling a mongoose.

"I ask you one more time," she said, her accent thick as she fumbled over the words. "I ask one more time … avant que je te tue." A lock of jet-black hair fell across her forehead as her thumb moved and she pulled back the hammer. Her finger moved to the trigger, and she asked again.

"Who the fuck are you and where the fuck is my sister?"

CHAPTER SIX

"My name's Phoenix," I grunted as I rose to my feet. "Phoenix Bones."

"Your real name. Tell me your real name. Or I shoot you." She waved the gun at my exposed crotch. "I shoot your balls off."

"That is my real name." Blood seeped from the wound around the knife in my gut, and it hurt like hell to talk, but I answered. "Grab me that, will you?" I asked, pointing to the dead man. But she didn't listen. She just stood there with the gun pointed at my junk and took another step closer.

"I swear, I'll use one gun to get rid of the other," she replied, and the heat of the recently fired barrel burned against the bare skin of my balls. "Where is my sister?"

I raised my hands slowly, palms-out, so she'd hopefully understand she really did have the upper-hand here. It wasn't like I was going to pull some crazy action-movie move and slide the knife from my gut and into hers. As cool as that would have been, I knew myself well enough to realize I severely lacked the strength to do something so badass. And besides, she was cute.

I might have even been turned on should this same scenario been played out under different circumstances.

"I told you, my name's Phoenix Bones. Don't believe me? Take a look in my—" I glanced over to the pile of ash where my clothes used to be. "Well, I had a wallet in there. As for your sister? I don't know who you are, so I don't know who your sister is. But if her name isn't Nancy Langenkamp, and I seriously doubt it is, I can't help you. Hell, I can't even help Nancy Langenkamp. Not anymore at least." I nodded to the blood-drained corpse hanging from the wall. "Assuming that was her, that is. Too late now."

The woman scanned the inverted dead girl, and her eyes went wide as the situation finally became real to her. God knows she'd already seen a lot of shit down there, what with the pile of bodies and all… but those were *dead things*. The girl … the girl had been a *living thing,* and now it too was a dead thing. And she'd seen it happen. She'd seen it happen and not done a damned thing to stop it. Not until it was too late. I'd seen that look before. Seen it in my own mirror. See it every damn day.

She dropped the gun, burst into tears, and collapsed in a sobbing heap onto the floor. I considered asking again for a bit of help, but she was out of it and she'd stay out of it for a little while. I only hoped the hysterics wouldn't kick in. That's when things got dicey. So, while she sat there, her tears dripping to the floor and mixing in with the various pools of blood, I knelt and began to strip the clothes off the man who no longer had a face.

He was a dirty, stinking mess—and not just from the blood. Everything he wore, from his jacket to his undershirt to his skivvies was caked in dirt, dead skin, roiling bugs, and old sweat.

But it was better than nothing, I figured. The knife wound, on the other hand, was a bigger problem. I considered calling it a day and stabbing myself through the chest so I could come back fresh, but considering where we were, I couldn't trust I'd come back where I left. You can't find a portal to Eitherspace just anywhere, but they do tend to center around darkness ... both literal and figurative. And this place? Even with the blazing light of the torches, it was still *dark*. If I popped myself then darted off to Eitherspace, I could deal with it and eventually find my way back home—safety line or no safety line. But I couldn't leave this woman here. Even if she'd gotten herself here on her own, there was no way she could have ever suspected this was the kind of mess she'd find herself caught up in. If the hysterics set in, or the delirium, she'd never find her way out of here. And then there'd be one more dead girl on my conscience.

Blood welled from the wound as I withdrew the blade from my gut, and along with the blood came some other stuff I didn't want to think about. Wherever he'd gotten me, he'd gotten me good. But still, I could move. I could help us find a way out. I could help save the girl.

Save the girl. Then save myself. Or die trying.

I stumbled over to the cinders where I'd burned myself up and sorted through the ash pile. Not much remained other than my set of keys and a few heaps of melted electronics. I swore under my breath as I shoved aside what remained of my PKE meter and my night-vision goggles, not wanting to think about how much it would cost to replace the damn things. Then I found what I was searching for. There wasn't much left of it, but the small piece of handkerchief that had survived my Ghost Rider act was still more than I needed. I balled it up, pressed it to the place the knife had been, and wrapped the dead man's belt around my abdomen, holding it firmly in place.

Might not be clean, but it sure as hell is sterile, I thought.

Off to the side, the girl was still crying, but she'd let up some. She watched me curiously as I slid my arms into the sleeves of the blood-soaked jacket. The crying gave way to sniffles as I started going through the dead man's pockets. When my hand found something cold, round, and metallic hidden away in his jacket, the woman's eyes finally met mine. She stopped crying altogether when I pulled out what I'd discovered: a golden amulet with an amber gem inside, dangling from a sparkling chain.

"What is it?" she asked.

Now fully clothed, I stepped over to the woman, took a seat beside her, and handed her the amulet.

"I don't know," I answered, as she gazed into the sun-shaped gem embedded in its center.

And that was the truth.

We sat there in the silence of the catacombs for what felt like hours. Eventually, her sobbing subsided, and the only remaining sound was the ever-slowing drip-drip-drip of blood from the dead woman's throat. The bucket had been knocked over in the fight, so what had been drained earlier now made a dark red slick on the stone, but with each drop of the fresh blood from the fatal wound, it spattered and made a kind of "plunk" while slowly expanding the puddle's reach until it neared the edge of our toes.

"What's your name?" I ventured. She wasn't about to give it up freely, not without some sort of prodding from my end. Or at least not until she finally broke out of whatever stupor all the shock had put her into. But we'd been down here long enough. Or at least I had. I'd lost track of time somewhere between the time I arrived and when I woke up from her conk on my noggin, but from the way my internal clock ticked, I figured it had been at least an hour or two. Chances were slim, someone else was coming any time soon as this looked like a solo operation. But you never can tell with these psychos. Sometimes they travel in packs.

"Sofi," she replied softly. "Sofi LeRoux."

"How'd you get down here, Sofi?" I asked.

"I was already down here."

How long? I wondered.

"Well, why were you down here? You said something about a sister. You asked me where she was. Is that why you're here? Are you trying to find for sister?"

"Who was that?" she asked, ignoring my questions and shifting her gaze again to the dead woman on the wall. "How did you ...? Who are you?"

The girl had a lot of questions, and I should have expected them. After all, this wasn't exactly a scene from your everyday life diary. Well, at least, not if you weren't me. I'd been through this before. Well ... not exactly this, but *the shit.* Some people say they've seen *the shit* when they're in 'Nam or Iraq or some other war. But I've been in a war all my own. Been in it as long as I could really remember. Wasn't time to dive into the gritty details now though. This called for the abridged version, that is, if we ever wanted to get out of there in a reasonable manner of time.

I sighed and started. "Like I told you earlier, my name's Phoenix Bones. What you saw? The fire and the burning and all that? Well, that's just something I can *do*. Don't ask me how. Don't ask me why. I don't have an answer to either question." I sighed again at my statement, not because I was telling her lies, but because I hated to say it. I hated to say it because it was the truth, and the truth was a damned bastard of a thing. Where I'd gotten my *abilities* was anyone's guess. They'd been there since the day I was born. Since the day I was dead. "I'm down here because I was following someone. Or something. And whatever it was, I'm pretty sure that pile of meat over there is the one I was after."

She scowled at the psycho's now naked body on the floor, seemingly floating in a pool of blood. Little critters scrambled across his bare flesh, darting in and out from the mop of greasy hair atop his head. Worms wriggled down into the hole where his skull had once been. He looked like he'd been rotting for weeks. Had looked that way when I stripped him down earlier too, but I'd been in too much pain to give it much attention. The smell was probably horrendous, but with all the other stench down here it wasn't something you'd notice. One thing I did know though, was the man on the ground was just that—a man. Not a zombie or a ghoul or even a ghost gone corporeal. No demon infested him, and he'd not been formed out of mud and voodoo. He was a man. Just a man. And now he was a dead one.

"Why were you following him?"

"He took someone."

"Someone you know?"

"No. Nothing like that," I answered. "Someone I was trying to help."

"If you don't know, then why bother?"

"Why? Why not? When someone's in trouble, you help them. That's what I was taught, at least. And sometimes people find themselves in the kind of trouble no one else can fix. Or if they did try to fix it, they'd end up in a big old mess of their own. Regular people aren't ready for the kind of shit I've seen," I hesitated, "the kind of shit *we've* seen. Because believe me when I tell you this: what you've seen here isn't normal."

She let out a nervous laugh—the kind you can't tell if it's because the person honestly thinks you said something funny, if they think you're nuts, or if they're just too damned spooked by whatever the hell situation they're in laughter is the only reasonable response. A chuckle of incredulity.

"I think I agree. This," she waved her hand around the room, "this is definitely not normal."

"So why are you here, Sofi LeRoux? Really. Tell me how you got here."

"I'll tell you. But first I'd like to leave this place. I'm sure my sister isn't here, and the stink is making me sick."

As to exactly how we were going to escape was another question entirely. I could pop back into Eitherspace. That'd be a surefire way to get out of there. Even if I had no idea where *there* was yet. But with the girl there with me and all the dead bodies stacked in a pile, I assumed wherever *there* was had to be somewhere close to other people. I surely hadn't popped out in the middle of some jungle cave in the middle of Paraguay. Or if

I had, this girl's trip to the tropics had gone badly off track. Though I suppose even the track it was on right now was badly off. No matter where we were, thousands of miles from home or ten steps from our bedrooms, this was some nasty shit.

If I popped back into Eitherspace one thing would have been certain: I'd have no idea where I was. Or how to get back home. The rope tethering me back to the bed in my house was long gone, so there wasn't much of a trail. Sure, I'd gotten lost in Eitherspace before. But that was when I'd been wandering. First time I died I ended up there, and I was certain it was some sort of hell. After all, what place other than hell would you find yourself lost in the inky dark with no up, no down, utterly isolated, and trapped in pure silence? It'd be enough to drive you mad. Luckily, after a period of stumbling around and nearly giving up all hope, I'd found a way out. Turns out it doesn't take much at all to leave Eitherspace. About as much as it takes to get there. But to know where you are? That's something I still haven't mastered, and I doubt I ever will.

Besides, even if I did know my way back, I couldn't leave my new friend alone here in this terrible place. Could I? I mean, she got there on her own, so for me to leave her behind to fend for herself and find her own way out really wouldn't be that cruel. She got herself into this mess, and she could get herself out.

Problem is, I'm not an asshole. And don't try to tell me I only did it because she was cute. Yeah, she was—an honest-to-God *looker*. But back then stuck in the mire it wasn't the right time or place to think such thoughts even if they were hovering in the back of my mind.

She got herself into this mess … she could get herself out. That thought echoed again in the caverns of my mind. No, I couldn't leave her here. But I could coax her to start finding her way out. Help us find our way out. However she'd gotten here, there must be a way to follow that path backward. All I had to do was convince her to follow it … and bring me with her.

"You said you were searching for your sister?" I asked again. "I assume that's not her?" I nodded to the now fully-drained corpse on the wall.

"No… not her."

"You know who it is?"

"Isn't it the girl you were looking for?" she asked.

"No, Not the same girl. This one's too old," I answered. "The one I'm after is much younger. Well, maybe not *much* younger, but younger. A teenager. And she wasn't wearing a dress. At least not the last time anyone saw her…"

"Saw her alive?"

"Yeah," I replied.

"I don't know who she is. But I have seen her before." She took a step closer to the dead woman, careful not to put her shoes into the pool of blood that spread out underneath. Crouching to the ground, she lowered her head as close to the floor as she could, attempting to get a view of the woman's face under her upside-down dress. The woman's blonde hair hung down in red-stained clumps, the tips dragging through the puddle. "I think I saw her at the party. Earlier. This woman looks like someone I saw there."

"Party? What party?" I stood up, wincing at the pain in my gut.

"Down here. Where they took my sister."

"They took your sister to a party?" I rubbed my stomach, and the pain shot fire through my abdomen. A burst of nausea slithered up my throat, but I swallowed it down. The room spun a little, and I took a breath and regained my composure.

"Not to a party. From a party," she answered. "That's where I was … where my sister was. Where *she* was." She took a few steps forward and put her arm around me, careful not to touch the place I'd been rubbing. "Come on, let's get out of here. Before anyone else comes. Before you die on me."

"Don't you want to look around more for your sister? She could be down here somewhere still."

"No, I already searched. Wherever she is, I do not think it is here," Sofi replied. "I have been down here for a long time now. Maybe days. And I only found this area now." She paused and peeked down the dark hallway where the man had come, dragging his bucket. "Down that hallway, where the man came from, there is nothing. But he was not there before. There is maybe a secret door, but I did not see it."

"We can give it a quick look, just to be sure," I said. But I knew there wouldn't be anything there. Wherever the guy had come from, it hadn't been from a door. There's more than one way to come and go from a place if you really know what you're doing. And based on how I got here … how I followed him here, I was fairly certain he knew what he was doing.

Still, he was human. And I'd never seen a human enter Eitherspace before. No one other than me, that is. But if you want to call me something other than human, maybe that's true too. I'm not like anyone else I've ever met, and chances are high you've never met anyone like me either. No, the only way in and out of Eitherspace that I'd ever heard of was to either be dead or undead. And this guy had been neither. I supposed now he was dead there was no telling where he'd gone. Hopefully, straight to hell ... though you never can tell for sure. Sometimes people like to stick around a bit—even after their body's lost its usefulness. Other times people stick around even if they don't want to. God knows I've met my share of pissed off ghosts in my time, and most of them were pissed for good reason: they didn't want to be stuck here on earth, even if they did have access to another plane of existence for convenient travel purposes.

Still, we proceeded with our search. If only to soothe any worries she might have still harbored in the back of her mind she'd missed something somehow. Nothing down that hallway of course. Nothing, that is, except a worn down trail of scraped stone, from what looked like countless trips back and forth by that man as he dragged his metal bucket back and forth. It ended in a corner. A dark corner recessed in the wall. And at first, Sofi mistook it for a door. Hell, even I did. But it wasn't a door, just a little space tucked away, big enough to hide in if you wanted to. And big enough to enter Eitherspace, if you *could* put a door there.

Satisfied her sister hadn't been tucked away in some unknown hideaway she'd somehow missed, we turned tail and headed out. But instead of following the submerged tunnel from this room into the next, Sofi surprised me as she pointed out an exit I *hadn't* seen. Similar to the dark space in the dead-end hallway, but only half as wide, she turned to her side and squeezed through the blackened crack in the stone wall. Her body halfway in, she paused and reached her left hand into her jacket pocket. When she retrieved it, she held my rusty old Colt .45. She offered it to me, but I shook my head.

"You keep it," I said. "Just in case."

"In case what?"

"In case we run into something else down here," I replied. "In case we run into something on the other side of that wall."

I didn't tell her the real reason I let her keep it. At this point I had become certain, should we come across anything *else* while we found our way out of this place of death, the gun probably wouldn't do us a lick of good. It only helped with living things. And as far as I was concerned, we were probably the last two living things down here … other than the rats.

I probably should have felt bad for using her as bait like that. But I wasn't about to let the chance to put someone else out there in front of me get away. If there was any monster — paranormal, human, or otherwise —on the other side of that wall, I didn't want to be the first to feel the brunt of the hit. Yes, I can revive myself after being killed. But no one ever told me if my special skills had an expiration date. For all I knew it could be something limited, like a cat with its nine lives. Many more than nine had been spent already, so I'd outlived any cats as far as chances go … but that didn't mean there was no upper limit on how many times the old man upstairs was going to give me to keep coming back here and doing whatever the hell I wanted. And if I was going to come back, there are worse things than dying. After all, I don't heal much better than anyone else does. Probably the same as everyone else, to be honest.

The stab wound in my gut was reminder enough of the human side of my being, and it burned like a goddamn fire in my belly. The knife had hit something inside me, probably intestines, but I was no anatomy professor, so I didn't have any certain idea of what it had sliced open. What I did know is the pain was bad, getting worse, and likely to continue until either I got better, or I died. What I didn't want would be for me to stumble along and then get an infection where I ended up paralyzed from the waist down or something worse.

Each time I come back to life, I come back pretty much exactly as I'd left. And that means any non-fatal cuts or scars or aging or anything else that happens to me *before* I die, stick. If someone cuts my arm off and I don't die from the wound? I'll come back as a one-armed man. Not exactly something on my bucket list.

So why did I let her go first? For one thing, she didn't argue. Could have been the shock still in her system, or the irrationality of wanting to get the hell out of wherever she'd gotten herself into. I didn't give a shit. As for the other thing … like I said earlier, I feel pain like anyone else. And squeezing my body through a crevice in the wall when for all I knew there could be a herd of zombies on the other side ready to claw into me, rip my guts from my chest and eat my brains, wasn't sounding like that great of an idea.

Besides, I've still never tested what happens if I something cuts me up into little morsels, much less eats me. I don't think I'm going to be like the liquid metal terminator from Terminator 2 and have all my little bits and pieces come back together into one piece after I die. I mean, what happens if someone gobbles me up and I'm completely digested? Would the crap that I'd turned into magically transform back into a person? Would I be a walking pile of shit? Not something I ever want to find out.

Of course, there was nothing on the other side of that wall. Or if there had been, I probably wouldn't have included Sofi in this story. Yeah, it was a bit of a dick move to use her as bait, but she was okay. If I'd used her as bait and she'd gotten killed straight up? I'd have cut her out of my narrative. No reason to bring up that kind of nonsense. Bad mojo is what I call it.

The tunnel she led to was like the one I'd appeared in when I popped out of Eitherspace. Skulls embedded in all the walls; racks of bones piled high in little openings. Every once in a while, a rat would scurry by, squeaking with glee at whatever prize it had found tucked away in the tunnels. One who raced by just missed my foot, and in the damp glow of my lighter, I saw what appeared to be a half-rotted finger dangling from his mouth like a macabre cigar.

For the first part of our journey, we traveled in silence. As we'd hit one dead-end or another, I'd hear her mutter something under her breath, though it was in French so I couldn't make it out if I wanted to. After about an hour of this, the wandering became hurried and more sporadic. Though I initially had thought since she'd found her way in here, she must know the way out, all the backtracking, grumbling and swearing made it clear her plan for exit was as good as mine. Still, as far as she knew, my exit would also just be a bunch of wandering. Once or twice I considered trying to snatch the gun back from her hands and putting a bullet through my brain so I could jump into Eitherspace and find my way out of here. Didn't matter where I ended up, so long as there was fresh air and a chance at sunlight. But I had enough on my conscience and wasn't about to add forcing her to witness the grisly sight of my suicide, followed by my magical disappearance into nothing. Add that shock to her already fragile system and she'd probably drop dead from a heart attack right next to me.

"Do you have any idea where you're going?" I finally asked.

She ignored me the first time I asked, so I gave it a few minutes and asked again. This time she stopped where she stood, spun to face me and gave me a glare I'd only seen on the faces of girlfriends I'd pissed off in years prior. "I know the way. I just have to find it," she answered, and went on leading us blindly through the bone-coated caverns.

"What were you doing down here anyway?" I asked. "Did you follow that guy? Were you tracking your sister?"

A snick of sound and a flicker of flame sputtered from her direction, and she lit a cigarette. Taking a puff, she offered the pack to me, and I accepted. For a few minutes, we stood there, again silent, and then she told me her story.

"I came down here with my sister," she began. "Her name is Camille, and we were down here for a party."

I almost interrupted her right there. The simple thought of anyone having a party in a place like this already sounded fishy, but she was here for *some* reason. I might as well let her go on.

"Crazy place for a party, yes? We have them here often. Away from the police so we can do what we want. We have secret ways into these catacombs. Ways they do not know and they cannot find us. Unless someone is followed," she took another puff of her cigarette and started to walk. "Our friends invited us to a party, and we came. When we got there, it was already big. Lots of music, lots of drinks, lots of drugs. A fun time.

"Here in the catacombs, it is like another world. We like to come here to escape from the one above. It is freeing. Cami and I partied with our friends, dancing and having fun like we do every time. But something was different. Something was wrong. I did not know what it was when I arrived, but the people who had the party were people I did not know. Cami did not know them. Our friends did not know. Just someone heard from someone who heard from someone else that something crazy was going on and we should follow the signs."

"What signs?" I asked. "I thought you said this was a secret party. Doesn't sound like much of a secret if you've got posters up all over the place advertising it."

"Secret signs. Only show up when you spray them with this." She handed me a small plastic spray bottle filled with a pale yellow liquid. "Glowing arrows on the walls, like painted by fingers. Pointing the way. You do not see them if you are not looking."

"Blood trails," I muttered, though I hoped I was wrong. I could only think of one reason to stack up piles of exsanguinated bodies … and that would be because you're gathering the blood for something. But now was not the time to start planting ideas of vampires into this girl's head. She'd seen enough already.

"We entered through a secret door. One in the old part of the city. Just a green door in a stone wall down an alley leading into an abandoned store. Down the stairs in the store, you will find a basement, and that basement is earth and stone and ancient time. But it is still only a store. Glass bottles cover shelves of wood planks. Cracked and rotted and dried away until only husks are inside. If you go to the last shelf, and you know to slide it the right way, you find the second door—the door to the catacombs.

"Everyone knows not to come down here alone. These tunnels wind like snakes beneath the city, twisting and turning. Dark secrets almost forgotten to time. But time has remembered them and now so do the tourists. And we stay away from the places the tourists go. Security and prying eyes like a children's game. We do not play games because we are adults and adults know better than to go lurking in death's shadow without a partner. This is why Cami and I came together. If she was not with me, I would not have entered, and if I was not with her, she would not have entered. Many times you hear stories of people lost in the catacombs. Entered and never coming back. But we go to a party, and we think everything will be fine. Lots of other people at parties, even if many of them are up to no good. I am often up to no good myself, so I am with people like me. No one to be trusted, but still a lot of love. If you can understand."

I nodded, dropped my cigarette to the floor, and crushed it beneath the sole of my two-sizes too big boots.

"When we arrive, there is much loud music. The kind of party I love. Music and sound echoing through the darkness so hard against your ears, you cannot hear anyone else. Just the music. The music and the lights and the drugs and getting lost in dancing like you are an animal. Because you are an animal.

"Only what came to us, while we were lost in our ecstasy … it was a true animal. They were true animals. The flashing pulse of bright light flickering in the darkness showed it in slow motion. People but not people, out of the dark corners wearing dark clothes but with faces white as Christmas snow. Grabbing others, tearing into them. Blood spray caught in the flickering light like an old film. Screams ripping through the caves out of the terrified throats of both the victims and the witnesses, yet buried in the volume of the song. I screamed and screamed as one of them appeared behind Cami and then as soon as he appeared, she was gone. The music kept pulsing, booming against the catacomb walls, and the flickering of lights stopped. Red and blue and yellow dancing lights returned, and the record came to an end. All around me, crimson death. Boys and girls ripped apart. A few still twitching on the ground. But nowhere I looked did I find Cami. Just dead brothers and sisters. I wanted to run, to scurry from this place of death like a rat does from a burning ship, but I could not leave Cami alone. She was not dead. I knew this as only a sister knows many things about her sister. As I know she is alive now. But where she is? That is a mystery."

"You're damned lucky to have lived through that," I said. "Vampires don't usually leave people behind. Not if they're fresh up with blood like you are."

"You are silly. There is no such thing as vampires," she gave a nervous laugh. "Those were something horrible. Maybe psychotics who have found homes down here. Vagrants who are sick."

"Oh, they're sick, alright. And maybe they were vagrants … at some point. Back when they were alive. But with everything you're telling me and everything I've seen so far? Those were vampires."

"But what about the man you killed. The man who…" she paused. "Who killed that girl. If he was a vampire, why did he die?"

"Wasn't a vampire. A familiar. A stooge. A lackey. Just someone who wishes he was a vampire, doing the dirty work for other vampires. Maybe there used to be a nest down here, and *maybe* those others were simply passing through, but that guy? He was setting up camp here to do something else. He was harvesting here like this was his home base. But where he was taking his bounty?"

"Who are you really, Phoenix Bones? Why are you here?"

"I'm here for the same reason you are," I replied. "Or at least a close enough match of a reason. I'm here to find out who took a girl and save her. You're here to find another girl and save her. And I'm pretty sure they're in the same place."

"How do you know this?"

"Because otherwise, we'd have found them in that pile of bodies back there. Or you'd have found your sister bled out at your party. Whoever took these girls had something else in mind for them. They weren't just cattle to be slaughtered. They were taken for something else and whatever that something else is, it led through here. Though it didn't end here."

"Where did it end? There is nowhere else to go. I would have seen them escape past me."

"There's more than one way out of a dark place," I muttered.

We kept moving, neither of us talking for quite some time—the only sound the echo of our footsteps against the stone floor and the occasional crunch of an old bone beneath my boots. Here and there the scurrying of rodents could be heard from the darkness, scattering as we drew nearer. We had no idea where we were going, and I knew it. And she knew I knew it too. But I let her keep leading. Let her have some impression she had any amount of control over the situation. The idea of popping into Eitherspace kept coming into my head, but I pushed aside time and time again like the cobwebs draping the corners of our path. Sooner or later, if we didn't start making any meaningful progress, I would have to take over. If I even had the energy to. But in the meanwhile, I gave her time.

As we passed from one tunnel to another, through archways and crevices connecting the underground labyrinth, we'd pause and listen. I knew what she was listening for, even if she didn't. Or maybe she did but wasn't quite ready to believe me yet. Either way, she remained on guard, and I was grateful. Eventually, we entered a new cavern, bored larger than the rest with less scattering of bones and other debris than the others had harbored. Even the air in this new space felt different. Cooler. Drier. Fresher somehow, but still with the same sickening sweetness of liquid decay.

As we entered the space, a sound like a rat echoed at our approach, though this one sounded bigger than any we'd seen so far—a chewing and slurping sound from the edges of the periphery. Sofi heard it too and remained frozen in place as the *chomp* and *shluupp* sounds continued, oblivious to our presence. A painful ache throbbed in my gut around the searing pain where the knife had gone in. It hurt to speak, but I spoke anyway.

"Your light," I half-grunted, half-whispered. "Hand me your light."

Sofi remained still, moving nothing but her arm as she reached back and placed the flashlight into my waiting hands. Her ears perked up at every sound, and if I were close enough to kiss her, I'd have felt the hairs on the back of her neck standing up straight. She didn't breathe.

I ventured a few steps forward, leaving her behind me for the first time since we'd teamed up for our journey out of this hellhole. No footsteps followed. As I stepped off, leaving her in the darkness, she remained rooted to her spot, listening. Waiting. Fearful and ready to die.

I cast the beam across the floor and walls but found nothing, so I continued. Pointing the beam ahead of me I could tell the space we'd entered was by far the largest of the tombs, as the light found no wall ahead but instead petered out into the inky dark. One step at a time, I crept forward and gave a slight jump when a gasp for air sounded behind me. The breathing continued, shaking and unsteady. Sofi's body had finally decided it needed air again if it was going to keep on living. The ragged in and out of her breath comforted me somewhat, knowing not only was I not alone … but I'd not let another girl die on my watch. I'd already had more than enough of those in my life, let alone today.

With each gingerly placed footstep, I crept forward like a ninja. A ninja with a flashlight though, so now that I think of it,

I wasn't being all that sneaky. Anything in there with me would have known I was there long ago. Would have known we were there the second we entered the room. But that fear reaction, it lurks within all of us. Even brave and stupid monster hunters like me. So, while I might have thought I was being sneaky at the time, the truth is I was scared. I didn't have anything with me to fight a vampire, let alone an entire nest of them, if that's what Sofi had come across. The cutlass wouldn't do me a lick of good other than to wound them. And if I had the gun, it would have made a few annoying holes—enough to piss them off—but it wouldn't stop them. I was thoroughly unprepared for this, and I should have known better than to have come this far without going home and stocking up. But I didn't expect vampires. And who knows if that's really what they were. I still hadn't seen one. Well, not that night at least. Been through my set of run-ins with the blood-sucking bastards before so I knew how to handle them … and knew I was in no way ready for them now.

After a couple more steps and a few more swipes of the flashlight, I finally found it—the thing making that horrible sound. And my suspicion had been correct: it was no rat. Down on the floor, a writhing mass of tiny pale bodies and translucent wings fluttered about, nipping and biting at one another in a fight for whatever lay on the floor beneath. I crept closer, and they ignored me, too caught up in their hunger. But as I closed in on them, nothing showed. Nothing at all to expose whatever it was they were fighting over. I crouched down and put my cheek to the floor, taking in their view. Tiny proboscises sucked at the stone.

"Come up here," I whisper-shouted to Sofi. "It's fine."

I shined the flashlight in her direction, its pale beam revealing her mascara-streaked face. There in the darkness of the catacombs, with only this meager light to illuminate her, she exuded death. I flicked the beam down, out of her eyes, and a dragging shuffle arose from her direction as she broke from her stasis and moved to join me. I kept the light trained on the floor, enough to cast the space between us in a dim glow bright enough to guide, but nowhere near bright enough to blind. When she finally reached me, I turned the light up and covered it with my hand, casting us in the faded red glow of light through skin and blood. Tiny beams splintered through the places where my fingers met one another, like cracks opening to hellfire.

"Your spray bottle. The one you had to find your signs to the party. Do you still have it?" I asked.

"I do," she whispered. She reached her left hand into her jacket pocket and retrieved a small mister bottle with a pump trigger and handed it to me. The gun remained in her right hand, barrel pointed down but her finger still on the trigger.

I turned and pointed the beam again to the parafairies, still sucking away at the stone floor. As it lit upon them, another sucking sound echoed behind me—that of Sofi taking a reactionary inward gasp of air. My hands full, I could do nothing to stop the scream erupting from between her lips. Their pointed ears perked up, and their eyeless faces snapped in our direction. The tiny hose-like proboscises retracted into their mouths as the skin around their mouths peeled back. Circular rows of tiny teeth spun like microscopic blades inside the suction-cup-like opening one could only call their lips, and their wings flung open.

This only made Sofi scream louder, and I cringed at the sting of her cries against my eardrums. The parafairies were about to take flight and attack, and with the situation we currently found ourselves in, the last thing we needed was to fight off an infection from one of their bites. They were notorious carriers, and the kinds of viruses they'd probably been exposed to were not the kind you healed from. Without thinking, I lifted a heavy boot from the ground and slammed it down onto the first. Another found its wing caught under my heel, and I brought my second foot up and down onto its screaming face before it had a chance to break free. The third, however, I missed entirely, and before I could bring my foot up and down again, it took to the air, directly toward my face. With one heavy swing of the flashlight, I clobbered it, and it burst with a sound like a baseball bat smashing a grapefruit. A cocktail of various fluids and fleshy bits exploded into the air, and its dead body slapped against the far wall with a wet smack.

Sofi's screams continued, even as I lifted my boot from the smashed remains of the other two flattened parasites. "Please, for the love of God… shut the fuck up," I shouted, as I spun and raised the flashlight over my head like a club. Her eyes met mine, wide with shock … and she began to laugh.

"You're nutty, you know that?" I asked as I lowered the flashlight.

"You were going to hit me," she said through her bellows. "I should shoot you."

"You shoot me, and you're never getting out of here," I replied.

"We are never getting out of here," she said and raised the gun. "We are trapped here with these monsters until we die."

"You want to shoot me, you go right ahead." I tried to shout, to knock her out of her new psychosis through the stern sound of reason. But the pain in my gut stabbed through me again, and I only managed to answer with a wheeze. I paused and took a few slow breaths. "How did you say you got down here?" I asked.

"We followed signs on the wall. Signs we see only with the spray the men give my sister."

"Do you know what those signs were?"

"Arrows. Painted with something invisible."

"Blood," I replied. "Arrows painted with blood, then washed away like they were never there at all."

From the mangled expression on Sofi's face, I could tell she was now stuck between the place between laughter and screams. The mere mention of blood seemed to remind her of what kind of a mess she'd gotten herself into, even if she couldn't fully comprehend it yet.

I knelt, held the spray bottle out before me and pumped a few squirts onto the stone surrounding the mashed corpses of the parafairies. The goopy mess that had gushed out of their insides when my foot brought them to their end immediately lit up with a bright iridescent blue, but soon the stone floor around them started to light up as well. I took a few steps away from Sofi, sprayed again, and took a few steps more. With each step, I squirted another mist from the bottle, and with each squirt more of the room lit up. Soon the entire space was aglow in a soft electric blue, some areas brighter than others, but all painted in spurts and sprays like a Pollack had decided to paint the room with glowsticks.

"I think we found your party," I said, grimly.

"But there is no one here," she replied. "Where are the bodies? Where are the speakers and the lights? This room is empty."

"It may be now, but it wasn't. You see all that?" I asked, gesturing to the ghostly glow all around us. "That's luminol. Your bottle was full of it. Glows when it reacts with blood."

Laughing and crying were now both well past Sofi. All her body wanted to do now was to wretch. To physically reject the place in which she now recognized. The place where she'd seen countless killed and her sister stolen from her. But, to her credit, she swallowed it down.

"We need to get out of here," she said.

"Do you know the way out now?"

"Yes. I think I do. Suis moi," she answered. "Follow me." Before I could respond, she'd snatched the flashlight from my hand and started off again.

I spun on my heel to follow, and that white-hot pain again seared through my gut. The tip of my boot caught on the stone, and I toppled forward, collapsing in a heap. Sofi returned to me and helped me back to my feet.

"Come. I help you. Not much farther and we are free home."

"I think you mean home-free," I mumbled. As she brought me to my feet, my world began to swirl. Wherever that bastard had stabbed me, it hadn't been someplace nice. But I wasn't about to let a slow death of infection and delirium take me. Not here. Now all I wanted was my gun back, so I could punch a slug through my brain and go through the whole resurrection process and start over fresh. But the words couldn't come, and my mouth refused to work.

From there on, all I remember are fleeting glimpses of flashlight beams over yellowed stone and stacked bone, down one tunnel after another. A door. The sickly smell of damp earth. Steps, another door … the twinkling of Paris streetlights.

Then, for a long while … nothing at all.

CHAPTER SEVEN

There was no way to tell how long I was out. Or how long it had been since I last saw sunlight. But when the morning came some several days later and peeked in through the crack in the drawn shades, I finally woke up. Not for long, mind you. Just a moment. And it was possible I'd woken earlier than this. Had maybe been awake time and time again since we escaped those hellish catacombs, but this was the first time I could remember being conscious.

It didn't last long, though. I shivered violently, sweat pouring down my brow and a piercing headache shrieked through my skull. I remember grumbling, trying to make out words ... to ask for someone to please turn out the lights. Nothing nowhere near that intelligible came from my lips though, if I'd managed any sound at all. Still, something signaled I'd woken, and a shadow passed before me, then drew the shades completely closed. I dozed off again, and again, I have no idea how long I remained out.

Time went on like this, in little bits of frenzied spasms of wakefulness—but wakefulness in name only. My mind reeled and spun like a monkey on a tricycle on a high-wire balancing an array of spinning plates. Ready to fall apart and crash at any point. Headaches, fever, and nausea wracked my every waking moment, and in time, I'd thrown up enough that all that remained between my grunts and moans were outbursts of dry heaving.

I do remember her, though, as she took care of me. Sofi observing me with pitiful eyes as she dotted my brow with a wet washrag. Why she brought me here, rather than leave me for dead on some hospital stoop, I had no idea. Then again, I couldn't ask. I couldn't form a single word, let alone quiz her on where we were and what she was doing with me.

I remember wanting to die. Many times, just wanting to die. To shut down, reboot, and start over again.

After what must have been days but could have been weeks for all I knew, I managed to take down some liquid—mostly water, but at times some broth. But I wasn't getting better, so much as acclimating to the ongoing pain. That stab in my gut, it had hit something alright and whatever it had hit had leaked all over my insides. Sepsis is what some call it—infection and rot from within. Maybe a doctor could have saved me, I don't know. What I do know is a regimen of ibuprofen and Perrier is not enough to cure a dying man.

"Let me go," I whispered—the first words through my lips since we encountered the cleansed massacre scene in the catacombs. Or, the first words I could remember speaking. My head had been filled with all manner of twisted dreams while in my feverish dying state, from memories of past run-ins with all manner of boogeymen, to nightmares of being lost in Eitherspace for eternity, to a dinner with my mother turning into a zombie film as my lost sister clawed her way from a hidden grave in our corner garden while dad roasted a pig over a pit to hell. Words surely came during those visions, but not conscious words. Just the raving mutterings and screamed obscenities of a man trapped in the violent throes of death.

"Let me go," I whispered again. "Kill me."

Sofi, seated on the bed beside me, reached her hand to my forehead. Though I knew it to be soft and warm, it felt like pure ice against my roasting skin. "I am taking care of you," she replied, her voice like velvet. "You saved me. Now I save you, Phoenix."

"Please…" I stammered, barely managing to form the words. "Don't under… die… okay."

"Shhh," she whispered and pressed her soft lips against mine. "You rest."

The next time I woke, it was to the sound of a door opening. My eyelids felt like steel shutters, but I managed to raise them far enough to make out the blurred silhouette of two people talking in the doorway. After a quick exchange of words, Sofi opened the door further and let the visitor into her flat. The door closed behind him, and the room fell back into hushed darkness. The two spoke again, a hurried, focus conversation wholly unintelligible to me because they spoke entirely in French. A pause, what looked like an exchange of money for something the man took out of his inner jacket pocket, and he left. My eyelids fell closed again, and sleep washed over me.

Sometime later, I again woke, this time to the gentle shaking by a hand on my shoulder. "Wake up, Phoenix," Sofi whispered. "I have medicine. It will help you feel better."

My eyes fluttered, catching a few fleeting glimpses of her concerned face, and then closed again. I again tried to speak, to create words to tell her to put me out of this misery, but only managed a pained groan. She responded by slithering her fingers into my mouth, gently prying my lips apart, and slipping in a pill. I tried to swallow, but my dry throat erupted into a fit of coughs. The lip of a glass found my mouth, and she poured a small amount of water in, and I managed to swallow it, and the pill, before falling back asleep.

As I slept, dreams hit me again. But this time they weren't so much fantasy as disjointed remembrances of past reality. With the fever and the drugs and me on the literal edge of death, it's hard to recall what all went through my head, but what I do know is it centered around Belinda.

We'd been kids at the time — no more than eight or nine years old. I can't exactly recall, even now in the lucidity of current hindsight. Either way, though, it didn't matter all that much. Just that we were young enough to be children still but old enough that Momma didn't mind much when we wanted to go off on an adventure. No, back then us kids were free-range. Momma loved us, that I know. But she didn't hover over us like some parents do today. Looking back, I can't tell if that was a good or bad thing, especially when you consider what ended up happening, but it there wasn't a lack of love in our family. Fact is, love is what let us be the kids we were—love and trust.

Must have been late summertime. In my memory, the trees are still dense with leaves and the air so thick and heavy with humidity you're almost swimming through it. Take too deep a breath and you might drown. The time of year bugs buzz about in swarms and you best watch where you step before you bring your foot down on a cottonmouth and it gets so damned pissed off it latches its fangs onto your ankle, and you scream and holler well past the time you've been taken to the hospital. Of course, that never happened to me, but I had friends who told me about their own friends whose feet found them sons-of-bitches. I'd seen a few in my adventures too, usually slithering off in some swampy land we knew better than to go mucking around in. But never been bit by one. I'm not stupid.

Far as I can remember, this was the first time Belinda and I ever came across something "not-quite-normal." Sure, she'd told tale of other strange goings-on she'd come across out on her solo adventures, but up until then I never seen nothing like that. Usually, I put it up to her wild imagination, and usually, I was probably right. But a few weeks back she'd come screaming through the screen door of our little house just about sunset, wild-eyed and out of breath. Yammering something about monster or wolf-man or something-or-other she'd seen tearing into a deer. From then on, she didn't want to go out in the woods alone, so we'd started going out again together. Mostly she tagged along when I was going out adventuring, but I didn't mind so much. Not that I was scared myself, mind you, but that I knew she was, and it felt noble to play the role of big brother … even if she was technically a few minutes older than me.

The sun was going down, sending little beams of light through the gaps in the summer leaves and branches, streaming down onto the forest floor like little spotlights. The western sky turned a wondrous shade of pink lemonade, and the two of us scampered through the trees on the path we'd worn bare through our countless travels. We hadn't been up to much of anything that evening. Just off on our own, hunting for whatever kind of mischief a few kids might find. The falling sun though, it was our cue to skedaddle and head on home. Dinner would've been well-past over, but Momma and Daddy knew better than to wait for us. We'd eat whatever was left over when we got home, and from the smell wafting our way on the summer breeze an hour or two earlier, Daddy had been grilling up something tasty.

This exploration had taken us considerably farther than we normally ventured, so the trip home took longer than we planned. Or at least that's how I remember it. Looking back at it now, the memory's quite a bit clearer of course … but when I was in Sofi's bed, sweating and fussing and delirious as a rabid cat, things didn't make quite as much sense. Back then, when the memory dream hit me, it hit me in bursts and spurts. The sun went down, and that signaled it was time for us to head on back home. But after that? I don't know if things started hitting me harder, what with that "medicine" Sofi had shoved down my throat and the continual slide into madness as the infection brewing in my gut took hold and ventured into my bloodstream, but after that, the memories started getting jerkier and hazier.

Thing is, even now I can't remember exactly what happened that night, other than it was surely a harbinger of things to come years later. The sun went down, and the bright sky turned from yellow to pink to murky purple dusk, and the trip home began to feel as if it were taking longer than it should have. Soon night fell completely, plunging the forest into complete darkness, and us without any flashlight had to try to figure our way home through the tangle of wood. Twigs crackled under our feet and a hoot owl started in with his questioning *who, who*? The forest erupted in a cacophony of bugs all around us, and we pushed on through it, sure home couldn't be much further. Never, ever much further.

At least that's what I kept telling my sister. She was alright at first, still high on the adrenaline from our scampering and playful jaunt through the woods. But as night fell, I witnessed a new realization hit her, and as much as she tried to hide it, fear was starting to settle down on her bones.

She managed to keep it to herself though, mostly … until the moon came up, full and bright and peeking at us through the breaks in the canopy. Shadows danced across our path like little demons scampering from tree to tree. The wind picked up as we moved and soon started to whip through the branches, letting out a series of horrible yowls, accentuated by the occasional crackle of a fallen branch.

And this is where things get murkiest of all. Even now, when I think back to it. Those sounds, they started to come from all around us, even when the wind didn't blow.

"Don't be scared," I told Belinda. "That's farther off, none of that ruckus is here. Just branches breaking off farther in the woods and it echoes a lot more cuz it's night-time."

I feel we must have been about home when *it* happened. Another crack, this time from behind us … and this time far too close for me to consider lying to Belinda. She might have wanted to believe my lies earlier, believe them because they made her feel safe. The time for false bravery left with that crack though. Because something was there, and it was just about on top of us. Belinda broke off in a run, screaming, in the direction I assumed our house was. I turned around, and something like a man rose from the brush about twenty feet away. Nothing I could make out, other than it was bigger than me. A silhouette against the moon. But another crash from my right distracted me, I turned to see, and found nothing, for the woods had become too dark and whatever made that second noise had hidden in the shadow.

When I finally made it back to the house, I expected a firm scolding from my father for being out so late and not taking proper care of my sister. Nothing of the sort happened though. Because Belinda hadn't come home. She didn't come home at all that night, and I spent near until sunup crying and worrying about her while Momma and Daddy searched the woods calling her name until their throats were hoarse. Still, sometime throughout the night, I did manage to nod off and it musta been while I was out that after Momma came home to check in on me. I woke to the sound of joyous screams as Momma found Belinda, safely asleep in her bed.

Next morning, when she woke, they scolded her and threatened her with a whooping for scaring them so much, but nothing came of it. She said she didn't remember coming home, just running off scared in the woods and getting lost on her own. Then waking up.

This wasn't the last time something like that happened to her. Belinda's little disappearances continued, off and on for years. Until the horrible day they stopped. But it was the only instance that hit me while I was dreaming away, sick and dying in that French girl's bed.

I must have been muttering her name while I slept, because as I woke and my eyelids crept open, Sofi stood above me, wet washcloth on my forehead, whispering softly, "Sofi, not Belinda. I'm Sofi… I'm Sofi."

Seeing I was awake, she took another handful of pills and shoved them between my lips. A gulp of water helped them down my screaming throat, and as they worked their way to my gullet and that horrible burning place I called my stomach, I tried to speak. Again, I mostly croaked, but I did manage a word or two before everything started to spin again.

"My… gun. Shoot."

But again, she ignored my plea, which when you consider the situation, isn't all that surprising. I mean, here she was with some strange man in her apartment … a strange man she probably by now was regretting having brought back here. Now though I was in her care. Her responsibility. A bullet through the brain was the last thing on her mind. No, she needed to save me. And as far as she could tell, whatever she'd been doing could have been working. My agonizing screams of pain abated, as the drugs she'd been dumping down my throat had seen to that. Mostly from there on out I slept, waking from time to time, and if I let out a whimper of pain, she shoved another pill in my mouth.

She must have thought everything would be okay if only she could make the pain go away. That's what you get when a junkie is filling you up with whatever cocktail of pills she manages to buy from her junkie friends. Because that's what she was giving me, though I didn't know it at the time. Problem is, junkies should know better. They should know better from all the junkie friends they see overdose.

That's what finally did me in. And I suppose I should be happy for it because she did do what I asked for, albeit in her own unintentional way. Each time she dosed me, she upped the count of whatever she had available. As I went into cardiac arrest, I remember seeing her staring at me wide-eyed, screaming and crying. She slammed her fist against my chest, put her lips to mine, and breathed the air from her lungs into mine. Doing whatever she could remember from TV and movies to perform some kind of CPR on me. Mascara ran in streaks down her face onto my failing body, and she screamed and cried and looked about ready to die herself. When nothing worked, she finally gave up and gave in to the inevitability of my death, she held me and sobbed. Her wet cheeks slid against my own, staining me with the black mascara. My breath long since over, my brain shut down, and I died for her.

Now, normally, when I've come back to life, the rebirth has been a pretty quick experience. Dead one minute, back to life the next. As I said earlier, however, I'd never died in such an extended way before. This was a natural, prolonged death. Not a sudden poisoning, stabbing or gunshot wound through the head. This wasn't a "he's fine" one moment, dead as a doornail the next. I'd been dying a long, excruciating death, made only a bit more bearable through the cocktail of drugs she'd given me. And it is for that reason, I believe, my resurrection was far from sudden.

As I started to come to, I heard her sobbing from farther away. From what I could gather, she must have taken a seat on the sofa in the living room area, a few yards from the mattress I'd turned into a deathbed moments earlier. But unlike the last times when I'd come back, I wasn't jumping up doing a jig, fit as a fiddle. This was a slow recovery, and though I could hear, I couldn't move yet. My muscles were pins and needles from the trickle of blood flow that had started to ooze along as my heart kicked back into motion.

There in the dark, she sobbed away. Why? I honestly don't know. It's not like we were old pals. I can only assume it was because she'd had enough of death and losing people, and it all finally had come crashing back down on her. That idea of if she could save me, then maybe she could save her sister, must have been loitering around the back of her cranium … even if she wouldn't have known it if you asked her. Now that I was dead, death was again all she knew.

I wouldn't have been surprised if she took her own life next. I've been around death and grieving enough to understand the pain it can cause. I needed to get myself back into action if only so I could stop her from doing something stupid. So, I did the one thing I knew how to do when I'd lost all else: I focused my energy inward, in a kind of corporeal meditation. As I lie there, stiff as a board, I willed the blood to flow and bring life back to my corpse. It hurt like hell, but soon enough I was able to flutter open my eyelids, allowing the cracked ceiling of the dimly lit room to come into focus. A few minutes later, my big left toe twitched.

I was so focused; I almost didn't hear the knock at the door. In fact, I very well may have missed the first one. But the one I did hear, the loud pounding of a heavy fist on solid wood, that got my attention. The thundering noise reverberated throughout the apartment, sending the framed pictures on the walls to rattle and shake against the plaster. A voice followed, "Hello, is anyone in there? Hello?"

By now I'd regained enough movement to allow myself to twist my neck enough to peek toward the door. Sofi remained balled up on the couch, her sobs subsiding, as her mind undoubtedly scrambled for a decision as to what she should do next.

"Sofi, let us in," echoed a second, familiar voice.

At the sound of that second voice, her head perked up, and she addressed the closed door, "Paul, is that you?" she asked.

"Yes, yes, it is me," came the answer. "I am here with a friend. Can we come in?"

Sofi paused and thought about this for a minute, then replied, "I'm sorry, Paul. Now is not a good time. There is something I am dealing with. Can you come back later?"

"Please, Sofi, this will only take a minute. Can you please come to the door?"

Sofi glanced in my direction then back to the door and sighed. "Yes, I am coming," she said. "But this must be quick. You cannot come in."

As the door opened the light from the hallway spilled into the room, casting the entryway under its bright glow. Sofi's shadow fell like a stickman across the welcome mat and connected to her feet, which connected to the soft silhouette of her body. I immediately recognized the man at the door: the very same man who'd come those days or hours earlier with her "medicine."

"How is your friend?" Paul asked, looking past her toward where my presumedly dead body lay.

"He is sleeping," Sofi replied. "He needs to rest."

"Can I come in and take a look at him?" asked the second man. As he spoke, he stepped into the doorway, exposing a frame just over six feet tall, dressed in a well-manicured suit. His hair slicked back, revealing a clean-cut, chiseled face, and eyes such a bright, piercing blue, I could see them from where I lay.

"No, like I said, he is sleeping right now."

"But, Monsieur, I am a doctor. Maybe I can help him."

"I'm sorry, but the answer is no. Perhaps I will call when he is awake, then you can come." She moved to close the door, and the taller of the two men stepped forward to the edge of the threshold.

"Perhaps you can invite me in now, as an act of goodwill."

Sofi shook her head and continued to close the door. The man lifted his arm as if to reach out and grab her, then stopped suddenly, as if he didn't want to break the plane separating the apartment from the outside world. It was then I realized what we were dealing with.

I wanted to scream and shout and tell her *Shut the door, Sofi. Do not let them in!* But my lips refused to cooperate. My gaze shifted from the man's hand, then to his eyes, as sudden realization overtook over his face. He wiggled the fingers on his raised hand, and slowly brought it forward, past the threshold and into the room. Sofi swung the door in an attempt to shut them out, but he took another step and blocked it with his foot. A loud crash against the door sent it flying open, as Paul slammed his shoulder against it, sending Sofi crashing to the ground. As the two men entered, their faces changed and became more contorted and angrier. The blue of their eyes began to sparkle, emitting a faint glow in the darkness, and a pair of *snikt* sounds echoed as they unleashed their fangs.

"Where is he, girl?" the dapper man shouted. "Where is Donal?"

"I… I don't know what you are talking about," Sofi replied, as she scurried backward, crab-style, until backing into her couch.

"He is here, and I know it. You cannot hide him," he shouted again.

By now the adrenaline had kicked in on me, but it still wasn't enough to get me moving. Not in the speed or manner I would need to do anything about what was happening. Still, it was enough to allow me to turn and let out a moan, which was enough to grab their attention.

"Is that him?" He sniffed the air. "No, he does not have Donal's stink."

Paul took a few steps forward and reached down, grabbing Sofi by the shirt and hoisting her into the air. "Just help, Sofi, and you will not be harmed. He has given me his word."

"And what will be done to her if she does not help, Paul?" the "doctor" asked.

"I'll suck every last drop of blood from your pretty little neck."

Unable to leap into action, my mind scrambled for anything I could do to help. Next to me, the red LEDs on a small clock radio read 4:50 a.m. I reached out, took the radio into my hand, and yanked the cord out of the clock. Then, I grasped those bare wires in one hand, pulled back the covers, and slammed the bare cables directly into my bare chest. Sparks flew, and my body shuddered as it was brought back to life, like a present-day Frankenstein experiment made possible only through the miracle of our modern electrical grid.

Of course, the crack of sparks and the smell of burning flesh and ozone got their attention immediately. Paul dropped Sofi to the ground, and she stared at me, surely shocked to see me up and moving again, but broke out of her amazement and made a break for the kitchen, just to the side of the bed.

"What are they?" she screamed.

"You damn well know what they are," I replied, as I stepped out of bed and planted my feet firmly on the hardwood floor. "And we're going to kill them."

Now, my miraculous recovery might have been enough to catch most anyone's attention. But these guys, they'd seen plenty of shit in their day. Or at least the older one had ... Paul? I was pretty sure he'd just been turned, and I felt like an asshole knowing I'd have to kill him on what was probably his first day on the job. Regardless, they forgot all about Sofi for the time being and focused in on me.

"What the hell do you think you're going to do, boy?" asked the elder.

"I'm gonna make like The Clash and send you Straight to Hell, boy," I replied.

"Phoenix, take this," came a shout from the kitchen. I turned just in time to see a large butcher knife headed my direction, and though I could have caught it if I wanted to, I let it go right past me and embed itself in the wall.

"They're vampires, Sofi. Not muggers. A knife won't do a damn thing," I shouted.

"Right. I will find something else," she replied as she started rifling through drawers.

Paul leaped at me, covering half the distance of the room in a single bound. The other vampire walked steadily forward, secure in knowing I had nowhere to go other than out the window ... and from the sound of traffic outside, we were quite a ways up. Definitely farther than most people could safely fall.

I dodged Paul's attack and rolled into the kitchen, backing up toward Sofi. We were cornered, but I wasn't worried. I'd dealt with vampires before and could take care of these ones ... but only if I could find something to take them out with. By now, all the kitchen drawers had been opened, and an array of knives, napkins, and cutlery were strewn about the linoleum floor and granite countertop. Nothing I could use. Even if the stuff was made of real silver, it wouldn't have worked, since although plenty of movies might tell you otherwise, silver doesn't do shit against a vampire. But then I saw it, sad and stained red with marinara sauce: a wooden spoon. Clutching it in my right hand, I cracked the end against the countertop, snapped the spoon part off the handle, and lunged at Paul.

Stupid bastard didn't think enough to dodge. Probably was still in that honeymoon phase where he thought he was invincible. His eyes widened in horror when my makeshift stake found its mark, as his heart exploded, and he realized maybe he wasn't so invincible after all. His undead body crashed to the floor and went up in flames, bubbling and boiling until POP, it burst like a water balloon, painting the rooms with little bits of French boy.

From behind me, the older vampire snickered. "Since you are not Donal, and Donal is not here, I can only assume you have it," he said, wiping a flap of Paul's ear from his cheek. "Give it to me, and I will not kill you. I won't even kill *her*."

"Duck, Phoenix," Sofi yelled, and I dropped to the floor. Something round and white flew above my head like a baseball and bounced off the vampire's face. Again, he sneered and began to advance on Sofi, unfazed. The bulb of garlic rolled along the ground, stopping a few feet away from me. I leaped to my feet, but the vampire was too fast for me, and the sofa blocked my other path. There was no way I'd reach Sofi in time to save her.

So, I thrust my right foot down, broke the wooden leg off the coffee table, kicked it up into my hand, and threw it across the room to Sofi.

"In the heart!" I shouted as she caught it. Her eyes narrowed as the vampire sprung in for his late-night snack, and before I knew it, he stumbled backward, caught fire, and exploded into a mess of undead flesh, as his apprentice had done before him.

I nodded to Sofi, and she returned a great big smile. Probably the first time I'd ever seen her smile like that. And she'd have looked damned pretty if not for the blood and guts dripping down her hair and face. "We need to get the hell out of here," I said. "Now. Before any more come."

She took three large steps in my direction and stood before me. Facing one another, she stood with her head at my chin level, but with the fire burning in her eyes, I couldn't help but feel small. "You were dead," she said. "You were dying on my couch, for days. I took care of you. I tried to save you, and I held you as you died."

"I told you to kill me." I didn't have time for this.

She didn't respond, not in words, at least. Instead, she balled her right hand into a fist, pulled it back, and punched me square in the jaw. I'd be lying if it said it didn't hurt.

"They know we're here," I said, wiping the stream of blood from my lip. "I don't know how, but they know. And there will be more of them. We have to go."

"I have just the place," Sofi replied. "But first let me grab some fresh clothes. For both of us."

"We don't have time for that," I argued.

"If we go out into the streets of Paris like this," she said, as she hastily shoved a few handfuls of clothing into a duffel bag, "we're going to attract the attention of much more than vampires."

I conceded. She did, after all, have a point.

CHAPTER EIGHT

As we stepped out the door of Sofi's apartment building and onto the streets of Paris, the sun still lingered well below the horizon, not yet ready to make its grand daily entrance into the world. The early morning darkness, while useful in hiding our noticeable appearances, did little to put me at ease. With night-time came the things that lurk in the night. And from what I knew already, Paris must have been swarming with vampires. Sure, they wouldn't be out much longer. Not when the sun was on the verge of rising. They didn't like that part—the part where they turned into undead human bacon strips. It didn't mean they'd gone into hiding already though, and they knew who we were. Or at the very least, the ones we'd done in did. There was no telling how far that information went, or who sent the death squad to Sofi's apartment, but one thing was certain—we needed someplace new to lie low.

This early in the morning, the streets were as dead as a graveyard. Far in the distance, a siren wailed, but other than that the streets were clear of traffic in the little part of the city Sofi called home. I'd never been to Paris before, though I admit I always wanted to visit ... albeit under preferably different circumstances. Where Sofi was taking me, I had no idea. The problem was I had to trust her. She was my only guide to the city and the only person I could trust not to have a pair of fangs ready to dig into my neckline.

As we traveled, we kept to the shadows near buildings. Careful not to expose ourselves in the streetlight, as even in a city that appears to be asleep, you never do know what might be awake. One sight of a blood-soaked duo skittering through the streets would be enough to send any onlooker straight to the telephone, and the police. Now, I have nothing against police … but I also had no way to explain this one. Sofi was right. We had to clean ourselves up.

"Where are we going?" I asked as I scurried from the shadow of a parked truck to the side of a dumpster in an unlit alley.

"Stay close, and follow me," she said. "And stay quiet."

I knew she had questions for me because I definitely had questions for her. But she was right, now was not the time for conversation. She darted off again, and I followed. We traveled this way, like gory Parisian ninjas, until eventually, we came to the edge of a large courtyard.

"There." She pointed to the center of the courtyard in which stood a large stone building, fronted by a statue of an angel. Wings outstretched, the angel's right hand held a crooked sword, while his left hand pointed up toward the heavens. Beneath him, a man lay conquered on at his feet. A man, but not exactly a man … but rather an evil man, with a tail. All of this perched on a stack of tremendous stones, over which poured a cascade of running water. "Hurry, into the fountain," she commanded, before she darted off, stripping her clothes as she ran, until she reached the fountain, fully naked, and jumped in.

With little other choice, I followed, stripping off my blood-stained jeans and underpants, and I too dove into the fountain. We rinsed ourselves hurriedly, the water quickly turning a deep red as we washed our bodies as clean as we could.

"I am sorry, St. Michel," Sofi whispered to the statue as she climbed out and onto the stone courtyard.

I followed, took the clothes she offered me, and hurriedly pulled them on. Though a bit snug around the waist and tight around the midsection, the faded jeans and black t-shirt fit well enough. The sneakers, however, were at least a size too large, and as I tied up the laces, I prayed we wouldn't have to go too far before I could pick out a new pair closer to my size.

"Come, we must go. Before someone sees us," Sofi urged, as she pulled a pair of fashionably torn jeans up over her hips. She slid into her usual leather jacket, now clean of the blood and gore from our time in the catacombs and ran off again into the shadows.

I moved to follow but first glanced back once more at the fountain in which we'd cleansed ourselves. Two winged serpents, like dragons with the heads of lions, stood solemnly at its base. Each spit a stream of cherry-red water, while the cascading waterfall beneath St. Michael and the vanquished devil pulsed the same wicked crimson. As if Satan had just fallen, and his minions vomited blood in the onslaught of wretched sickness that came from the realization their king ruled hell no more.

"How are you alive?" she asked, kicking the tip of her right shoe absently at a stone lodged in the worn ground. We sat together on a bench, shoulder to shoulder, as the morning sun broke the eastern horizon. Neither of us looked at the other, our eyes transfixed on the dawn of the new day. "I saw you die. Twice now, I have seen you die."

"Technically, I didn't die in the catacombs. I only burned up on the outside. There's a difference," I reached to my pocket, found it empty and remembered I wore someone else's clothes. "Speaking of which, do you happen to have a cigarette?"

Sofi took her bag from the ground and placed it on my lap. "Should be some in there," she replied. "But you were dead. In my apartment, you were dead. And how do you mean you *burned up*. People do not *burn up*. And if they do, it is from a fire, and they are either dead or very badly scarred. There was no fire near you, and yet you were on fire. Then you were a man of ash, then like new. This is not normal, Phoenix."

"I know, Sofi—it's not normal. A lot about me isn't normal."

"You mean there is more beside the fact you can come back to life like Jesus, and you somehow are trained in the art of killing vampires that is not normal?"

I laughed as I lit the cigarette I found in her bag. "Well, when you put it that way, I guess you're already aware of some of my weirder quirks," I said and inhaled a deep drag of the sweet tobacco smoke. "I don't know how it works, to be honest. It's just something I do—something I've always done. I die, and I come back to life. No magic healing powers and I feel pain and get sick like anyone else. But when I die? I come back, usually better than I was when I left. But this time was different."

"How is resurrection different one time from the other? They are all crazy." She took the cigarette from my hand and took a drag herself. "You are crazy."

"You don't know the half of it," I muttered. "This time was the first time I've ever died from a prolonged sickness or injury. Every other time, it was boom! Here and alive, then dead, then back to life. This time hurt like hell, and it scared me just as much. I told you to kill me, but did you listen? Hell no."

"I tried to help you. I thought you were delirious."

"You saw me burn like a marshmallow! You should have known something was off then."

"You are off, Phoenix. I do not kill people. Even when they ask me too."

"You had no problem killing those vampires."

"That was different."

"How? How was it any different? It was a hell of a lot messier than killing me would have been, that's for sure. I don't flare up and explode in a burst of mangled guts when I die."

"How was I to know this? You already flared up. And besides, I was helping you."

I thought back to the various trips in and out of consciousness I'd taken while the infection from the stab wound ravaged my body. I remembered the man who came. I remembered the pills Sofi gave me. And with that memory came a screaming pain in my gut, precisely where I'd been stabbed by the serial killer we'd taken care of down below the streets of the city. No death-wound had ever bothered me before, not after I'd come back and it healed itself. This was something new, and it hurt like hell.

"Do you have any more of those pills? The medicine you gave me?"

"Now is hardly the time for a party," she replied. "Coffee and breakfast. That is what we need."

The pain stabbed at me again, and I buckled over, clutching my stomach. "The pills, Sofi. Do you have them?" I spoke in slow, deliberate words.

"Yes, yes. In the bag. Just… just give it to me, and I will find them."

As she rummaged through the bag, several more spasms rattled my gut. I winced as each one tore through me, and as soon as she handed me a couple of pills, I wolfed them down. Sofi tried to speak, but I brushed her away. The pain had moved into my head, and a throbbing headache racked my brain with each beat of my heart. She returned to searching the bag, taking inventory of whatever she'd managed to grab from her apartment in our hasty exit. I, meanwhile, hunched over and put my head in my hands, waiting impatiently for the medicine to do its work. After a few minutes, the pain subsided, and a wash of mental relief flooded through me like an ocean wave breaking at the surf.

"What exactly did you give me?" I asked, my head swimming.

"Same thing I gave you before. Cocktail Paul recommended. Special K, Vicodin, oxy. Just a mix."

"Jesus Christ, Sofi!" I shouted. "All of that? I took all of that?"

"Well, I think what you just took was only oxy. And I'm pretty sure we ran out of Ketamine."

I almost shouted again, but the drugs had already taken hold, and it was a little hard to stay mad like that. Still, I knew a cocktail like that could be dangerous, and while I was still angry, I managed to keep my response relatively relaxed. "Who was Paul?" I asked.

"The friend of mine you killed," Sofi replied.

"First off, he wasn't a friend. He was a vampire. Or at least he was when I took him out."

"Killed him," she corrected.

"No. You don't kill a vampire. A vampire is already dead. You can't kill something that's dead. It's just not possible."

"You told me to kill you. And you're dead," Sofi replied.

"That's different. I'm not dead. I'm alive. I just die a lot. But each time I come back, I'm 100% living. Nothing like a vampire."

"Kind of like a vampire…"

"Fine, maybe kind of like a vampire. I don't care how you define it. But I'm no monster, and your friend Paul? He was a monster. So was the guy he brought with him." I paused, taking a moment to think through the events. "Who was the guy he brought with him?"

"No idea. I never saw him before in my life."

"Then why was he with Paul?"

"I do not know. I also do not know why they were vampires. When he came over earlier to bring your drugs, he was not a vampire. But now he is… or was."

"Did you… invite them in?"

"No. I thought you were dead on the couch. I would not invite in a friend, let alone a stranger, when there is a dead man on my couch. I am not stupid."

"Then how did they get in?" I wondered aloud.

"They walked in. When I told them no, they just came in anyway. Vampires do not seem to be very good listeners."

"That's not how it works, though." I shook my head. "A bunch of the stuff you know about vampires, the stuff from the movies, a lot of it's a load of horse shit. But some of it is true. Like when you threw the garlic at the vampires? Yeah, garlic doesn't do anything other than give them bad breath. Crucifixes? Normally don't work. Haven't tried holy water. Definitely haven't tried consecrated ground. But what I do know is they can't come into a residence unless they are invited in. Weird rule and I'm sure there are plenty of odd workarounds, but as a general statute, it's true. Same with a stake through the heart. That kills them. Sunlight? Deathly allergic. Silver bullets? Pass right through them—only work on werewolves as far as I'm concerned."

"Well, I did not invite them in. So, I do not know how to answer you. This is not something I would lie about. After all, they still have my sister."

Not wanting to tell her that her sister was probably already dead … or undead, I changed the subject. "Speaking of ways to kill vampires, you didn't happen to bring any of my stuff in that sack of yours, did you?"

Sofi reached into the bag again, now not taking nearly as much time to sort through it as we'd left our blood-soaked rags behind and now wore the clothing that previously took up most of the space and produced my charred Colt .45. I grabbed her hand and pushed it back into the bag.

"Not here. Sun's up and people will notice. Just keep it safe in there for now."

Sofi put the gun away, and we sat silently as the sun continued to rise, bathing the city streets of Paris in its warm glow. A stray cat strolled by. Birds chirped, and people left their apartments to head off on their daily routines.

Finally, Sofi spoke, "You're still going to help?"

"With what?"

"With finding my sister. You're going to help me find my sister, yes?"

"I'm going to—" I hesitated. "I'm going to hunt down these vampires and rid them from this world. If we happen to save your sister along the way, so be it."

"Then I am coming with you."

I saw this coming, and I also knew better than to accept a new sidekick. But the life of a monster hunter can get lonely … and I didn't speak any French. Or have any money. So, I didn't argue.

"Fine then. But first you need to learn the very first rule of monster hunting: never hunt on an empty stomach. Let's go find some breakfast and figure out what to do next."

CHAPTER NINE

Since I'd never been to France before, let alone Paris, she let me choose breakfast. And though it felt a little cliched to suggest, if I didn't have crepes while I was there, I'd end up regretting it later. I considered suggesting baguettes or croissants, just because they were the only other French words I knew, but I figured she wasn't in the mood for that kind of stupid this early in the morning—especially after everything she'd been through. That also meant French toast was out of the question … though I did make a mental note to request we go out for an order of Freedom Fries and Budweiser later that night once we got our shit in order.

So, we headed off into the heart of Paris on foot, in search of some little creperie she liked. Whether it was honestly a *good* creperie wasn't something I could judge, but it was a cute little place with only a few indoor tables and a few more outside. At this stage in my life, I'm so out of touch with "cool" that I really can't tell if something is or not. So, either this was a cool, hip little joint, or it was a bit of a dirt hole. I didn't care all that much though, because I was famished. And besides, I'm not one to talk. Have you seen my house?

"What's good here?" I asked as I searched the menu, unable to choose between the blueberry and strawberry. When my eyes hit the croissants, I held back a snicker. God, I'm such a damn American.

"You asked for crepes, so I bring you to crepes. Order whatever you see… is délicieux."

"What are you having?" In instances like this, where I find myself unable to decide on what to order, I've found it's best to let someone else order first. Then you order whatever they're having, or maybe the alternate version. I figured if she chose strawberry, I'd go with blueberry. Easy enough.

"I am having waffles." She took her cell phone from her pocket and began to scroll through it, leaving me to make this important decision on my own.

Before I could make up my mind, a young waitress stopped by our table. Dressed casually in jeans and a white button-up shirt, she addressed the two of us, briefly making eye contact with me before I smiled and she looked away.

"Bonjour. Vous voulez un café ?" she asked.

"Il ne parle pas français." Sofi nodded in my direction, not bothering to take her eyes from her phone.

"I speak coffee," I replied, gruffly. "Yes, I'd like un café, por favor."

Sofi groaned. "Just tell her what you want to eat… and try not to speak any more French."

I still hadn't decided which kind of crepe I should order, and the decision was driving me mad. For all I knew, this was the only time I'd ever get the chance to eat a real crepe in Paris. With a pack of vampires tracking us down, God knows *how*, the likelihood of seeing another morning was becoming slimmer and slimmer. Yes, if they killed me, I would probably just come back. But what if they didn't kill me? What if one of them *turned* me? Then I'd still be some version of undead, but now with the added complexity of becoming deathly allergic to sunlight. That meant nothing but night-time food from here on out. Maybe they had a Waffle House around here, or some other restaurant that serves breakfast all day and all night … but I didn't know for certain. And Waffle House doesn't serve crepes. I'd be stuck eating waffles.

Jesus, I wouldn't even be eating waffles. I'd be drinking blood. Forever. How the hell do vampires do it? I make lasagna and I have a hard time eating the leftovers the next day, I'm already so sick of it. But the same thing every day? For eternity? It's like being a dog or cat, every day eating the same old chow. At least a dog gets to *die* someday.

"Blueberry crepes," I answered.

"Et vous… ?"

"Waffles. And scrambled eggs. And orange juice."

"Un café, no?"

"Oui, un café aussi."

"I can't tell if French girls are all gorgeous, or if the accent just tricks me into thinking you are," I muttered, as I watched her walked away.

"We are all gorgeous," Sofi replied, as she set her phone on the table and waved away my comment with a brush of her hand. "But I am not interested."

For a while there, we didn't talk. With this first bit of calm we'd had since our meeting, I think we both realized we didn't know the first thing about one another. Let alone why we were working together or what our goals were. Sure, I knew I wanted to save Nancy, and she wanted to save Cami, but by this point neither really had much of a chance for a happy ending. Days had passed, and if there was one thing I've learned through my time hunting them down, monsters don't tend to keep things alive for very long. At least not without a purpose. Given the disasters we'd encountered so far, these vampires we'd come across weren't much different. The thing that gave me hope, though, was we still hadn't found either body. So between that twinkle of a chance to save the day and the opportunity to spend some time with a pretty French girl (even if she didn't seem to be all that interested in me, other than for thoroughly utilitarian and selfish reasons), there was enough in my mind to keep on going. Besides, I didn't have the heart to tell her, her sister was probably drained and rotting in some ditch somewhere.

"So, where do we start our search?" Sofi asked. I'd been wondering the same thing.

"I think the first thing we need to do is regroup here and figure out what we know so far. Then go from there. Follow the clues."

"I thought you were a monster hunter. You did not tell me you are a detective as well." Her lip curled up at the edge as she spoke—a slight grin of amusement. I'd seen it before—plenty of times. And no matter how many times I've seen it, it still pisses me off. No one takes monster-hunting seriously these days.

"You can't hunt unless you know where your prey is. To do that, you need to track it. Unlike what you might have been expecting, there's a lot of work that goes into tracking down monsters. They generally don't like to be seen."

"I feel they are doing just fine coming to us so far," she answered. "We have not had to search for them. They have been hunting us."

"And there's the biggest clue," I replied. "Some of this is following standard vampire protocol, but not everything. Missing people, massacres in the dark, even a familiar who's hunting down livestock for his masters—that's normal. But the ones that came to your apartment. That was new. And the fact you didn't even invite them in, but still, they could enter. Also new. Something about this is important and we need to figure it out."

"It is like an episode of Scooby-Doo," said Sofi. "Or a comic book. *World's Greatest Detective.* Are you the world's greatest detective, Phoenix? Are you Batman?"

"You need to take this seriously, Sofi. Your sister needs you. And I will help you. But first you have to understand this is all very real and although you may have just met me, you need to trust me."

"I trust you," Sofi laughed. "But it is all so fantastic. Tell me, how does someone become a "monster hunter?" Did you go to monster hunter school?"

I didn't want to delve into my history. But if I wanted her to understand what all this was about … if I wanted her to *truly* trust me … I needed to tell her. Tell her what it takes to be a monster hunter. Tell her what it takes to put your life on the line. Tell her what it was like the first time I sacrificed myself for someone else … not knowing then that a sacrifice was something I could come back from.

CHAPTER TEN

I didn't start my life as a monster hunter. Though I suppose no one does, assuming there even are others out there like me. I wanted to be a veterinarian. Maybe a zoologist. Something with animals, I knew that much. And when I was in my senior year of high school, that was my plan. Focus on science and biology, earn as many early college credits as I could, then head off to some university and get my degree. A lot of this stemmed from the time I spent outside as a kid, I think.

My sister and I, we would while away the hours out in the woods around our house. A lot of that time was spent climbing trees, but we'd head on over to the creek that ran through plenty often, usually with our nets and a few buckets so we could go scoop up some frogs or tadpoles. Maybe a few crawdads if we could find them. But that was all when I was younger—before we lost Belinda. After that, after she disappeared, I didn't spend much time out in the woods. My mom said they were full of haints, and that's what happened to Belinda. Dad wasn't as superstitious. Nonetheless, he preferred I stay close to the house too. And I did—for a few years, at least. As I aged on and the memory of Belinda turned from an open wound to a patch of scar tissue, I started venturing back out there into the forest, and I was soon reminded why I loved it so much.

Eventually, time in the woods behind our house wasn't enough. I needed to spend more time outdoors, exploring and discovering life that maybe wasn't as common as close to the city as we lived. It was about that time I started heading out to my dad's hunting shack, spending weekends out there even when it wasn't hunting season, just myself and nature, getting to know one another.

Off a few miles to the east of Dad's shack, the land joined up with a national forest. Over time I got to know the few miles surrounding the cabin and would start venturing further and further east, into those woods, which went on for hundreds of square miles. Occasionally, I'd come across another hiker, though it was fairly uncommon. Mostly I communed with nature and started to learn all about her and the creatures that dwelled within. I'd gotten to the point where tracking any sort of reasonably-sized animal was second nature, I could name pretty much any bird from its call and how to set up a little campsite in under five minutes. While the other kids in school went out on dates, I spent my Saturdays alone in the woods, with a patch of stars and the hooting of owls my only company.

One of those Saturdays, I found myself miles from home as the sun started to come down and decided to set up camp. I identified a little place high enough up off the swampy areas that I wouldn't have to worry about a gator coming through and snacking on me while I slept, lit a campfire and read some Faulkner by firelight. Just as I was beginning to doze off, a swishing in the brush woke me.

Now, I'd spent a lot of time in the woods, and I'd heard a lot of different creatures rustling around at night. And this wasn't like anything I'd heard before. Too loud to be a raccoon or a deer, I assumed it was probably a black bear. I'd run across a few over the years. But they tended to stick mostly to themselves, and I'd never heard one make the ruckus this thing was making. Not much was visible outside the low glow of the dying fire, and I hesitated to do it, but I brought out my big flashlight and started to sweep the clearing around me. The last thing I needed was to deal with some bear wanting to root through my bags to gobble up whatever food it could find. But as the beam of my light caught the thicket of brush to my left where the sound had come from, the noises stopped. The branches shuffled lightly, still agitated from whatever lay just beyond my vision. After a minute or two of silence, I assumed whatever it was had gone back off into the woods. But before crawling back into my sleeping bag, I decided to give one final sweep of the area, to be sure.

And that's when I laid my peepers on it. To my left now, instead of my right, it had circled me silently. And when I first saw it, I had no idea what it was. Just a pair of big red eyes staring at me from inside the brush line. As I held my light in its direction, the eyes rose to what must have been seven feet in the air, and a terrible howl like some mix between a bobcat and a wolf tore from its lips. Then it sprang at me.

As it bounded across the clearing, I had no time to think, let alone take in what I was seeing. All I did was react. As much as I didn't like the idea of killing animals, I was no idiot. I knew what kinds of things lived out there in the woods … or at least I thought I did. Every time I ventured out, I made sure to bring my gun with me. Thankfully my father took hunting seriously, as he did self-protection—especially after the incident with Belinda. So, he trained me the best he could. Out back behind our house, he taught me how to use and handle a gun. And though it would probably be frowned upon these days, on my sixteenth birthday, he gave me a handgun of my very own. I'd already had a few guns for hunting—it was how he and I had originally bonded as I crept into manhood. But those, he argued, were for shooting things when you were the hunter. A handgun, that was for when you needed to protect yourself. I'd never fired it at a living thing before, but that night all my time with Dad paid off and I had it out of its holster and in my hand, its barrel aimed straight at the ferocious, snarling snout of this demon. Before it had closed half the distance between its hiding place and where I stood, I fired. Where I hit it, I didn't know, but I did hit it. That bullet found home somewhere on the beast and pissed it off something fierce. I followed with a second shot, this one likely catching it in its shoulder, though I couldn't be sure as it didn't run like a bear or a wolf, but more like the swinging lope of a gorilla. That second shot was enough to force it to think again, and before I managed to get a decent look at it, it darted off into the woods.

In the dark of night, it would be impossible to track the thing. But I knew I hadn't killed it, at least not outright. So, I spent the rest of the night on guard, stoking the fire with as much wood as I could to light up the space and keep it or any other potential predators at bay. At first light, I packed up and began to track it.

Breakfast consisted of nothing more than a nutrition bar and a few gulps what remained of the cold coffee in my red and white striped thermos straight out of *The Jerk*. I knew I should be more hydrated, and coffee wasn't the best thing to be filling up on before I headed out on my trek, but the sleepless night wore me down. While the caffeine did its magic, I packed up what was left of my campsite, tucked it away in my backpack, and prepared to head out.

Rather than go off straight into the woods in search of the beast's trail, I first took a few minutes to survey the campsite. A spray of blood marked the tree line where the creature had run off, but before that break in the undergrowth, I found what I was searching for: a set of footprints. Now I'd tracked a lot of animals over the years, and I'd come across the prints of countless others. My field guide to the wildlife of Mississippi had worn out long ago, ultimately finding retirement in a swamp where I'd plucked it out to try to identify a snake I hadn't come across before. But by then, I'd already marked off every other creature and print in its well-worn pages. The common creatures I knew by heart and could sketch the prints straight out of memory if needed. The others I'd at least recognize and have a respectable guess as to which they were. One thing was certain though, if it had paws or claws and lived in Mississippi, I'd recognize the print.

I didn't recognize these prints.

CHAPTER ELEVEN

The night before, when the creature tore across the clearing at me, I couldn't place what it was. And now, I still couldn't. Too big to be a wolf and too … humanlike … to be a bear, the only thing I could compare them to was a cast I'd once seen of a gorilla's print. And alongside the prints, spread out evenly between each set, another set of prints spaced farther apart … but less prints than indentations. Upon closer inspection, they took on the shape of four symmetrical lines each, with a separate impression slightly offset toward the creature's center. I assumed they were the creature's front paws or knuckles, which it had been using to bound itself forward, again like an ape.

Now I don't know how much you know about the wildlife of the south. Or even of North America. But we don't have apes. A few monkeys down in Central America. But apes? Big ones? Not unless they escaped from the zoo. And besides, I've seen enough documentaries to recognize a gorilla or a chimpanzee … and even if I didn't get a proper view of it as it came at me, I still knew this wasn't either of those.

Curiosity, as they say, got the best of me. I had to find this thing.

I slung my backpack over my shoulders and returned to the break in the trees where the creature had run off. Blood marked the leaves dotting a growth of shoulder-height young oaks, their branches cracked and broken where the thing had pushed through in its escape the previous night. This was the place to start. And given the hurry in which it had run off, along with the fact I'd injured it, following its trail was much easier than I would have thought.

But then again, with something this big and this prone to attack, maybe it didn't worry much about keeping itself hidden. When you're the one at the top of the food chain, unless you're the one hunting, why bother?

I followed the trail for about a mile before it hit a stopping point at the edge of a creek running through a rocky ravine. The opposite side of the creek spread out into a wide stone-covered expanse, likely remnants from a time when the creek had been a much larger river, or the wash where the water rose up to in times of flood. Very little grew on the stony plain, making it extremely difficult to see exactly where the creature had run off to. So far it had traveled in a fairly straight line though, so while it could have taken to the water to hide its trail, I thought it best to cross the stream and assume the trail went on in a line from where it left off.

As I neared the edge where the empty riverbed rose to earthly land, a horrible, rotten odor began to permeate the air. With each step forward, the scent became stronger, until it filled the air so thoroughly, I could taste it. Swarms of flies rose from the forest's edge, where the sun fell to shadow, making the darkness swell and squirm as if it were itself, alive. I considered turning back, the smell was so strong. Maybe find another way around. But glancing back across the creek to where I'd come from, this was indeed a straight line connecting the end of the creature's trail to the place where it had likely continued. I stepped gingerly, careful not to lose my foot in a pile of dung or the rotting corpse of a dead animal.

Just as I was about to cross the barrier into the brush again, I stopped my foot short, narrowly avoiding placing it directly onto the decaying remains of a human hand.

I should have turned back then. Should have gone and found some help. Some kind of authority. Maybe a park ranger. Or the police. Or the army. But I was young full of stupidity misinterpreted as bravery, so I continued into the trees, careful with each step not to land on some other piece of human remains.

When I entered the dense brush, it took a few seconds for my eyes to accustom themselves to the lack of sunlight. But once they did, I became all-too-aware of what I'd come across. Scattered amongst the trees and branches were chunks of what could only be disemboweled humans. Intestines draped from the branches like macabre moss—strips and scraps of clothing caught in the lower branches like birthday streamers. And all around me, the leaves were stained dark with drying blood. Another step forward and a murder of crows erupted from the thicket. As they flew off, an eyeball dropped from a beak and landed with a sickening plop on my boot.

This was the way the beast had come, though this mess wasn't from the night before. Whenever this had happened, it had been several days at least. From the bits of fabric I could identify, it seemed to be the remains of some hikers or campers.

Very little in terms of supplies, other than the shredded remnants of a tent a few yards further in.

I again contemplated my options. Did I press on? Find whatever did this and pump a few more bullets in it and put it down? Or was I in over my head? Would my handgun do any damage to this beast? If the night before was any indication, it'd at least give it a new hole or two. But take it down? Either I needed to go back to the cabin and grab something more powerful, or I had to report this and bring in someone much better equipped.

A shrill scream like that of a woman or child tore through the air, piercing my eardrums and making the decision for me. I would do neither. Someone up there needed help … and they needed it *now*.

Through the brush and thicket, I ran, part of me hoping to hear the cry again to offer some guidance and assurance I continued in the right direction … the other part of me wishing for pure dead silence. Not hearing it would mean whatever was about to happen had happened. It would mean I could still turn around, go back to my cabin, and do my best to forget about everything I'd seen and heard. Unfortunately, it would also mean whoever let out that scream had likely seen the last of his or her days, and I'd failed to do a damn thing to stop it.

As I continued, low branches and rough twigs scraped at my arms and tearing rips in my jeans until finally, I spotted the tell-tale signs of the thing's blood trail. The massacre I'd come across earlier had already started to fade over several days' worth of decay, and I feared I'd gotten off the recent trail by being distracted by the remnants of its previous kill. But these spatters of blood, some still sticky where the sun hadn't had a chance to break through the leafy canopy and dry them, they encouraged me to keep moving on. Bounding over fallen logs and splashing through mucky puddles, I discarded any concern I might have had earlier for the more common threats of these southern woods, like cottonmouths, rattlers or the stray gator, and pushed onward. Another cry broke through the air, sending up a murder of crows from the tops of trees some twenty yards ahead.

So, on I went, though my legs throbbed, and my chest burned. Onward in the direction of the deathly shriek. Onward along the leafy path dotted with freshly spilled blood.

I almost ran into it before seeing it, it was hidden so well behind a thicket of brush. Luckily, I noticed the cave entrance in time to duck low enough to not catch my head on the upper stone of its entrance. The trail led here. Into this crack in the earth, filled with nothing but black silence and the unmistakable stink of death.

CHAPTER TWELVE

I dared not enter. Even as a teenager, I knew better than that. Memories of a book my mother read to me as a child, where a family went off on an adventure through fields and rivers and woods until they finally found a cave ... where they went "tiptoe, tiptoe, tiptoe" into that cave ... and found the monstrous beast they'd flippantly set out to find, returned to me. A pair of furry ears ... a big wet nose. A chase back home. All the while pursued by the beast until I could hide away under my covers, safe as it lumbered back into the wilderness. *I'm never going on a monster hunt again,* I'd whisper to myself.

But that scream. And what I'd seen. Last night's encounter and the death and dismemberment this morning. None of that could be ignored. Not at this final moment. Not when I could finally do *something*. Something I felt, deep inside, that I was *meant to do.*

So, with my right, I took the trusty six-shooter from its holster and held it before me, while with my left I pointed the beam of my trusty flashlight into the dark, cavernous maw the creature likely called home.

Tiptoe, tiptoe, tiptoe I crept. Silent, but painfully aware that even if my footsteps remained hidden, the glare of my light would give me away well beforehand. I considered switching it off and stowing it in my backpack, going on further into the cave, relying on my other senses to guide me. This, however, I knew to be foolish, as I was just as likely to trip over a fallen stone and announce my presence, thereby negating any advantage the darkness would give me. Besides, anything in here was bound to have keener senses of sight, hearing, and smell than a lowly human such as I. Any chance of creeping up on a bear, wolf, or murderous gorilla, was nonexistent. I could only hope to catch it either asleep or otherwise *occupied.*

I continued onward, further into the cave until eventually, I lost complete sight of the entrance through which I'd come. Roots dangled from the ceiling like strands of witches' hair. Bugs flitted through the air, lighting gently on my face and arms, careful to disguise their eagerness to find out of if I were some manner of snack. I envisioned nests of brown recluses above, the deadly little arachnids waiting until I stepped below at the right place so they could drop down onto my neck and bite me—just because they could.

Another scream rang out, this time horribly close. The walls seemed to tremble under its echo. My goal lay close ahead.

I'd like to say there was a big faceoff. Some huge battle as I pitted myself majestically against this foreign beast. I'd like to … but I'd be lying. Instead, I turned a corner in the cave, and the creature knew I was coming well before I saw it. Crouched low, it waited for me to appear following the reckless beam of my flashlight. And as soon as I was in view, it pounced—or, rather, sprang, at me. Lips peeled back in a snarl of hot breath and putrid teeth, it attacked. Before I could react, the beast was on me, its wicked jaws snapping at my face, trying to rip my face to shreds then gobble me up like it had the campers in the woods.

Snapping and growling like Old Yeller in a tantrum, I held it back for only a few seconds before it finally overpowered me, sunk its teeth into my throat and ripped my jugular from my neck. In those final moments, I managed to fire my remaining bullets into its hide. Its dead body collapsed onto me, and I bled out on the floor and passed from this world to someplace altogether different.

Some people talk about how they hover over their bodies when they're dead, in some out-of-body experience. Their souls kind of floating there while they make the decision to either head up into the light or go back down into their bodies and stick around a bit longer. That's not at all how it works though. At least not for me.

For me, when I die, I just kind of stop being here and end up somewhere else. A dark place that's here, but also not here. Another plane of existence parallel to our own. It's where true darkness lives, and I think it's the place where souls go when they're lost. When you see a ghost, what you're really seeing is one of those souls breaking through the layer of Eitherspace into our reality. But they never quite break through all the way … that's why they appear so ethereal.

Me, on the other hand, I do come back all the way. Somehow, I'm able to do it. My soul goes off into wherever the hell souls go to when they don't go anywhere else—where they go when they're stuck in the almost here. The difference is, I can come right on back. That's what I did in your apartment … and why I begged you to let me die. I know you meant well, but all you really did was make me suffer. And it sucked.

So next time, when I ask you to let me die, just let me die. Okay?

And if I tell you to kill me … you don't hesitate to put a bullet in my head. My brains'll blow out, and it'll make a goddamn horrible mess. But I'll be back.

Like I said, I always come back.

CHAPTER THIRTEEN

"What was it?" Sofi asked. She still hadn't touched her breakfast, and from the look on her face, I didn't think she ever would. "Did you find out what the monster was? What was the screaming? How did you get away?"

"Stories for another time, my dear. Now you know enough about me. Enough at least to have a bit of an idea of what you're getting in to. It's time for you to tell me what I am getting into. I could just as easily do the rest of my job alone. In fact, I could do it much better alone." I finished off my coffee and reached to my pocket for a cigarette, realized I had none, and eyeballed Sofi.

"There is no smoking here, Phoenix," she said dryly. "You are a strange fuck of a man, and I have nothing to tell you that is "special" about me. I wanted to be a model, but I am not. Or not yet. There are many beautiful women in Paris. So, I do what I do, and what that is, is no concern of yours. What you must know is that I am coming with you. It is my sister we are after—"

I cut her off right there. "Now get this straight, little lady. I'm not after your sister. I'm after Nancy, and I'm after whoever these bastards are who took her. Turns out they took your sister too, so if we find her, we'll save her. But she's not my top priority."

"No, she *is* top priority," she said, clutching her butter knife in her hand. "We will save her, and you are going to help me. I helped you, and I will continue to help you."

"All you did was knock me over the head, tie me in a chair, get me stabbed, pump me up with drugs, and extend my suffering until I died." I squeezed my coffee cup so hard it cracked. "You didn't help me a damn bit."

"You will be quiet now and listen to me," she scolded. "I have a friend. A friend here in town. I send a photo of this." She reached into the bag and removed the talisman we recovered from the dead man in the catacombs. "My friend may know what it is. But we must bring it so it can be examined."

"A friend of *yours* is a specialist in supernatural artifacts?" I asked incredulously.

"Yes. A friend. One you have not killed yet. And you will trust me to go there. He will help."

"You're full of shit," I said.

"I am full of nothing. Who did you think I was texting here while you were figuring out what crepe is best? Now you will sit there and let me eat my waffles. Then we will go see my friend."

I almost stormed out of the restaurant then and there, but somehow managed to keep my cool. All my life I'd been doing this thing alone. Some research online and some time spent in chat groups and subreddits, along with plenty of lessons from boots-on-the-ground experience had taught me quite a lot about hunting monsters. And none of it taught me to go make friends. A lot of the times I saved people. But never when someone was with me. Saving people was one thing—without my interference, they'd probably be monster chow. Having a partner or a sidekick was out of the question. This lone wolf hunted alone.

But that amulet. And all those bodies down in the catacombs. How that dapper vamp tracked us down ... and turned Sofi's drug dealer. How the hell they got into the apartment uninvited. I was wrong. *None* of this was following standard vampire protocol. Besides, other than lodging a bullet in my head and taking the Eitherspace Express back home in defeat, I had no idea where to go next or what to do.

A few more hours in Paris couldn't hurt. Worst-case scenario, I'd have the chance to eat a few baguettes and snarf down some escargot. Maybe see the Eiffel Tower or take in The Louvre. A little bit of culture.

I interlocked my fingers behind my head, leaned back, and watched as Sofi tucked into her plate of waffles. She was very pretty, I had to admit. I could see her being a model. As she delicately chewed each bite, my mind wandered back to the city of lights and what I should try to take in before finally heading back home to my daily life of dogcatcher and raccoon patrolman.

Of course, I never got to do any of my planned sightseeing. Because soon after, shit got even worse.

CHAPTER FOURTEEN

On our way to meet with her friend, we took some time passing the amber artifact back and forth between us, scrutinizing it closely for any indication of what the thing might be. The murderous familiar had kept it close, and it sure as hell looked old. But other than some carvings of characters I couldn't recognize—possibly Egyptian--there was nothing all that spectacular about the thing. Just a chunk of amber about the size of a golf ball lodged in a larger piece of brass or copper on a similarly constructed chain. At first, I'd thought the housing had been made of gold, but that had been under the poor lighting of the catacombs. Now, out in daylight, it still shone and sparkled some, but there was a dullness below the sheen, and the spaces deep in the crevices of the carving had tarnished considerably with age.

"Do you think it is magic?" Sofi asked.

"Could be. Though it sure doesn't seem very magical."

"It looks like a piece of junk."

"Yeah, it does," I conceded. "But I still think it's important. Funny as it sounds, I think this is whatever they were after when they came to your apartment."

"They asked for Donal. I think he is what they wanted. Not this hunk of garbage."

"I think Donal was the name of the guy I killed," I replied.

"You mean, I killed."

"You, me, whatever. He's dead, and we took this thing from him. Maybe they were looking for him because they thought he'd have it?"

"But why would they think he is in my apartment? I do not think anyone followed us."

"No, you're right." I conceded. "I don't think anyone followed us. At least not while we were down in the catacombs. Maybe they tracked you after we got out though. I was pretty delirious at the time."

"I am a beautiful woman living in Paris. I have learned to recognize when I am being followed. Otherwise, I would be a beautiful dead woman in Paris. There was no one following us. I would have known."

She had a point there. Paris, I'd already discovered, wasn't much different from any other city. Sure, it was beautiful and held tremendous history, but the same people filled the streets here as any other major metropolitan area. Unless you were in a tourist spot, the place didn't look all that safe. And to be honest, I couldn't even say the tourist spots were very safe-looking since I still hadn't had the chance to check any of them out.

"Maybe it's magic."

"It is ugly magic."

"Maybe that's part of its charm," I paused, waiting for a laugh, or a groan. "Charm. Get it?"

"I get it. But I do not want it," she replied, tucking the amulet back into her bag. "There is our destination. You will follow me, and you will not speak French. I will take care of us."

I grunted in dissatisfied agreeance and followed her through the front doors of Musée des Arts et Métiers. As we first entered, I had to admit I was a bit underwhelmed. For such a fancy name, I honestly expected a bit more. Especially given the grandeur of the stone architecture of the building's exterior. Instead of opulence, we were met with a bit of surprising modernity. Bold red display cases dotted the far wall of the front entrance, meeting up with a cherry-bomb-red information desk, marked clearly in English as *Information*, and the gift shop.

"So, do we wait? Or—"

Before I could finish speaking, a mouse of a man scurried our way between the security gates separating the entrance to the gift shop from what I assumed was the museum, proper. Dressed in an ill-fitting tweed suit with a pair of full-moon glasses perched on the tip of his nose, he couldn't have been more of a stereotype museum curator if I'd made him up myself.

"Bonjour, Sofi!" he exclaimed and leaned in to give her a small kiss on the cheek.

"Hello, Ralph. It is good to see you again."

"Ah, we are speaking English!" he exclaimed, then turned to behold me as if he hadn't noticed me standing beside her when he first came over to greet us. "Who is your friend? American?"

"Phoenix," I replied. "Phoenix Bones."

"Ah, it is excellent to make your acquaintance Monsieur... Bones. We do not get many Americans here at Musée des Arts et Métiers. They seem to prefer The Louvre and our Eiffel

Tower. So happy to greet you. Though you may find you are one of the few "bones" in our museum today."

"And why is that? Are they on loan?"

"No, no, no, Monsieur," he replied, nodding his head vigorously. "Surely Mademoiselle has told you? We are a museum of art and science!"

I turned and glared at Sofi, disappointed she'd bring me to an art museum. We needed a real museum. With real curators and experts. Not someone who liked to gawk at pretty pictures.

"So, you're an expert on vampires?"

"Moi? No. I am no expert. I am only a student of scientific history. I research and catalog older scientific instruments, like the calculators we have of Monsieur Pascal or our wonderful astrolabes and telescopes," he replied. "I am a friend of Sofi, but I do not know anything about your *vampires.*"

"Why the hell'd you bring me here, Sofi? I thought you said your friend could help us."

"My friend can help us. But not this friend. I have many friends," she replied. "Ralph, can you take us to see Rousseau?"

"But of course!" Ralph turned and started off back through the security gates and into the museum. "Pas de problème. Ils sont avec moi," he said to the woman behind the information desk.

Sofi and I followed closely. And as soon as we left the gift shop and entered the museum, I finally saw what all the fuss was about—and why we were here.

As we snaked our ways through the hallways, I became aware this was unlike any museum I'd been to before. No dinosaur bones or sarcophagi or collections of ancient weapons.

But also, not an art museum, at least not in the traditional sense. Instead, this museum more closely represented a steampunk fever dream. Various items from throughout our technological history sat safely encased in glass, but rather than purely historical artifacts, these items all possessed a deeper beauty inherent in their design. Early model cameras, vintage typewriters, printing presses and looms marked the more recent progressions in our civilization's technology, while beautiful brass astrolabes and telescopes and calculators marked our earlier days. These, juxtaposed with more modern advances such as a moon rover and even a DVD player showcased how far we'd come in such little time. As we passed a full recreation of a late 18th-century chemist's laboratory, I found myself pausing to explore the details—only to be rushed along by Ralph on his hurried trot to Rousseau's office.

While truly a remarkable collection, what struck me most was the innate beauty each of these objects possessed. More than pure function, they were built with an eye toward aesthetics that imbued more value in these items than their pure utilitarian qualities—something possibly lacking in our culture today, though perhaps renewed through the devices companies like Apple had built their modern empires around.

Even the museum itself felt much different than any other museum I'd visited. No dark, dusty hallways. But also no modern blank minimalist chic. These spaces were open and filled with light, but built primarily around core elements such as stone, plaster, natural wood, and industrial metals. With each corner we turned, I expected to discover one of Da Vinci's famous machines, as they would not be out of place in this collection of curiosities.

As we made our way through the various exhibits, Ralph and Sofi chattered on in French. Clearly, the two were old friends, but nothing more. They'd exchanged kisses earlier, true. But only in greeting. The fact I kept peeking back to them to see if anything more than a friendship existed, something I could perhaps pick up in their body language if I couldn't understand their actual language, gave me pause. The girl was considerably younger than me ... and remarkably beautiful. Despite the sturdy exterior walls she'd erected between her and I, it was clear she possessed much more love and empathy than she cared to let on. She could have let me die down there in the catacombs—not that it would have mattered to me—but she didn't. Yes, I brought value to her. Or at least hope. But seeing her with her friend, those walls were nonexistent.

Eventually, our tour took us to a closed doorway which required Ralph's keycard to open. He held the door open and we passed out of the main exhibits, into a plain narrow hallway marked with closed doors. "She is down there, Sofi. You know the room."

"Merci, Ralph," Sofi replied. "À la prochaine."

And with that, the door swung closed behind us, and we were once again, alone.

"Friend of yours?" I asked.

"Yes. A friend for many years. Since children."

"But he's not who we're here to see?"

"No. He is a smart man, but he does not know what we are asking. Rousseau. Rousseau will know."

"How can you be so sure about that? This place is remarkable, but it's also not quite the same type of collection I'd expect to have curators who are experts in the occult or paranormal. This is all… science."

"Do you truly believe there is a world beyond science, Phoenix? Maybe what you think is magic is science you do not yet understand." Sofi took my hand in hers and pulled me along behind her as she continued down the hallway. At the third door on the right, she stopped, rapped her knuckles loudly on the door, and entered.

Loud rock music blared through the room at such a volume I doubted Sofi's knock had even been heard. In sharp contrast to the rest of the museum, this room was dark, aside from a single lamp perched on a desk. Between us and the desk, crouched over an array of brass and gold instruments in one state of disassembly or another, sat a silhouetted figure.

Sofi put her finger to her lips, smiled, and crept forward. Why she felt the need to be quiet in this racket was beyond me since I don't think anyone could have heard an elephant fart in all this noise. But she tiptoed forward until she stood mere inches from the stranger I assumed to be Rousseau, leaned in close to the person's right ear, and shouted, "Boo!"

The figure leaped from its seat, clutching a screwdriver like a knife, and revealed the closest thing to a mad scientist I'd ever come across in my life. Dressed in a dirtied white lab coat, she stood about six feet tall, though a few inches of that were disorganized tousles of bleached blonde hair that shot out in every direction—much like Einstein in the famous photo with his tongue sticking out. Unlike Einstein, however, she appeared to be much younger—likely in her mid-30s, though it was difficult to get an immediate gauge with the pair of magnifying goggles strapped to her head. They gave the appearance of bug-eyes when she blinked I half-expected to see one set of eyelids close over the other. Of course, they did nothing of the sort, and once she removed them from her face, the aura of mad scientist diminished a bit. But still not much.

"Sofi!" she shrieked, and the two exchanged a quick hug. "Are you hurt? Let me get a look at you."

"Not hurt. But definitely shaken. Back at the flat, there was such violence. But I am safe."

"And you," Rosseau continued, now speaking to me, "I suppose you are to blame for the danger of my poor Sofi?"

"Sorry, ma'am, but I had nothing to do with it. All I did was save her life."

"After I saved yours," Sofi interjected.

"That's… debatable," I resisted the urge to explain to her again how my whole *dying isn't that bad* thing worked and instead addressed Rousseau. "Sofi tells me you're an expert in the supernatural. We were hoping you could help us crack a little riddle we have."

Rousseau rolled her eyes at Sofi and replied, "I am no such thing. I am a scientist. But I do know about things others do not. Such things that the science in our books does not attempt to describe, for fear of ridicule."

"So, you're a supernatural scientist," I replied.

"You do not understand me," she paused. "What was your name again? I seem to have forgotten it."

"Phoenix Bones, ma'am. And we don't have time for idle chat. Either you can help us or you can't."

Sofi let out a little huff and glared at me. "When I sent you the photographs, you said you might be able to help."

"Might? I thought you said she was an expert! If you dragged me here on a *might,* then we're wasting our time."

"Do you have a better idea?" asked Rousseau. "Some other plan to find your... what did you call them, Sofi? Vampires?"

Sofi nodded, and Rousseau continued, "There is more to reality than what you might think, Mr. Bones. Much more."

"Trust me, I already know."

"What you do not understand are the complexities. Sofi tells me you are some sort of... *chasseur de monstre.*"

"You mean monster hunter? Only in my spare time. My day job is much less glamorous."

"What if I told you there are others in the world who also hunt monsters? What if I told you there are many, many bad things out there you do not know of, and there are people not so different from you who are charged with keeping them at bay?"

"I'd say I'm not surprised. Not that I've come across any... but I've seen enough evil I can't explain to think that at least a few others might have had the genius idea to hunt these bastards down."

"That is oversimplifying things, my dear *monsieur.* These creatures may be different from us, but that does not make them inherently evil. To say they are *bastards to hunt down* is the thought of the bourgeoisie." She stepped around to the back of her desk and gestured to a pair of metal folding chairs in front. "Please, take a seat. We have much to talk about."

Half of me wanted to head for the door and leave this bullshit behind. But she was right. I had nowhere else to go. No wallet, no credit cards, no identification. The best I could do was take my gun from Sofi's bag, head off down the hallway in search of a broom closet, and blow my brains out so I could take the Eitherspace express back to my shitty old house in Mississippi. Problem was that wouldn't save Nancy … if she could even be saved anymore. Wouldn't do a damn thing to help Sofi's sister either. And for all I knew, these abductions would continue. Even without their Donal out there snatching people from their homes, unencumbered by the "you must ask permission" clause the vampires were somehow forced to abide by (except for at Sofi's…) they'd find a way to continue. Maybe by exposing themselves more than they cared to, or maybe just by finding some other vampire-wannabe to enlist as their next intern familiar.

I scraped the chair across the hardwood floor and took a seat next to Sofi.

"Can we get some goddamn lights on in here at least?" I asked. "It's like we're back in the catacombs."

"Ah yes, the catacombs. That is where you found the… specimen?"

"And where they took my sister. And where we found a pile of dead bodies. And where I killed a killer. And where this guy," Sofi pointed at me, "managed to burst into a ball of flames and live to talk about it."

"You have to admit I do look pretty sexy for a guy who recently burned to death."

"And died from a stab wound on my couch," Sofi added.

"I'm still not convinced I died from the stab wound," I replied. "I'm starting to think that cocktail you gave me might have been the real culprit there."

"You would have died without it."

I died with it, I thought. And as the memories of agony in Sofi's apartment came back to me, so did the stabbing ache in my gut. "Do you have any more of those pills? The pain's back."

While Sofi searched through the bag, Rousseau spoke again. "How is Paul? I have not heard a word from him in several days. The last we spoke, he told me he was helping you with a problem." She paused for a moment and glared at me. "I assume Mr. Bones here was the problem."

Sofi handed me a pill. As I swallowed it down, she answered Rousseau's question. "Paul is dead."

Rousseau's jaw dropped and her eyes widened nearly as big as they'd first appeared with the magnifying goggles on. "Comment ? Qu'est-ce qui s'est passé ? Une overdose ?"

"No... something much worse. I think he became a vampire. He came to me with a strange man I have never seen before. They came in to and attacked us."

"We staked 'em," I replied. "Boom! Up in flames. Nothing left of them anymore."

"Or of my home."

"Did you let them in, Sofi? Did Paul trick you?"

"No. Nothing like that. Phoenix had just died, and that's when Paul and the other man appeared at my door. If it had been only Paul, I may have let him in, perhaps to help me with the body."

I huffed. Being referred to as "a body" felt insulting. But I left it alone and kept the rest of my commentary to myself.

"If they were vampires, they could not come in without you inviting them first. Everyone knows this, Sofi. So, if they came into your home without an invitation, they could not be vampires."

"Oh, they were vampires alright," I interjected. "As I said, they popped as soon as we shoved some timber through their undead hearts. And they had fangs. So, unless you all are hanging out with the types of people who file down their teeth and have a strange tendency to explode and then spontaneously combust when stabbed, I'm pretty damned sure they were vampires. The thing is, vampires I can handle. I've done it before, and I'm sure I'll do it again. What I can't handle are vampires that don't follow the rules." I reached over, took the bag from Sofi, and retrieved the amulet. "Or who have familiars who carry around weird shit like this thing."

"Ah yes, the charm from the photo. May I see it?"

I looked at Sofi. When she nodded, I placed the amulet on Rousseau's desk beside a half-assembled spyglass and slid it across to her. She took it into her hand, popped her goggles back on, and began to examine it.

"Yes, this definitely appears to be vampiric in origin," she began. "Those markings. They are a manner of cuneiform. Egyptian, I believe. They speak of the goddess Sekhmet—the one often referred to as the first vampire of them all."

"So that thing belongs to an ancient Egyptian goddess?" I asked. "Egypt? Is that where we need to go?

"Highly unlikely," Rousseau replied. "She is likely no more than a myth. And even if she is not and did exist, I find it unlikely she still would today."

"But if she's a vampire, she can live forever. Why wouldn't she still be around?" asked Sofi.

"It's as valuable a lead as any, right?" This journey just became a lot more interesting. The simple idea of facing down an ancient Egyptian goddess piqued my interest. I'd never fought anyone so *historical* before. And a trip to Egypt? Double the fun. Another place I'd never been, and again much better than catching strays or pulling raccoons from attics back home. Besides, how bad could she be?

"Perhaps… but again, unlikely. If this were, in fact, hers, she would not have given it to some familiar. Even if he was responsible for important business. It does, however, explain how the vampires entered Sofi's home. If a vampire's possession is in a place, taken there absent the will of the vampire, it is then assumed the vampire may enter to retrieve its property. No permission is required."

"So, they *were* after the amulet. But how did they know it was there? Some sort of magic?"

"I do not believe in magic, Mr. Bones. I believe in science. To simply "know" where something is would be *natural* psychic ability, and though it is possible your vampires possess a psychic ability, I am not sure that is how they found you. Nonetheless, you are asking the wrong questions. True, this is old. And it is clearly vampiric. But why did your killer have it? What use would a relic be to him? Those are the questions you should be asking."

"Well, do you have the answers? Because I sure as hell don't."

"I am sorry, but I do not. Though now that I have seen this up close, I believe I may know of another who might. May I keep this a bit longer? I would like to examine it closer and make a few calls with some colleagues. It should not take long. In the meantime, you can explore our museum."

I hesitated to answer. The last thing I wanted was to give up the one clue we had, if only for a few minutes. I didn't know this Rousseau, and although Sofi appeared to trust her, she still hadn't won that privilege from me. "Are you sure there's nothing else you can tell us? Maybe give it one more look right now?"

Rousseau sighed but conceded. "Very well. I will inspect it once more if only to assuage your curiosity." She took the amulet back to her eye and inspected it carefully. First the side with the etchings that tied it back to Egypt and that vampire goddess, then to the other side, where Sofi nor I had noticed any markings or other obvious curiosities.

"Now this is curious," she muttered and leaned in closer. She picked up a small screwdriver from the table and began to poke and scrape at the relic's unmarked backside. "Yes, I think I have found something very interesting indeed."

"What? What is it?" asked Sofi as she reached across the table to try and snatch the amulet back.

Rousseau pulled away, and as she did so a small piece of metal broke from the amulet and landed with a soft tinkle on the wood surface of her desk. "I believe I know how they found you."

"How? Some sort of charm? A magic tracker? A blood curse?" I asked.

"Nothing of the sort," Rousseau replied. "That, Mr. Bones, is a GPS tracking chip."

I reached out to pick it up and see for myself, but before my fingers managed to touch the thing, a loud explosion rocked the building.

Rousseau sprang from her seat and took the chip into her hand. "I will destroy this. You two, take the amulet, and get the hell out of here!"

"No, Rousseau, you must come with us."

"As long as they do not see me with the two of you, I will remain safe. You two they will recognize. I am just a person working in a museum. It is you they are after."

"But how will we—"

"Just go!" She dropped the chip back onto the desk and reached for one of the telescopes. Heaving it above her head, she brought it down on to the chip, utterly obliterating it. "They cannot track it now. You are safe with it, but first, you must escape if you want to live! If you want to save your sister!"

Sofi took the amulet and stuffed it back into the bag, and the two of us ran from the room. Once in the hallway, out of the soundproofing of Rousseau's office, screams of terror rang out as another explosion rocked the building and the lights went out, and the red glow of emergency lights kicked in.

CHAPTER FIFTEEN

Even with the lights out, the museum remained well-lit from the light of day streaming in from the many windows. The very idea vampires would attack in broad daylight again went against all the vampire logic I possessed. Either they were desperate, or they'd hired someone else to do their dirty work again. Regardless, from the smoke and the screams choking the hallways, we needed to get the hell out, and quick.

"Do you know the way out of here?" I shouted over the blare of alarms.

"Yes, I have been here many times. Follow me."

And so, I followed. Back through the maze of exhibits, past scores of terrified museum visitors locked in indecision between cowering and escaping. No one dead yet. That was a positive sign. But the screams continued. Some from the visitors we passed, bellowing in fear at the sudden idea of a terrorist attack on the building. But the other screams … the ones from far away corridors, those were screams I recognized all too well … for they were screams of death.

As we neared the front door, my heart sank. The entire entrance had been blown up. Impossible to exit. Scores of bodies scattered bloodied in the rubble, dead from the explosion. More blood and bodies streaked the walls and hallways—a grisly mess of dead people with their throats ripped out.

It was vampires, alright. And we were trapped in here with them.

"How do we get out?" screamed Sofi. "The doors are all blocked."

My eyes darted around the space, searching for another exit. "The windows. We break the windows."

We ran to a wall of windows across the entrance, remarkably unbroken by the explosion. I lifted a chair and hauled back to throw it through the glass when out of the corner a dark shape lunged at us. Dressed in black jeans, a long-sleeved black shirt, black gloves, and a head covered in a black ski mask, all I could make out in his flash of movement was a snarl of razor-sharp teeth through the mouth hole. I shoved Sofi out of the way and dodged the attack.

"The gun, Sofi! Shoot out the window with the gun!"

But it was too late. Two more vampires appeared, seemingly out of nowhere, and began to circle us, snarling. "Give it to us. Give it to us now," they hissed.

"Fat chance, fucko!" I shouted and kicked a chair in their direction. Sofi fired off a shot, catching the one who spoke square in the chest. Even with his ski mask on, I could still see him smile.

"There has to be another way out. Just run, Sofi. Run!"

I admit, at that moment I wished I had the bag in my hand. That I had the amulet and my gun, so I could escape on my own and leave her to them. I could always regroup. Come back later once I'd figured shit out. If one of those bastards got his teeth into me, all my coming back from the dead would be useless. I'd just be a damned vampire when I woke up. I was sure of it. And with nothing on me to fight with, my best chance of survival was to kill myself and run away.

But she had the amulet. And with as little as Rousseau had helped, I still felt it was important. To give it back to these bloodsuckers would be a mistake, and likely one I'd live to regret.

Besides, the girl needed saving.

"I fucking said run, Sofi! Go!"

"I'm not letting you die for me," she shouted back, as the vampires continued to close in.

"I'm not dying for you. That's why I'm telling you to run. Run, and I'll follow, and we'll figure something out. Just not here. Here we're trapped."

Sofi regarded the window again, reconsidering our previous exit strategy. But the vampires now stood between us and it, the bright light of midday streaming through but doing nothing to harm them, shielded by their cover of protective clothing. She then turned and ran, back through the gift shop, and I followed. We hooked a left and passed through a large archway into a room that appeared to be a converted church. Ancient airplanes hung from the ceiling, and a large pendulum swung above a sort of round glass table. A miniature statue of liberty gazed at us from the far end of the room. Behind it, a large red door.

"Down there!" I shouted. "Through the door!"

We bolted down the length of the church, past a series of metal platforms that formed a staircase to the airplanes, past the cutaway of an early automobile and through a series of what looked like old bicycles. As we reached the Statue of Liberty, another loud explosion rocked the building, and the door in front of us blew inward, knocking us back and to the ground. As the smoke cleared, three more black-clad vampires entered and strode menacingly in our direction.

I glanced behind us, hopeful for a means of escape, but the other vampires had followed. We were trapped, and the only direction we could go was up. I surveyed the metal trellises, the ceiling, and the old airplane. Maybe if we could get to it, we could fly out of here. Just need to blow that stained-glass window at the end of the church, and we could fly off to safety. Or at least out of this hornets' nest.

How we were going to blow that window was another question altogether ... and one I didn't have an answer to. At least not yet.

"Follow me!" I shouted to Sofi, and the two of us began to scramble up the metal scaffold. The vampires gave chase, their footfalls landing nearer and nearer with each desperate step forward we took. As we reached the top level, one of them leaped up from the level below and cut us off. I considered throwing Sofi onto the plane and urging her to start it up and escape—to save herself—but now up, close, it was clear the plane was far too large to fit through the window without breaking the wings off first. Besides, what were the chances they kept it fueled? Or if the damned contraption would even fly? I cursed under my breath. We were trapped.

"What happens when a vampire gets caught in sunlight?" Sofi shouted. "Do they burn, like in the movies?"

"They burn, and they explode," I answered. "But these ones are protected. They're safe from the sun."

"Not if you can pull off their masks, they're not."

She had a fair point, but to do so meant close combat with a vampire. And without any sort of weapon, that would be a pretty short fight. Besides, even if I could manage to take care of one, another half-dozen would be right behind him.

"How far can you throw a man?" she asked. "Can you throw him there?" She pointed to the window I'd hoped to escape from.

"I have no idea! I don't generally toss vampires! But if I had to guess, yeah I probably could. At least that small one." I pointed to one of the new vampires who'd recently reached the top of the stairs. Must have been a kid when it turned. Now it was just a blood-sucking monster.

"I have an idea," Sofi shouted. "When I say go, you grab him, rip off his mask, and throw him that way."

I had to give her credit. Even if it was a stupid idea, it was still an idea. And I ran out of those the minute I saw the plane was too big. Still, although I could probably throw the little fucker to the window, I doubted I'd be able to do it with enough force to break through the glass. And the sunlight coming through the decorative display was probably not strong enough to do any real damage to him. Direct sunlight? Yeah, that'd burn him to a crisp and set him off like a miniature nuke. But this? This was stupid.

Still, stupid was better than nothing. And when she shouted "go" I lowered my shoulder and charged. The vamp hadn't been expecting that, and the force of my impact almost sent him flying off the platform, but I grabbed him by his shirt, catching him before he could tumble to the floor below. With my free hand, I snatched the ski mask from his head, narrowly avoiding his fangs as they snapped at my wrist. I let go of the mask, grabbed him with both hands, and tossed him as hard as I could in the direction of the stained-glass window.

An ear-splitting crack rang out behind me, and the glass shattered where the bullet from Sofi's gun hit. A stream of sunlight broke through, catching the flying monstrosity's snarling face. The shock on its face quickly disappeared under a bubbling mass of burning flesh, and a split-second later the whole thing exploded into chunks of seared vampire flesh. The rest of the window shattered outward in thousands of pieces … but we still had no way to escape.

"Phoenix, here! Into the plane!" Sofi urged.

"It won't fit through the opening!" I shouted back.

Sofi looked at me like I was crazy, then to the plane and to the window, finally realizing what I had in mind. "You are stupid if you think this would fly. Besides, we would need a runway. Just jump in. Trust me!"

So far, her plan seemed to be working, but that explosion wouldn't buy us much time other than a few seconds of shock from the vampires. They'd already turned their attention back to us and were again lunging in our direction. I leaped out of the way of their oncoming attack, and onto the wing of the plane. Sofi took the gun, pointed it to the ceiling, and fired once, then again. I winced when I realized she was almost about out of bullets but probably didn't even know it.

"Brace yourself!" she screamed as she shoved the gun back into the bag. "We're going down!"

A piercing screech tore through the cavernous church as the cables, weakened by Sofi's shots, began to stress and break. A few quick judders and the plane plummeted to the ground twenty feet below. It wasn't a soft landing, but it was soft enough that we survived it. But still, the question remained, how the hell were we going to escape?

"Take this and draw them away." Sofi tossed me the bag and ran off to the end of the room where the red door had once stood. "I have a way out, but I need a few minutes!"

"The door is blocked, Sofi! I saw it from above. The explosion, it brought down some stone. We can't get out that way."

"Oui, je sais ! Give me time!"

Before I could respond, one of the vampires dropped down from above, landing between Sofi and me. He took one look at the bag and knew I was the one he needed. I gave him a little smile, then turned and ran. The rear of the old church-turned-museum ended with an area sunken lower than the rest, down a few stone stairs, and straight into a wall. I searched frantically for any place to hide, escape, or otherwise draw them off. But again, I was trapped. A few glass cases dotted the area, but none of them held anything of much use ... a few telescopes, a chunk of old stone, an instrument that looked like some kind of trumpet ... and some odd wooden contraption.

I reached into the bag, took out my old single-action Colt. 45 and checked the chamber. As I expected: only one bullet left. I pointed it at the glass case, turned my face, and fired, shattering the glass. I reached into the case and took the contraption, said a little apology, and smashed it on the floor. From the destruction, I retrieved what I'd been hoping for all this while: a *real* weapon. One of the pieces of wood had broken off into a stick—perfect for a makeshift stake in a situation like this. The stake in my right hand, bag in my left, I bounded up the steps and onto the glass platform where the pendulum swung gently back and forth.

Three vampires circled the glass on which I stood, each one waiting for the other to make the first move. "Well come on," I taunted. "Which of you wants to go first?"

And all three lunged onto the platform together.

The first one I took out with a simple thrust, straight into the chest. He hadn't been expecting it, so it was easy to catch him off-guard. But as blood spurted across the glass tabletop and he burst into flames, the other two quickly caught on to the fact I was now armed. I kicked him away, and he exploded before hitting the ground. The other two now circled, careful not to get caught up in the string of the pendulum. Each snarled incessantly, and their nasty-ass vampire breath made me want to gag. But it was all show, as each of them waited for the other to make the first move. I dropped down to one knee and did a sweep kick 360, knocking them both onto their backs. Before they could react, I sprung at one and plunged my stick into his heart, then vaulted from him to the other and stabbed him too, just as the glass broke beneath the pressure and all three of us came crashing to the ground. I scrambled away, cutting my palms on the shards of broken glass, and managed to get out of the blast radius before they exploded.

"Phoenix, come! We must go!" Sofi sat on the seat of some strange bicycle—a bicycle with wings. Like a foolish flying contraption. "Climb on!" she beckoned and pointed to a second, tandem seat.

The remaining vampires were closing in, and absent any idea of what else to do, I hopped on to Sofi's ridiculous flying machine, and began to pedal.

"Does this bike really fly?" I asked.

"It is an aviette. And yes, it will fly," she answered, as we steered us toward a long metal ramp running the length of the room.

"How can you be so sure?"

"Because if it does not, then we are dead," she replied. "Now pedal!"

It was a stupid idea, but when you're all out of ideas, even the stupid ones are worth trying. So, I tried. I pedaled as hard and fast as I could, and Sofi did the same. Up we went, along the length of the ramp, the pedal pushing not only the gears on the bike wheels but also a small propeller at the fore of the little bike-plane. I dared not look back over my shoulder, though from the heavy clang of footfalls behind us, I knew the vampires were gaining ground. Still, I pedaled. I pedaled until my legs burned. Just as we neared the end of the ramp, the machine lifted off the ground, and we were airborne.

As I kept working my legs, Sofi pulled back on the machine's yoke and took us higher, until we flew through the shattered stained-glass windows of the church of Musée des arts et métiers and onward into the red glow of a Paris sunset.

CHAPTER SIXTEEN

"Where to now?" I asked as we soared above the buildings of Paris. "I don't know how much longer I can pedal this thing."

"I do not know how much longer this thing can fly before it falls apart."

"We need to land. How about the Eiffel Tower?"

"It is too far, and too conspicuous. We would be on the television."

"Where then?"

"There," she replied and pointed to our left.

"The Louvre? You've got to be kidding me."

"No, not The Louvre. Over there. Behind us and to the left."

I scanned the city beneath us, my eyes following from The Louvre to the Seine River and its series of bridges, then even further until they lit upon an island smack in the middle of The Seine.

"Notre Dame?"

"Yes, Notre Dame. We will claim sanctuary."

"I think that's only in the movies."

"It was a book first. Besides, maybe we can get help from your friend, the hunchback."

"I'm pretty sure that was only a story, Sofi. But yes, Notre Dame looks as good a place as any. Especially if we want to land this thing."

And so, we pedaled as hard as we could, though our legs ached and burned from the effort. As we neared the fabled church and the covered remains of its charred roofs and grand spire, our energy continued to wane until our legs gave out and the aviette became nothing more than a gliding bicycle. Sofi aimed us at the rooftops, but as we neared them it became clear we were coming in much too fast and too high to land.

"We're going to have to jump."

"I know," she replied and leaped from her seat down to the rooftop of Notre Dame's fabled North Tower nearly twenty feet below.

I followed and hit the ground close beside her. Remarkably, neither of us was seriously hurt from the drop, other than a having a bit of wind knocked out of us. I scooted on my butt up next to her and put my arm around her, as we watched our flying bicycle crash into the Seine below.

"You are awfully close," she said, and I made to take my arm back. "But it is cold tonight. And I am tired." And she rested her head on my shoulder as the sun set and the rest of the vampires came out to play.

The two of us shared a cigarette as we contemplated our next move. Security had likely been alerted to our presence, so we couldn't stay here forever, but after the exhausting ride from the museum to the rooftops, our legs burned, and the idea of climbing down several stories of old staircases didn't much appeal to either of us.

"It is beautiful, no?" Sofi asked as curls of smoke escaped her lips.

"It sure is," I replied, not taking my eyes off her.

"Paris is the city of love for good reason. There is no other place as beautiful."

"Or anyone," I whispered.

"Look there, to the East," she said, ignoring my compliment. "It is lit up like that every night, and every night is more remarkable than the one before."

I took my eyes from her and scanned the city. A few miles to the east, the Eiffel tower sparked to glowing life.

"This place must have been amazing as well," I said. "Before it burned."

"It is still beautiful. Beneath all of that, there is much to behold. Not everything was damaged in the fire. And we are French. We will rebuild."

"Is that why there's no one up here?" I asked. "I expected to come crashing down on a crowd of tourists."

"Tourists can only access the South Tower," she replied, pointing to an adjacent tower very similar to our own, but with a massive metal cage wrapping the walkway. "But it has been closed since the fire."

"Then who's that?" I asked as a flash of movement caught my eye. Then another. I leaped to my feet and ran to the edge of our tower for a closer look and was met with pair vampires hissing in our direction from the opposite tower.

"Looks like you two picked the wrong set of stairs," I said, laughing. "Good luck breaking through those bars."

One of the vampires grabbed ahold of the metal cage holding them in and shook it fiercely like an ape trying to escape from a zoo. The second reached through with his arm, then shoulder … then somehow managed to force his head through too, before getting stuck. Sofi joined me by my side, saw their predicament, and began to laugh as well.

"You silly monsters," she shouted. "We will pick you off one by one."

I was about to tell her we were out of bullets and remind her they wouldn't do a lick of good anyway when Sofi's bag began to ring. She reached inside, retrieved her phone, and took the call.

"Allo ? C'est moi, Sofi," she answered. After a few seconds pause, she handed the phone to me. "It is for you. Rousseau."

"This is Phoenix. What's up, Rousseau? Sorry about the mess. Are you okay?"

"Yes, yes, I am okay. They are gone. There is no time to chit-chat. They are coming for you."

"They're already here," I replied.

"Then listen to me. I will be quick. I reexamined the photos Sofi sent me and have deciphered more of the inscription. Though I do not understand what it means."

Behind me, Sofi screamed. I took the phone from my ear and turned to see what happened. The other two vampires across the way had given up their struggle to reach us, and now stood staring our direction, their gazes transfixed on the sky above us. I eyed Sofi, saw she too was now transfixed on the sky … and I followed her gaze up into the night. A cloud of smoke hovered a dozen feet above us and dropping quickly. As the smoke cleared, a man in jeans and a hooded sweatshirt emerged.

"I have to go, Rousseau. We have trouble," I hissed into the phone.

"Wait! Just listen. The part I made out: it says *The blood key leads to the path of shadow.*"

"Blood key. Path of Shadow. Got it." And I hung up just as the man touched down in five feet in front of us.

"You have been a major pain in my ass, Mr. Bones," he snarled. "As have you, Miss LeRoux."

"And who are you?" I asked. "The Flying Dutchman?"

"I am not Dutch," He took a pull from an electronic cigarette and blew out a cloud of thick black vapor that once again engulfed him. "I am German. And I am here for the amulet. Give it to me now, and we will go our separate ways. Resist, and I will tear you apart."

"You seem to know our names; shouldn't we know yours?" I assume Sofi was attempting to buy us some time while I came up with a plan. But with a bag full of nothing but some drugs, half a pack of cigarettes, Sofi's purse and a gun with no bullets, I was completely out of ideas.

"My name is Wagner. David Wagner. But you may call me Deathbringer."

"You are serious now? Deathbringer? This is maybe your PlayStation name? I think I will call you Vampire Dave instead," Sofi replied. "Well, I have the news flash for you, Dave. Mon ami, Phoenix is a master vampire hunter. He has killed dozens of your friends. He will have no problem killing you."

An empty gun. A bag of drugs. A purse ... and the amulet.

"Is that so?" Vampire Dave snarled. "Well, Mr. Vampire Killer. I admit you have made quite a mess out of my friends. But they are nothing compared to me. Now hand me the amulet or I will rip your artery from your throat and throw your twitching corpse off this tower until it crumbles into a mess of mangled meat on the pavement below."

The amulet ... blood key ... path of shadow. A plan started to form in my mind. A stupid plan, but the best I could come up with.

"Sofi, give me your hand," I said.

"Are you not going to slay me, vampire hunter?" He took a step forward. Then another. "Have your movies not prepared you for this?"

Sofi put her hand in mine and slowly backed away from Vampire Dave, tugging gently at her arm as I coaxed her to follow.

"There is nowhere for you to go up here," the vampire continued. "Frodo and his gargoyles will not be coming to life and singing a song. It is just you and I."

"His name is Quasimodo," Sofi corrected him. "And the gargoyles don't come to life. It is the chimeras. You'd think a powerful vampire like you would know the difference."

"I trusted you before," I whispered to Sofi. "Now this time, you have to trust me."

Sofi nodded, and the vampire moved closer.

"Very well. Though I hate to make such a mess of this place." He pulled the hood of his sweatshirt up over his head and frowned. "It has already suffered enough."

"Blood washes off," I replied, and took another step back.

"I guess we will find out," said the vampire, and he rose a few inches from the ground and sped toward us, teeth bared, as we turned and ran the other way.

We raced across the rooftop, to the edge of the tower, and off into the night sky. Sofi screamed as we fell. I took her hand to my mouth and bit down, piercing the skin and drawing blood. Down we fell, the stone sidewalk below rushing closer and closer with each millisecond. I pulled the bag from her hand, tore it open, and pulled out the amulet.

"See you soon," I whispered, as I shoved the amulet into her bloody hand, and she disappeared.

Moments later, I hit the ground with a sickening thud, feeling my bones crumble and my skull crack as I exploded like a water balloon onto the streets of Paris.

Then, everything went black … just like I hoped it would.

CHAPTER SEVENTEEN

Once again dead, I counted my blessings that I'd managed to target my fall accurately enough to hit the shadowed enclave at the base of the tower. If I hadn't, there would have been a bit of a mess to explain once I got up, since the only way in and out of Eitherspace is through darkness. The people across the street would have probably called the police, and then there'd be a whole mess of *new* problems to deal with. Then again, they probably still called the police once my body crumpled onto the sidewalk and disappeared. The sickening crunch of my bones breaking still echoed in my head loud enough for me to know any passers-by would have seen it as well. How they were going to explain the explosion of blood and the lack of body was beyond me, but I didn't give a shit since I had more important things to deal with.

For one, since I hadn't come back to life yet, my body here in Eitherspace was in pretty rough shape. With more broken bones than I could count and a fractured skull with brains leaking out and floating in the blackness around me, it was a miracle I could move. But like I've said before, things work differently here, and though I was a mangled mess of an undead corpse stuck in limbo between worlds, I managed to move around anyway like some sort of sluggish blob.

My first order of business was to find Sofi. If I understood Rousseau's translation correctly—and from the way things panned out on our way down, I did—Sofi's blood had activated the amulet, which had sent her straight into Eitherspace. I spun my floppy body in a series of cartwheels, like a circus acrobat in the space station, and found her floating above me (or below, or to the side, since there isn't any up or down in Eitherspace) and flapped myself on over like a boneless bird.

Her eyes were as wide as moons, and her mouth was open in what looked like an eternal scream, though no sound emanated from her lips. When she saw me approaching, a little whimper escaped from her mouth, but she did not blink.

"Sofi, are you okay?"

"Are… are we dead?" she asked.

"Well, it's complicated—"

"—because you look dead. You are all smushed. We are dead. We are in hell."

"Listen carefully, and I'll explain. Me? I'm dead. But I'll come back once we get out of here. We're in a place called Eitherspace—kind of a limbo between the living world and the dead world. Almost like a parallel universe that exists beside our own. This is the same place I went when that monster killed me in a cave all those years ago. And now it's kind of my personal commuter lane."

"So, I'm dead?"

"No. You're not dead. You're alive. Don't ask me how you're here and alive, but you are… and it has something to do with that damned amulet. I think it's some kind of key that unlocks doorways between reality and Eitherspace."

"My hand… it's bleeding. Wait a minute… did you bite me? I seem to remember you biting me." Her thin voice echoed in the emptiness as if she were both miles away and inches from my ear simultaneously.

"I had to. It was the only way I could think of to make you bleed. Somehow the blood interacts with the stone and opens a portal. I don't know. It doesn't make any damn sense, but nothing does lately, and so we're just going to go with it."

"How do we get out of here?" she asked.

"Getting out of here's easy. But the question is, *where?*"

"What do you mean, where? Back to life. Back to reality."

"Vampire Dave's probably still right there on waiting for us. And there's nothing left for us in Paris."

"Perhaps nothing for you. But for me, there is my life. And Cami. We need to find her."

I searched the darkness, twisting my entire body to do so since my neck was broken and fairly useless. One place we could go would be back to my house in good old America. But there wasn't much we could do there, other than regroup. I put the idea in the back of my mind, in case nothing better came along. Then I saw it—a thin, gossamer trail of light, leading from Sofi's hand out into the empty space.

"I don't think Cami's in Paris anymore…" I said absently. "But I think I know how to find her."

"Where? Where is she? Let's go now and save her! We must before it is too late."

"It's not as simple as that, Sofi. I don't know *exactly* where she is, but I do think I've found a trail that will lead us much closer to her. You see that?" I asked, pointing to the thread of light. "That's coming from the amulet. And I think it's a kind of ghost trail. A remnant of the paths taken previously by whoever held the thing... and I'll bet dollars to donuts the last person to use it was your good old boy, Donal."

"We follow the trail, and we find where he went."

I nodded and continued, "Something like this... this amulet. It's not normal to be able to cut a hole in one reality and into another. I suspect when we reach the end of the trail, or at least the place we're trying to find, there will be something there. A marker... a scar."

"So, what are we waiting for? I want to be back alive." Sofi slung her bag over her shoulder and turned to swim away. "This place... it is cold, and it is dead. I do not want to be here any longer."

I didn't want to keep her here any longer than necessary either, especially since I had no idea what kind of effect being here while alive could have on someone. We followed the thread, she swimming through the inky goo of Eitherspace, me flopping and twitching my way along like the mangled blog of goo I was. Eventually, she had enough of my spastic movement, latched her free hand onto my shirt, and dragged me along behind her.

I have to admit, it was kind of sweet.

By the time we reached the end of the thread, it was impossible to tell how far we'd traveled. Could have been ten feet, could have been ten miles. Didn't really matter. What did matter was I was right: there was a kind of scar there, where the thread ended. A kind of shimmery jagged edge of light trying to break through the darkness. This had to be the last place he'd gone through, and I was about to take us back out, when I realized it wouldn't help.

"We are here. How do we get out?" She reached for the scar with the amulet, and it began to glow and throb, cracks slowly spreading out from its center as it threatened to burst.

"Put it away!" I shouted. "This isn't the right door!"

She pulled the amulet back, and the throbbing subsided.

"This would only take us back into the catacombs. That's the last place he used it. I'm sure of it. He was using the catacombs as a home base, I think. A place to bleed the bodies of the people he captured… then he'd take his bounty to its final destination via another trip through Eitherspace."

"But we did not find Cami there. Or your Nancy."

"I know… I know." I tried to shake my head but with a broken neck I just kind of jiggled. "But it doesn't matter. We need to find the door attached to this door."

Sofi and I both stared together at the crack in space, and with a sinking feeling, realized there were literally thousands of additional filaments of light sprouting off in all directions.

"I think you are right about it being his base. See how many paths he has taken," said Sofi.

"I see them. Give me a minute to think." How I wished I could find a bar in this place. "Sofi, hold the amulet close to the crack. But do not let it touch."

She moved the amulet closer again, this time much more slowly than before. As she approached, the crack began to grow and tremble, but something else happened I hadn't noticed … so did the strings. The closer the amulet came to the threads of light, the brighter they became, with some much more brilliant than the others.

"I think Eitherspace can heal," I said, my eyes darting from one thread of light to the next. "Don't ask me how, but that's what it looks like. See the thread we followed? How it's brighter than all the others? I think it's marking the most recent wound— the one that's healed the least. We need to find the next brightest thread. That will take us to the next doorway."

"Won't that take us back to where he captured your Nancy?"

"No. Like you said, Nancy and Cami weren't there. He took them somewhere else. We follow the right thread, and I think we find where he took them."

"But Phoenix, there are more threads than I can count. And they all look the same."

"They're not the same," I snapped. "You need to find the brightest one. I'm not able to move around very well right now, in my… condition… so, just look. And don't let the amulet touch the crack."

Sofi crept closer to the fissure of light, careful not to bring the amulet too near. Her fingers danced across the various trails, which quivered at her touch like ripples of light on an astral pond.

"I think I found it," she said. "But I am not certain."

"How certain are you? On a scale of one to ten."

"I am… I am a seven."

Seven would have to be good enough.

CHAPTER EIGHTEEN

Turned out, seven was more than good enough. It was perfect. When we reached the end of Sofi's thread, all it took was for her to touch the amulet to the fading scar in Eitherspace and drag it along the wound to tear it open again. After that, it was as simple as passing through the opening, and we were back in the real world, where I was fully alive with all my parts back where they belonged.

When we came through, we entered darkness, but not the same level of dark we'd left in Eitherspace. That's the difference between darkness and a void of nothingness. Here in the real-world black isn't really black—not if there's any hint of light creeping into a space, like there was where we popped out. Still, the place we'd entered upon returning to the real world didn't give up its secrets easily, so Sofi took out her cell phone and activated the flashlight, casting our location in a ghastly white glow. As the light revealed the space around us, I groaned, for it strongly resembled the catacombs where Sofi and I had first met—stone walls, stale air and the musty stink of wet death. A few more sweeps of the space, however, and I realized my mistake. This place *was* someplace new. Another place of death, yes … but one different than the one we'd visited beneath the streets of Paris.

"Follow me," I commanded, as I took the phone from her hand. "The exit should be…" I licked my finger and held it in the air, feeling for the direction of airflow. "… down this way."

As we crept through the gloom, my foot came down on something dry and brittle, which crunched beneath my feet like dry leaves. I knelt, felt for the floor, and found the broken wings and crumbled body of a desiccated parafairy. "He went through here, alright. Dropped this on the way."

"What are those things?" She kicked at what was left of the creature. "Why do we keep finding them? I have never seen them before, and now they are everywhere."

"They feed on the blood of the undead. But sometimes they'll hitch a ride on the living. Donal spent enough time around vampires he must have picked some up."

"They are disgusting," she replied, before stamping her foot down on the tiny corpse and grinding it into the floor beneath her heel.

I couldn't very well argue with that. "Come on, let's get the hell out of here."

We found ourselves at an ancient wooden door hung on large hinges to the stone walls of our tomb. For that's what it was, where we'd come through—a tomb, or perhaps a crypt (I never can tell the difference). With a heavy push, we shoved the doors open and stepped out into the moonlit night of a cemetery.

"I wonder where we are…" I said to myself. "Looks Christian. But old."

Sofi snatched the phone back from my hand and studied her screen. "Ravadinovo. Bulgaria. It says so here on the map."

"Bulgaria… Lots of vampires in Bulgaria. Guess it doesn't surprise me." I scanned the cemetery, searching for any sign of movement, but nothing moved aside from wind's scattering of autumn leaves covering the ground. "That map of yours. I don't suppose it tells you where to go next?"

"It is a bit of a walk, but there is a village nearby."

A crackling of twigs sounded from behind me, and I spun to face it. A rabbit hopped away in the moonlight and wiggled its body into a burrow beneath a rotting stump. When I turned back to Sofi, she'd already started on her way out of the cemetery, and I hurried to catch up with her.

"Wait up, will you?"

"You are too slow, Phoenix. You must be quick, like me."

"Where are you off to in such a hurry?"

"Phoenix. It is night, I am a thousand miles from home, and I have not eaten since breakfast. Where do you think I am going?"

My stomach rumbled and spoke to me in a language only I could understand.

Roughly translated it said, "Shut your damn mouth, follow her, and feed me already."

CHAPTER NINETEEN

The town of Ravadinovo was as small as it appeared on Sofi's phone map, and according to what we found on Wikipedia as we made the short journey, had less than a thousand full-time residents. Quaint in an old-world way, with a combination of paved and gravel roads, stone buildings built possibly centuries earlier, and surrounded in every direction by countryside and distant mountain ranges, the place sure seemed like a prime location for a secret vampire cult to set up camp.

We followed Sofi's map into the heart of the village, straight to the only restaurant that had a website. Nothing fancy, just a kind of bar and grill type place where you'd imagine rustic travelers stopping by for a drink and a bite before venturing off to the castle to jam a few stakes into some undead hearts. Before entering the front doors, the smell of grilled meat danced through the air straight into our nostrils. As we strolled down the light-lined streets, I imaged a trail of ghostly aromas swirling through the air like in an old episode of Scooby-Doo, luring us into a treacherous, yet delicious trap.

We left the street, went under a stone archway, and up the path to the restaurant. Once inside, any earlier ideas the town was dead this evening disappeared as loud music and happy voices filled the air. Sofi and I took a seat at a table, an old slab of wood scarred with the memories of countless dinners and ales.

"You buying?" I asked. "My wallet got roasted, remember?"

Sofi signed, plopped the bag on the table and sorted through the contents. "If they take credit cards, yes. Unfortunately, I forgot to pack my Bulgarian money."

Within a few minutes, a young man in an apron came to our table. "Dobar wecher!" he said, as he took the two of us in.

"Parlez-vous français ?"

"Oui, Madame," he replied, with a gentle curtsy. "Un petit peu."

"Fuck this shit," I grumbled. "Do you speak English?"

"Yes, I do speak English. Much better than French. You are American?"

"Yeah, and a long way from home," I replied. "Are you still serving food?"

"Yes, best food in Ravadinovo. What would you like? Our kebapche is first-class."

Obviously, I had no idea what the hell a kebapche was. Or the slightest idea of what they ate in Bulgaria. I assumed some sort of goulash, but as long as it wasn't freshly-drained blood of a virgin, my stomach didn't care much.

"Yes, we will have two," Sofi replied. "And a few beers."

"Zagorka?"

"Peu importe. Comme vou voulez."

A few minutes later the man came back with our drinks. "To new adventures," I said, toasting to Sofi. She didn't return the toast, but instead tipped back the beer and swallowed the entire glass in one drink.

"Whoah, whoah, take it easy," I said. Unless she'd been sneaking snacks while I wasn't paying attention, she hadn't eaten since breakfast either. With no clue as to where we were, other than somewhere in goddamn *Bulgaria*, much less who we could trust or where we'd even sleep this night, the last thing I wanted to deal with was a drunk French twenty-something.

"No. I will not *take it easy*." She slammed the glass on the table so hard I thought it would break. "Now that we are not running for our lives or in a cemetery or dead in some kind of black hell, I will enjoy myself. And you will tell me everything you know."

Problem was, I didn't have much to tell her. Not much she didn't already know. And from the tears hiding behind her angry eyes, I really did want to have answers for her. To tell her we were hot on the trail and in a few more hours and she and her sister would be back home in Paris, like none of this had ever happened. But I couldn't give her false promises. She had already proven too strong and too smart for those. All I could offer was truth.

"I... I think I'm in over my head here," I answered, unable to meet her eye. "This is all way bigger than anything I've dealt with before."

"I thought you were Phoenix Bones, Professional Monster Hunter."

"Professional is a bit of a stretch. I've hunted monsters." I paused to swallow another painkiller. "Plenty of them. But it's always been one or two here or there. We've already come across dozens. And that guy who flew? That vamp up on Notre Dame? I sure as hell haven't seen that before."

"You have not seen the movies? I think he is maybe the king vampire. Perhaps that is why he can fly."

I considered her theory. It was as sound as anything I'd come up with—even if she'd gotten all her ideas of vampires from the movies. I made a mental note to watch more of them whenever I finally made my way back home.

"I think we're in the right place though. Or at least on the right track. What we need is to find someone who can help us out."

"What we need is a place to sleep. I am so tired, Phoenix."

The waiter came back with two steaming hot plates of a kind of minced meat sausage with French fries. The smell was divine, and I dug in before he left the table.

"Une autre biere," Sofi said, handing him her empty glass. "And another for him too."

As he left to grab us another round, Sofi reached across the table and took my glass. A few gulps later, and it was gone.

"You're tired because you're drinking too much," I said.

"I am tired because we have traveled thousands of miles and I have seen you die twice already since I last slept." She snatched the fresh glass from the waiter's hand and addressed him. "Is there a place we can sleep? A hotel?" She took another drink and brushed him away. "Never mind. I will find it myself."

I munched on my dinner, washing down each bite with a drink of my beer. I'd never had Bulgarian food before, but I made a mental note to have it again. This was way better than any goulash I'd ever had. Sofi scrolled through her phone, absently taking a bite here and there. Every once in a while, she'd squint, mumble something like *punaise!*, scrunch up her nose, and scroll again.

"I could not help but overhear your conversation." A man in an official-looking uniform dragged a chair from the table across from us and pulled it up at the end of ours. "What brings you to Ravadinovo? Are you here for our castle?"

Castle? Hell yes, I'm here for the castle, I thought. If there's one place that vampires can't stay away from, it's castles. Castles in Bulgaria. Jesus, Sofi was right—this was like a movie. My fingers twitched as I imagined a freshly carved stake in my hand.

"We are visiting. We were looking for…" *play it cool, Phoenix* "… a friend. A friend of ours might have been here."

"A friend? In Ravadinovo? Maybe you were thinking of Sozopol? That is where the Americans go. Only here for our castle, but they never come into town."

"I'm sorry, but you are who?" Sofi interjected.

"I am Aleks," he replied, offering his hand. "I am… police."

Immediately my mind began to race. Questions of papers and permits and how did you get here without a car sped through my mind. But I took another peek at him and his recently shaven baby face and concocted a quick story. It wasn't much, but I prayed it would work.

"Yes, yes, we are here from Sozopol," I answered. "We came to see your castle and were supposed to meet a friend here, but we didn't find her… and we missed our ride back. I don't suppose you know someplace we can stay the night?"

"Yes, my friend was supposed to be here," added Sofi. "She came here days ago, but we have not found her."

"Have you heard of any strange happenings here in town? Any crime?"

Aleks shook his head vigorously. "No, no, we are a peaceful village."

"No… vampires?" Sofi asked.

I had to hand it to her, she went straight for the jugular when she needed to.

"Vampires?" the policeman laughed. "You tourists always with the vampires. Yes, we had vampires a long time ago. Or what people thought were vampires. But those were imaginations. We do not believe in that anymore." He paused and leaned in, lowering his voice to a whisper. "Though now you bring it up, there have been some strange things happening lately."

Now he had my interest. I took a sip of my beer and leaned in closer to hear what he had to say. "What kinds of strange things?"

"You will not tell the tourists in Sozopol?"

Sofi placed her hand on his shoulder and slid her beer across the table to him. "Your secret is safe with us."

"Few days ago, farmer died. It is mystery, but I am told it was heart attack."

"That doesn't sound so mysterious," I replied.

"That was only part of the mystery. Before that, his daughter went missing. Several weeks earlier. We have not found her, but we thought she left our little village to go find someplace new. Someplace fancy like Sozopol. The farmer very scared, and we tried to help him … ease his heart. Then one night, we find him dead. In the cemetery."

I raised my eyebrows at Sofi. "What was he doing in the cemetery?" I asked.

"Again, we do not know. But now we are getting reports of animals. Dead animals, at the farm."

"Isn't anyone there taking care of them?" Sofi asked.

"No, no, you do not understand. They are not dying. They are killed. We find them, and they are dead… and no blood."

"Some sort of disease? Something that's getting them sick and killing them?"

"No blood *inside*."

Yeah, that sounded mysterious, alright. And it sounded like the next logical place for us to continue our research. Apparently, Sofi was on the same wavelength.

"Forgive me, Aleks, if this is too forward." She reached out and stroked the back of his hand with her fingertips. "But we need someplace to stay, and it sounds like you could use some eyes on this farm of yours. I don't suppose…"

"In old times, we could rely on the vampirdzhija." Aleks turned down his eyes and shook his head solemnly. "They could rid us of ustrel. They know the ways of fire. But today? Nothing."

"Ustrel?" asked Sofi.

"Bulgarian vampire," I replied. "Eats cows. Though maybe they eat goats. Never met one to ask."

Sofi nodded. "It sounds like you know who did this, Aleks. Why don't you go arrest him?"

"You cannot arrest ustrel! Invisible beast. The vampirdzhija of old, they could destroy. But arrest? You are thinking you are a comedian!"

The first time he said the word, I wasn't sure I'd heard it right, the man's accent was so thick. But the second time the word "vampirdzhija" rolled off his tongue, I knew if I was going to ever come clean about our true purpose here in Bulgaria, now was the time.

"This… vampirdzhija… it is a vampire hunter, yes?"

The troubled police officer raised his despondent eyes to mine and nodded slowly.

"I have a secret to share with you, Aleks. I am a vampire hunter."

Aleks began to laugh, then stood from his chair. "You are making cruel joke of me. I think it is time for you to leave Ravidonova."

I held my hands up to him like he'd pointed a gun at me and ushered him back into his seat. When he didn't budge, I continued, "I am serious, Aleks. I hunt vampires… well, actually, I hunt all kinds of monsters. But the reason we're here? Vampires. I swear."

He turned his eyes to Sofi as if expecting her to burst out into a fit of laughter at any second. But she contemplated him solemnly and said, "It is true, Aleks. We are vampire hunters, and the trail has led us here, to your town."

"Yes, I think it is time for you both to leave," he said again. But as he spoke, he also began to lower himself back into his chair, a morbid curiosity starting to creep across his face. "Unless… unless you have proof?"

My mind immediately began to race. What kind of proof could I offer that we were here to hunt down some vampires? I could have shown him the amulet, but what use would that do other to show him we had some old hunk of metal? Tear open a hole into Eitherspace with it? Yeah, it'd be a cool trick … but still not proof of vampires. Kill myself and come back to life? Another cool trick, but still not a vampire.

"I have proof." Sofi unlocked her phone and gave it a few taps, then handed it to Alex. "Watch this video if you do not believe us."

As he watched the screen, his eyes widened. Reflections of the scene playing out before him danced across his pupils, and I moved to his side of the table to look myself. There on her display, played a video of a handsomely grizzled, man, leaping and dancing his way across the floor of an old church, as other men dressed entirely in black gave pursuit. Battle ensued, and the ridiculously handsome man slammed a wooden stake through the chest of one of them, then kicked him away just before he burst into flames and exploded.

"I look awesome," I announced. Sofi rolled her eyes. "What? You have to admit, that's pretty bad-ass."

"This? This is you! You are vampirdzhija!" Aleks cheered.

"Yes, yes. Vamprdzhija," I whispered and put my hand on his shoulder. "But be quiet. We don't know who here might be a vampire."

"No one here is vampire!" Aleks said, chuckling. "But you are right. We must keep this secret. Please, tell me more of your adventures."

While finishing our dinner and enjoying a few rounds of drinks, Sofi and I filled Aleks in on the journey so far. As we spoke, he listened with rapt attention, never once stopping us to ask questions. As far as he was concerned, everything we said was true … and the crazy thing is, it all was. Anywhere else in the world, you tell stories like this, they think you're nuts. Apparently, things are a little different in Bulgaria.

By the end of the night not only had we found a friend, but a place to stay.

"I have idea," Aleks began. "We trade. You will stay in farmhouse. Tonight. It is out of town and no one is there to watch it. You will watch the house, and we will let you stay there. Tomorrow you kill vampire."

Not having anything better to do, Sofi and I both agreed, and that settled it. Luck was finally back on our side. Not only had we managed to escape the immediate threat of Vampire Dave, but we'd gotten back on the trail and were closing in on him. A few rounds later Aleks before took us to the farmhouse.

We stumbled through the door, and I collapsed on the couch. Sofi took the bedroom. We were both out before his car left the driveway.

CHAPTER TWENTY

It was well past midnight when the sound woke us. A heavy pounding on the front door. Sofi was the first to wake, or perhaps she'd already been awake, and I just didn't know it. She's what pulled me from my slumber—her shaking my arm and poking me in the face with her finger. Whisper-shouting, "Phoenix, wake up, Phoenix. Something is outside and I think it wants to come in."

With how groggily I opened my eyes and the amount of time it took for me to recognize what she was saying; I should probably be ashamed to call myself a monster hunter. A real monster hunter wouldn't sleep through a monster banging on the front door.

A real monster hunter wouldn't rely on the person he was protecting to wake him up, so he didn't get turned into monster chow while he was passed out drunk on a dead man's couch in rural Bulgaria.

"Who's there? Get the door," I mumbled. "Tell them to go away. I already have some." Before the last syllables slurred from my mouth, my head was back on the pillow, and I was again dead to the world.

Sofi shook me again, but I didn't budge. So, she stuck her finger in her mouth, gave it a sloppy lick, and shoved it in my ear.

That woke me. But it was the following set of heavy knocks, followed by an ear-piercing screech, that got me out of bed. Now I was alert, or as alert as I could be after downing half a bottle of plum brandy. I leaped from the couch and searched the room, at first unaware of where I was. One glimpse of the wood-paneled walls, rickety kitchen table, and empty stone fireplace reminded me soon enough. And if it hadn't, the dusty odor of dried goat shit floating in the air would have surely done the trick.

"Quick, grab something. A weapon. Something to defend ourselves." My eyes darted from corner to corner until landing on a broomstick propped up against the wall in the far corner. "Grab that and bring it to me." I pointed in the general direction, summoning all my concentration to simply hold my hand from wavering too much she wouldn't know what I was pointing at.

As she darted across the room, I collapsed back on to the couch and closed my eyes. I was almost asleep again by the time she came back and dropped the broomstick on my lap.

"Right. The weapon. Who's there? Go peek outside and see who it is," I said, as I fumbled with the broom. "Ask him if he's a vampire."

"You are stupid when you are drunk, Phoenix," she replied, then mumbled something under her breath. "I am not asking if it is a vampire. Wake up and find out yourself." She reared back her hand and slapped me across the face. That woke me up.

Back on my feet, broomstick in my hands, I slammed it down across my knee and broke it in two. I took one of the jagged makeshift stakes into my left hand and offered the other to Sofi. She eyed it like it was a dead snake, then reluctantly took it. "In case I need backup," I said.

The two of us crept to the front door, careful not to disturb a loose floorboard. Though in hindsight with the racket I'd already made snapping the broomstick, I'm rethinking our desire to approach stealthily. I leaned against the door, and its dry cracks of paint tickled my ear as I rested my head against it and listened. Silence. Not a sound aside from Sofi's frantic breaths and the steady thump of my heart against my chest.

"Go over there and take a look." I motioned toward the drawn shades of the front window. "See if anyone's out there."

Sofi responded with a shake of her head that said *no way in hell, asshole.*

"Just get over there and check. I think whoever it was is gone."

"What if he breaks through the window?" Sofi whispered in a tone that would have made a poltergeist shrink.

"If it's a vampire, he can't come in unless we let him," I whispered back. "So, he can't come through the window. You'll be fine."

"But we still have their amulet."

Shit. "Okay. I'll open the door and look outside. If something comes at us, slam that through his chest. And use enough force. If you hit a rib, you've got to be able to break the bone." I lifted my stake and made several stabbing motions at the door, and she nodded. "Okay, on three."

Sofi spread her legs apart in a wide football player's stance, bouncing on the balls of her feet. The look in her eyes—like a gunslinger waiting to draw and cut down her opponent—that look was enough to tell me she was as ready as she could ever be. I reached out with my free hand, twisted the knob, and threw open the door.

The chirp of bugs and the rustle of wind through the trees was all that greeted us. I poked my head out the door, scanned the length of the porch, and still saw nothing. No sign of anyone having been here. Not even faded footsteps on the front stairs.

"All clear," I announced. "Now, can I go back to sleep?"

Before I could shut the door behind me, Sofi hastily rushed forward and pushed me out of the farmhouse and followed me on to the front lawn. "We will look for it."

"Look for what?" This lady was nuts. No way in hell was I going to go traipsing around some Bulgarian farm in the dead of night trying to track down a *possible* vampire—especially half-drunk and armed with nothing more than a busted broomstick. "We can do it in the morning. When the sun's up. Safer then."

I took a step toward the farmhouse, but she held up her stake and threated me with it. "I am scared, Phoenix," she said, and as tears began to well up in her eyes, she lowered her stake. "I do not like to say it, but I need you. I need you to protect me."

In retrospect, I probably shouldn't have believed her and her damsel-in-distress schtick. But I have to hand it to her—it worked.

"Fine…" I sighed. "Grab us a candle or a flashlight or something so we can at least see where we're going."

"We will use my phone," she said, and out came that damned phone again. I swear, it's like it was permanently attached to her. She flicked on the flashlight mode and held it in front of her, casting the yard in its ghastly glow.

"Doesn't that thing ever run out of batteries?" I asked.

"I brought a charger," she replied and gave me a shove from behind. "You lead. I will follow with the light."

"But what if something comes up from behind us?" I asked, stifling a laugh. "It'll bite you in the ass."

"That would be a very lucky vampire," she said and gave me another push forward.

For the next half hour, we traipsed all over the yard and didn't find a thing. I considered venturing out deeper into the fields, in case something lie in wait farther out, but my head was starting to hurt, and it sounded like too damn much work when all I wanted to do was sleep, so I didn't bring it up. Other than the grass had grown much too high with no one around to take care of the place, nothing seemed out of the ordinary—just a dark night on an abandoned farm in Eastern Europe. Eventually, Sofi became tired of the search as well and relented with her mission to track down the dreaded doorknocker. We returned to the farmhouse and back into our separate beds.

I made myself a promise to spend the rest of the night awake, listening for the intruder to return. I gripped the stake firmly in my hand, ready to spring into action in case my princess needed saving after all.

CHAPTER TWENTY-ONE

Turns out I wasn't as good as staying awake and on guard as I thought I would be. Somewhere through the night, I fell asleep, and I didn't wake until the sun's rays crept in between the crack in the front window drapes. When I finally rolled out of bed, it was to the sound of gently scraping wood.

"Sofi?" I called out. "Is that you?"

"Phoenix, come see what I have done! You will be proud."

My stomach rumbled again as I rolled out of bed, and a wave of nausea washed over me. I prayed what she had to show me involved scrambled eggs, orange juice, and a gigantic cup of coffee. What I found was something altogether different, though no less impressive.

"They are good, no? For our battle."

Legs splayed out on the kitchen floor, Sofi leaned with her back against the refrigerator, knife in one hand and a chunk of wood in another. All around her were stacks of broken chair legs, most of them whittled down to sharp points. She scraped the knife against the one in her hand, shavings dropping to her lap like yellowed snowflakes.

"The apprentice has become the master," I joked. "Seriously, Sof. Those are amazing."

A smile crept across her face, and she brushed a lock of hair from her eyes, careful not to stab herself in the face as she did so. "I do not know how many there will be, so I am making sure we are prepared."

"Are you sure you're up to this?" I asked. "I'm the monster hunter here. Not you."

Sofi threw a scowl my way that would turn Medusa to stone.

"Okay. You're a monster hunter now too," I conceded, and her smile returned.

CHAPTER TWENTY-TWO

Later that morning, after a breakfast of dry cereal and stale coffee, another set of pounding fists shook the front door. Sofi immediately took a stake to her hand, but I motioned for her to put it back down. "It's sunny out. No vampires," I said.

"Phoenix? Sofi? It is Aleks," a voice boomed. "I am here to help you hunt the vampire."

I looked at Sofi, sighed, and begrudgingly opened the door.

"See that, Aleks? That's called the sun," I said, pointing at the sky. "Vampires can't go out in the sun. So, it's not vampire hunting time."

"I am not stupid man," Aleks said, brushing my rudeness aside. "I am here to help you to hunt. To find the trail. Give to you clues. Come outside, and I show you."

Sofi tossed her stake onto the pile, grabbed her coffee, and scurried to the door. The three of us stepped outside into the bright sun of a late Bulgarian summer, with Aleks leading the way. In the daylight, the yard seemed much less ominous than it had the night before. Yes, the grass was still in need of a cut, but besides that, the view was nothing short of magnificent. Rolling hills stretched out in every direction, with a long gravel drive cutting through it all leading out to the main road. In the distance, the hills gave way to mountains. Birds sang, and goats bleated. *If it weren't for the vampires, Bulgaria sure would be a nice place to retire.*

Aleks led us across the yard and around the back of the farmhouse, up along a worn path to an animal pen and barn. A few goats wandered around aimlessly, chomping away here and there at any stray grass they hadn't yet managed to eat.

"This is where we found it," Aleks said. "The dead goat."

I took a step closer to the fence and leaned over. Other than a few piles of goat shit, nothing caught my eye. "What did you do with the body?" I asked.

"I burn it. Like the vampirdzhija would. To destroy the ustrel."

"I see," I replied, not having the heart to tell him goats don't turn into vampires. "Do you think it worked?"

"Well, we have no more dead—"

"Phoenix, over here!" Sofi shouted from the barn door. "Aleks, you too! Come quick."

We rushed over to Sofi's side and immediately saw what had prompted her to call us over in such a frenzy. There on the floor of the barn, the body of a goat lay, a swarm of flies buzzing around its motionless body. I unlatched the lower half of the door and stepped in, careful not to land my feet in any of the stray piles of crap that dotted the ground.

"I tell you there is vampire!" Aleks shouted, shaking his fists triumphantly.

"Well, either that or El Chupacabra," I replied. "But we're a little too far from Mexico for that one."

As Aleks and Sofi joined me, the three of us knelt and examined the goat. Its body was cold but still limp. I checked the neck and found a pair of puncture wounds, each dotted with specks of dried blood.

I stood and addressed Aleks. "Last night you said there's a castle around here. Where is it exactly?"

"Oh, it is near. Just outside town. But there are no vampires there."

I rolled my eyes at Aleks, shook my head, and put my hand on his shoulder. "Who's the vampire hunter here, Aleks? I know vampires. It's my job. And if there's one thing I know about vampires, it's that when it comes to setting up lairs, they can't resist a good castle."

"I do not think you understand—"

"—that's where we're going. Sofi and I. That's the next logical place to investigate." I took Sofi by the hand and began to march back to the house so we could gear up, then stopped. "I don't suppose you have a car we can borrow?"

Aleks sighed. "Keys in the farmhouse. Car in the garage. But you will not find anything there. It is not what you think."

"Thanks, Aleks. But I'm a professional." I replied. "You keep an eye out here. Protect the village. We'll take care of the vampire."

Ten minutes later, we were on our way to stab some vampires at Castle Ravadinovo.

CHAPTER TWENTY-THREE

What a goddamn waste of time that was.

I should have known before we got there this wasn't going to be the right kind of castle. I mean, who builds a castle out in the middle of a farm field? Any good vampire castle will be tucked away in the mountains. Ideally, with some cliffs for a jilted lover to throw herself to her death, so the vampire stalks the nearby village as it suffers an eternity of mourning for its lost love.

At the very least, when you hear "Bulgarian castle" you'd think it would be scary, right?

Castle Ravadinovo was none of these things. What it was instead, was the weirdest damned castle I'd ever seen. Think of if Disneyland had an honest-to-goodness life-sized real castle in the middle of it. It would be basically indistinguishable from Castle Ravadinovo. No bats, no belfries, no dungeons, and no caskets. Not even a creaky old doorway.

Instead, the place was absolutely beautiful. Like out of a storybook. Built only about twenty years ago, it's now basically a tourist attraction perfect for photo opportunities and wedding shoots. Peacocks and swans roamed the lush grounds, and thick vines of ivy crept up the stone walls of the towers. Fountains and statuaries were everywhere, along with an unusually large number of Jesus statues and crucifixes. Hell, even the castle itself was shaped like a cross.

"Try and enjoy yourself," Sofi urged. "It is not every day you are in a fairytale. And I think we could both use a break."

"There has to be more to this place," I argued. "No one just builds a castle anymore. This has to be the work of vampires." But as we explored the grounds, nothing seemed amiss. When Sofi clapped her hands with glee as a couple trotted by on a pair of horses, all I could think was the horses were probably vampires. How they were out in the daytime, and why they were horses, I didn't know. But they had to be vampires. Everyone here had to be a vampire. It was too damned weird.

"Take a picture, Phoenix," Sofi urged, as she leaned in to kiss one of the many stone toads dotting the castle grounds. "Perhaps he will turn into a prince since today you are a grump."

"Or maybe he'll turn into a vampire…" I muttered and took the photo.

Things finally started to look up when we entered the castle itself. A grand arched dining hall straight out of *Game of Thrones* perked me up a bit, but when I noticed it was roped off, I was reminded this whole damn thing was nothing but a carnival attraction. The wine cellar likewise piqued my interest, until I realized the stalagmites in the "cave" it was "carved from" of were all nothing more than painted concrete. Still, I stuck my head down every closed-off hallway and surreptitiously picked the lock of every locked door just in case the façade was all part of their plan.

Nonetheless, Sofi had a great time. And once I gave up on any hope of finding a vampire there, I did too. It was pretty magical, especially if you could ignore all the tourists there posing and taking photos. Maybe even a little romantic. As we strolled through the gardens a second time, I took Sofi's hand in mine, and she didn't pull away. The path eventually led to a bridge, which for some reason had waterfalls coming out of the bridge itself, and as we stopped and watched a pair of black swans gliding across the water, I leaned in for a kiss. She turned her head, and I caught her on the cheek. Not what I was aiming for, but still, progress.

On the drive back to the farmhouse, we both remained silent, lost in our thoughts. Again, we'd hit a dead end ... and other than a murdered goat, I had nothing to go on. Perhaps the next day we'd unearth a hot new lead. Maybe Aleks had discovered something or remembered a tip he'd forgotten. But that was for the next day. After the letdown at the castle, I was too damned depressed to hunt vampires and sure as hell not in the mood to hear the Bulgarian version of "I told you so."

CHAPTER TWENTY-FOUR

"Why do you want to find her?" Sofi scooped a spoonful of beans into her mouth. After the day at the castle, I hadn't been in the mood to drive into town and find a restaurant. Instead, we decided to rustle up a meal from whatever food we could find in the farmhouse. Everything in the fridge had rotted or gone bad, and the loaf of bread in the bread box was now a mossy garden, so our options were limited to the nonperishables. Whoever the previous owner had been, he sure had a thing for beans. Half the cupboards were stacked with cans of them: kidney, cannellini, black, pinto, and even a few cans of lima beans. Either the guy loved beans or hated them so much they'd accumulated to the point where they overflowed the shelves. Regardless, they're what we had for dinner.

"Find who?" I replied, through a mouthful of mashed pintos. "Cami? Nancy? The farmer's daughter? Any of the other unknown number of girls who are missing we don't even know about?"

Although she could tell I was upset, Sofi gently prodded. "All of them, I suppose. Though I was referring to Nancy..." her voice trailed off, and she stirred her beans in quiet contemplation.

I'd been wondering the same thing lately. Why was I so damned determined to find this girl? I didn't know her. I didn't know any of them. Because I could? Because it was my destiny? Sounded like more of an excuse than a reason. Of course, I'd had these questions before. Every time I'm on the hunt and hit a wall, the questions come up. Who was I to go out into the world as some kind of rogue monster hunter? That's what we have police and armies for—to catch the bad guys.

Problem is, they don't always find the bad guys. And they particularly don't find them when they don't know what they're looking for.

"Belinda," I answered. "In the end, I think it all comes down to Belinda."

"Your sister…"

I nodded. "My *twin* sister. She went missing when we were kids. Twelve years old."

Sofi reached her hand across the table and placed it on mine. "I'm sorry, Phoenix. Did they ever find her?"

"No. Never. No one knows what happened." I took a deep breath and peered into Sofi's eyes. In them, I saw something familiar—the same vision of heartbreak, loss, and desperation that had plagued my face for nearly three decades. I couldn't let it scar hers. "Actually, that's not true. I know, or at least I think I do."

Sofi gripped my hand tighter and leaned in. Even after the beans, her breath still smelled sweet.

"When we were kids, we used to play in the woods. We'd make up games and have all kinds of adventures out there. It was the place we could escape from everything else and be ourselves," I said. "All kinds of things live in the forests where I grew up. Wild pigs, coyotes, bears, alligators, and even panthers. But they tend to leave people well enough alone. You make enough noise, and they won't come near you. Just have to stay out of their way. One night, when we were on our way back home, something else came out of those woods... and it took Belinda."

"Was she kidnapped? A child predator?"

"Oh, it was a predator alright. But not the kind you're thinking of."

"Then what was it?"

I hesitated to answer, knowing how stupid it sounded. Everyone I'd ever told my theory to had either laughed or patted me on the back to tell me they heard what I said, but that I was nuts. "Bigfoot. It had to be Bigfoot. That's the only thing I can come up with that makes any sense."

Sofi lifted her hand to her mouth and shielded a smile. At least she had the polite manners to hide her reaction. "That's why you spent so much time in the woods growing up?" she asked. "You were searching for Bigfoot?"

I stood from the table and carried my bowl the sink. Water ran from the faucet, rinsing away the gravy and leftover bits of beans, and I stared out the kitchen window onto the fields as they slowly darkened in the setting sun. Behind me, I heard Sofi rise from her seat and pad over to where I stood.

"I'm sorry, Phoenix. I am trying not to laugh," she whispered from behind me. "I have seen the things you have seen now. And I believe you."

"That thing in the woods I told you about before. The monster." I turned and faced her; our bodies dangerously close to one another. "I thought that was it. Back when I tracked it down, I thought that was it… and maybe it was. But I never found Belinda."

"But you saved the boy." Sofi raised her hand to my face and stroked the mess of a beard that had grown on my chin over our journey.

"I did. I saved the boy. And I died doing it," I answered. "That was the first time I ever entered Eitherspace, and it scared the hell out of me. But afterward, after I found myself safe at home, I turned on the television and saw the boy had found his way out and was safe. I knew then that even if I couldn't help my sister, I could help others."

A lone tear formed at the corner of Sofi's right eye, and she wiped it away silently. Then, taking a step back, she clapped her hands together and exclaimed, "That's it. Tonight, we will have fun. We will forget all of this for a few hours and enjoy life. Then tomorrow, we will save them all."

She put her hand into her pocket and took out a pair of pills. She popped the first into her mouth, then pressed her body to mine, put her fingers to my lips, and slid the other pill between them.

Before I knew it, she'd run off to the bedroom. I could hear her rummaging through her bag, and less than a minute later, she was back in the main part of the house, holding her phone high above her head like a trophy. "Dance with me, Phoenix!" she shouted over the music that began to blare from her phone's little built-in speakers. "I chose this in your honor. It is from the best French band ever. They are a national treasure. Can you guess what it is?"

Some synths over a house-y kind of rock beat kicked in, followed by the plucking of a guitar. I had to admit it was catchy, and before I knew it, I was at Sofi's side, dancing along to the rhythm. "Do you give up? It is a band called... wait for it... *Phoenix*!"

"Damned fine name," I exclaimed over the tinny speakers. "I dig it!"

That song flowed into another and another, and as we danced, the drugs took hold. Everything was right again—or if not right, at least put into perspective. We couldn't do anything for those lost girls tonight. Not without stabbing randomly into the dark. So why let that get us down? We were alive, and we were healthy. And Sofi ... Sofi was beautiful. We danced for what must have been hours. Just giving ourselves over to the music felt so damn freeing.

And then it came back—that horrible, stabbing pain in my gut. I dropped to my knees, clutching my stomach, and Sofi hurried to my side. "Phoenix, what is wrong? Is it the beans?"

I've had plenty of bad gas in my life, but this wasn't gas. The stabbing was in the wrong place to be the kind of pain that could be healed by conjuring a Class IV booty vapor. This was higher up and more specific. This was in the place where I'd been stabbed and, for some reason, it hurt like hell.

"Hurts," I grunted. "Have to lie down."

Sofi helped me to my feet and helped me over to the couch. I laid down on my side, squinting as the shots of pain tore through my abdomen, and she ran off, back to the bedroom. A few seconds later she was back at my side, a handful of pain pills in one hand and a glass of water in the other. As she tried to put them into my mouth, I pushed her hand away.

"Take them," she said. "They will help."

"Already have enough drugs in me. Not ready to overdose again. Died enough lately."

"You'd need to take a lot more than this to overdose. They'll make you sleep, but that is all." She brushed the back of her hand across my forehead as she spoke. "And the pain will be gone."

Another stabbing pain ripped through my gut, and I took the pills. As I swallowed them down, Sofi crawled onto the couch in front of me and wrapped my arm over her.

"Hold me, Phoenix. Just hold me, and everything will be alright."

I tried to stay awake, to enjoy the sensation of her body next to mine. But with the ecstasy and the pain meds all mixing together, sleep came much sooner than I would have liked. Still, it was a restful sleep. One free of the terrors and pain that had wracked so many recent slumbers.

It would have been the perfect end to a shitty day—if that damned banging on the farmhouse door hadn't come back and woken me up *again*.

CHAPTER TWENTY-FIVE

Along with pounding on the door, a low moaning sound echoed against the wooden walls of the farmhouse, so loud and close I could have sworn it was coming from someplace inside. The door rattled again under the heavy fists or boots slamming against it from the other side, and I rose from the couch, only to discover Sofi was nowhere to be seen. Another groan followed, and now that I was sitting, I was certain the groaning was coming from inside.

"Sofi! Sofi, where are you?" I shouted over the raucous beating. Another groan rang out, as if in reply, and a huge ripping sound like a duck being stepped on by an ogre tore through the house.

"I am in here," Sofi yelled back from the direction of the bathroom. "My stoma---" but another horrible fart cut her off midsentence. "Is there someone at the door?"

I bounded to the bathroom door and, catching a whiff of the damage our bean dinner had inflicted on Sofi's bowels, tried not to breathe. "Whatever was here last night… it's back," I whispered. "Hurry up and finish whatever you're doing in there. I need you."

The pounding continued, each bang louder and more vicious than the last. Sooner or later, whatever was on the other side was either going to bust the door down or give up and leave. Neither of those sounded like smart options. Leaving the rotten stench seeping through the bathroom keyhole behind, I dashed back across the farmhouse to the front window. This time when I pulled the curtains back, our visitor remained in view. A pale man, not much older than me, and dressed in a dirtied suit stood on the porch. He held his clenched hands in fists above his head and brought them down on the door, this time hard enough to knock a mirror crashing from the wall to the floor.

"Who is it?" I jumped when Sofi spoke. I hadn't heard her leave the bathroom … or flush … or wash her hands. But with what was going on I figured her hygiene was the least of my concerns.

"Vampire, from the looks of it. Only one way to find out for certain though." I strode to the front door and put my hand on the knob. "Go grab the stakes," I said to Sofi. "We might need them." As she did so, I cleared my throat and shouted through the door. "Who is it?"

At the sound of my voice, the pounding stopped, and I could hear heavy breathing from the other side of the slab of lumber separating us from our new guest. From across the room came the rattling of loose wood as Sofi gathered the stakes.

"Pusni me vǔtre!" a gruff voice on the other side replied.

"I'm sorry. You're going to have to speak English," I answered. "Me no speak vampire."

"Let me in," said the voice. "You are in my house."

Sofi handed a stake to me and took up her defensive stance again, much like she had the night before, and raised her stake like she was ready to throw it like a spear the second I opened the door. "Don't stake him. Not right away," I commanded. "First, let's see if he's of any use to us. He's the only lead we have."

I turned the handle and opened the door.

The man on the front porch stared at us coldly, then took a step forward to enter the farmhouse. Upon reaching the threshold, however, he screamed out as if in immense pain and fell back onto the wooden boards of the deck with a thump. From his collapsed position, he reached toward Sofi and me and asked, "You help please?"

Sofi made a move to give him a hand, but I thrust my arm in front of her before she could make it through the doorway. "Vampire. Can't come in unless we invite him," I said.

After clambering to his feet, the man took another try at the door, and again collapsed in pain the second his body reached the threshold. "What have you done to me? This is my house! Let me in."

"It's under our jurisdiction now." I ran my tongue across my teeth. Must have been sleeping with my mouth open. Everything inside felt dry and mossy, and I could only imagine how bad my breath must have smelled. "Means you can't come in unless we invite you in."

"But... but it is my house!" the man stammered and stamped his feet on the rickety floorboards.

"Sorry buddy, I hate to tell you this... but you're a vampire. And we aren't letting a vampire in here."

"I am no vampire! I am farmer, and you are in my home. Now leave before I find police."

I considered telling him to go out and find the police. See what good that did him when he showed up walking around town when he'd been buried a few days earlier. Maybe old Aleks had a few stakes of his own stored away in case his vampire dreams came knocking on his door someday. Would have saved me the trouble, that's for sure. I wanted to get back to sleep. Problem was, I couldn't. Not with this gift horse staring me right in the mouth. Middle of the night or not, this was our best chance to finally make up for the wasted day at the castle and hopefully stab a few more vampires while we were at it.

"I hate to tell you this, but you're dead—died a few days ago. They buried you." I gestured toward his filthy suit. "You wear that thing every day? While you're out milking goats or whatever it is you do? I'm thinking that's only for *special* occasions."

The man didn't answer, but instead simply stared at us with his glassy eyes, apparently thinking this over. Deep in thought, he chewed at his lip---poking a hole right through with his exposed fang. A slow trickle of blood dripped from it and plopped onto the dusty porch.

"What is the last thing you remember?" Sofi stepped forward, even with me but still on our side of the doorway. "I am told your daughter went missing."

At the mention of his daughter, the man's eyes lit up and darted back and forth between Sofi and me. He absently wiped the trickle of blood from his chin and spoke, "Yes. Days ago.

My princess. I try to find her. In cemetery. Then… then I do not remember. Then I am here."

"That was quite a while ago," I replied. "Days for sure. What have you been eating? Where have you been sleeping?"

He stared back at me with a blank and said, "I do not know."

I took a minute to think things over. Try to figure out our next move here, since obviously, this guy didn't know a damn thing about where the other vampires were. He didn't even think he was a vampire. Though I guess I couldn't blame him. It can take a few days or even a few weeks for the whole vampire thing to take hold completely. Usually, when people are just turning, their body switches faster than their mind. Full comprehension of what you've become is a gradual process, and he was still in the midst of it.

"Sofi, grab the keys. We're going for a drive," I said. "You, you're going to take us back to the last place you can remember. Back to the cemetery."

"And if I do not?"

"If you don't…" I hefted the stake in my hand, feeling the weight of it, and pointed it at him. "If you don't, I'm going to shove this chunk of wood right through your chest and laugh while I watch you die."

CHAPTER TWENTY-SIX

Less than five minutes later, we were back in the dead man's car, me in the front driver's seat and Sofi in the back with our vampire farmer. I considered asking him his name, then decided against it. No point in getting too personal. It's a lot harder to stab someone when you have an emotional bond.

"So, here's the deal," I said, over my shoulder. "We're going to go back to the cemetery, and you're not going to give us any trouble. Then you're going to take us on a little tour. Show us anything that might seem familiar. Maybe someplace that *calls* to you. While we're driving, you're not going to give us any trouble, or my friend back there will *take care* of you."

Sofi, sitting to the man's left, held a stake out a few inches in front of his chest. She brought it forward slowly and pressed it against his shirt, digging it through the fabric into his flesh. "You fuck with us, I will stake you," she said, pulled the stake back, and wiggled it threateningly.

"I tell you, I am no—"

"Just shut the hell up," I commanded. "You'll talk when I tell you to talk."

"Yes. You listen. Otherwise..." This time she ground the stake harder against his chest. So hard, in fact, that tears of blood began to well up in his eyes.

"You see that? You're crying blood. And you say you're not a vampire." As we turned off the driveway onto the main road, I hit the accelerator. Although we appeared to have the upper hand here, I didn't trust the situation. Any vampire with full faculties wouldn't be so ... understanding. Even if his afterlife was on the line, a fully-formed vampire would never do what we were asking. Victims of a hive mentality, where the one rule you don't break is *never put the leader in danger*, you could never force a vampire to lead you where I wanted this one to go. For now, we were safe. But if he progressed any further, we'd have a bloody battle on our hands—one Sofi was very likely to lose.

A few miles down the road, a pungent odor began to waft through the car into my nostrils. The only thing I'd ever smelled with such a terrible stink was a rotting corpse or a vampire's breath. But the vampire in the back seat had followed our orders completely, not even opening his mouth to breathe. Just as I thought I couldn't take it anymore, the vampire gagged and coughed.

"Please, open the window," he begged. Then he turned to Sofi and said, "And you think I am the dead one? You are sure nothing is dead inside of you?"

Sofi blushed and rolled down her window with her free hand.

"That was you?" I asked, choking on the air. "Jesus, Sofi. That's disgusting."

"I am not good with beans."

Not wanting to risk breathing in any more rancid air, I didn't answer. Instead, I held my breath, rolled down my window, and kept driving until we finally rolled into the cemetery parking lot. As the car pulled to a stop, tires crunching on the dusty gravel, I swung open the door and hopped out. Maybe my eyes were playing tricks, or maybe it was the ecstasy still swimming through my system, but I swear a green cloud of noxious gas poured out the open door behind me. Sofi climbed out of the car close behind, and I considered shutting slamming the car doors shut and leaving the vampire to stew in Sofi's broth. A kind of chemical warfare torture device, if you will. But even I can't stoop that low.

In the full dark of night, lit only by a waning moon slipping in and out of clouds, the cemetery exuded a much ghastlier presence than when we'd first arrived here a few days earlier. In the dying light of a late summer's day, even a graveyard can be beautiful. Perspectives change, however, when the ambiance switches to the silent death of night. Especially when your only company is a drugged-out aspiring model on a revenge mission and a dazed rookie vampire under the impression he's still someone's daddy. Thick tendrils of fog snaked between the worn gravestones, a wolf howled in the distance, and I swear the flutter of batwings surrounded us from above.

"Where to, Hoss?" I jabbed my stake against the vampire's back, figuring, at this stage, he would know the difference between the positioning of a fatal stab and a painful poke.

"I... I do not know. You bring me. I only remember cemetery."

"How about you show us where they buried you?" Sofi cracked her stake against the poor fool's head, the sound of wood on bone like a baseball cranked straight out of the park. Any man would have howled in pain, but it didn't faze him. I think this might have been the point where he realized things were considerably different in his world than he previously imagined.

"I wake up in box in dirt. But that is not where you want me to take you."

"Oh no?" Sofi wound back her stake again, preparing to land another blow to the guy's noggin, but I grabbed it and took it from her.

"Let's stop beating the vampire, shall we?" I offered the stake back to Sofi but as she reached to take it, I pulled it away and raised my eyebrows at her. She let out a sigh and nodded, and I returned it gently to her outreached hand. "Now, take us where you *think* we want you to," I said to the vampire.

"I do not know who scares me more. Him, or you," the vampire said to Sofi. She kicked him hard in the ass, and he started moving. He led us on a sure and direct path, through the stone markers announcing the dead beneath our feet, straight back to the crypt where we first arrived the other night.

"When I wake, I am… drawn… to this place. I do not know why. I go in, but I find nothing. Just an empty crypt. And I feel I am brought here often. It is baffling."

In the light of Sofi's cell phone, the place was as I remembered it the last time we'd been here. Just a crypt. Creepy as hell, since it's a crypt and you know … dead bodies and all that shit. But still, really nothing more than a dirty old stone room. The parafairy corpses littering the floor were gone now, but since it had been a few days, it didn't surprise me. Tasty little snacks like that tend to be gobbled up and disappear down the gullets of scavengers. A place like this, you expect a lot of those. Particularly rats. Nasty little fucking rats. I shuddered at the thought.

"Search the room. There has to be a secret button or a hidden doorway or something." Sofi handed me her phone and started rubbing her hands against the walls, frantically scraping nails through layers of dust and spiderwebs. Here and there she'd stop, rap her knuckles against the stone, shake her head, and move on. The vampire and I must have watched her for at least a minute before I decided to tell her to stop making such a fool of herself in front of our guest.

"You watch too many American movies," I said to her. Then to the vampire, "Just show me where the damn door is."

"I know nothing of door. This is empty room. Nothing to see here."

I took a few steps forward, dragging him behind me until we stood less than a foot from the back wall of the crypt, where a small iron cross hung from a hook in the stone. I reached forward, pinched the long side with my finger and thumb, and gave it a twist. As the metal scraped against rock, the cross swung on a pivot until completely inverted. It clicked into place and a tiny needle-like protrusion shot up from the center of the cross.

"Prick," I said.

"Who is prick?" the vampire replied. But before he could say another word, I snatched his hand and slammed his palm against the needle. He stared at me with that shocked expression of "that should have hurt … but it didn't … but I'm also still offended you did that" and pulled his hand away. A tiny drop of blood trickled from the needle, but before it hit the floor the wall began to rumble and move forward. I took a step back, dragging the vampire with me, the wall slid open to reveal a doorway. Beyond the door, an empty room appeared, its stark white walls blinding us as a series of fluorescent lights flickered on, one by one.

"After you, my dear," I said, bowing to Sofi.

As she entered, she turned to face me and asked, "What about him?"

In one swift move, I spun on my heel, tossed the stake in the air, and gave it a good, strong kick into the sad bastard's chest. The whole thing was super graceful—and super badass. Like a ballet dancer fucking a ninja while a gas tanker explodes in the background.

From the look on the vampire's face before he popped, I could tell he was as impressed as I was.

I wiped the spray of vampire guts from my face and flicked them to the ground with a sickening plop. Sofi rolled her eyes at me and continued her way down the secret corridor. I followed, each step leaving a bloody footprint in my wake on the white tile of the floor. As the door closed behind us with a heavy scrape as it dragged against the stone, I licked my lips, spit a coppery wad of red and yellow onto the wall, and didn't say a word as we ventured onward.

CHAPTER TWENTY-SEVEN

The air from the sterilizer units whooshed past us with a pungent chemical blast, and a few parafairies dropped from my clothes onto the floor. Must have been attached to the vamp before I popped him and attached to me in the explosion. One of them near my foot wiggled a bit, twitching in the final throes of death, and I stamped his life out under the heavy heel of my boot. His little bones crunched easily under the weight, but I gave my boot a hard twist for good measure.

"You didn't have to kill him." Sofi picked at her nails and squinted as she chastised me.

"Was gonna die anyway." I strode forward in her direction and the direction of the door from the makeshift clean room. Every other step, my foot threated to slip on the mashed parafairy guts marking the soles. But I kept my cool composure, careful not to slip, so as to retain my badass image.

When I finally reached her, she gave me a hard kick in the shin and scowled. "He wasn't hurting anyone. He only wanted to save his daughter."

"Then maybe you shouldn't have tried to gas him to death," I mumbled and pushed her aside.

"Listen to me, Phoenix." She stopped and spoke at me from behind in a stern, unwavering voice. I couldn't help but be reminded of my third-grade teacher, Mrs. Spellman, and how she would scold us for passing notes in class. "You are a great hunter. But you cannot just go around stabbing and murdering any old monster you come across. Perhaps they are nice. Maybe they are misunderstood."

"Just shut up and follow me," I replied, not breaking step. "They know we're here. You don't build something like this and not have any security." Sofi didn't reply, but from the footsteps behind me, I knew she heard me. I pressed a button on the whitewashed brick wall to the right of two gleaming steel doors, and they slid open, revealing an elevator. As soon as Sofi cleared the doors, I pushed the only button inside, and we began our descent.

How far down into the depths of Bulgaria our little metal box took us, I have no idea, but the trip down took much longer than I expected. To break the silence, I hummed "The Girl from Ipanema," while Sofi scowled at me. Just as I was about to apologize for stabbing her new buddy, the doors opened, revealing another blank white corridor—this one lined with doors.

"Be on your guard." I raised my stake and scanned the hallway—nowhere for anyone to hide, though we could easily be ambushed from any side doors. At the far end, at least thirty yards off, another set of doors mocked us, their inset windows staring like glazed-over eyeballs.

"I will take left. You take right," The stakes in Sofi's bag clacked against one another like a sack of firewood as she swung them over her left shoulder. She raised the stake in her right hand and marched forward.

One after another, we tried a door handle, only to find it locked, and we'd move on to the next. Two … four … six … whatever they were hiding down here, they appeared to have locked it up good. Either they knew we were coming, or they were paranoid. Perhaps a little of both. Still, with every rattle of a knob from Sofi's side, I couldn't help but cringe a little. I imagined her grasping one of those handles, twisting it, and the door opening to reveal a horde of bloodthirsty vampires, huddled in the darkness ready to swarm over us. Against a vampire or two, I could hold my own. Hell, after Paris, I figured I could easily handle a half dozen. But this was a nest. I was sure of it. And that meant there could be dozens or even hundreds of vampires down here. It all depended on what the hell they were cooking up in this underground hideaway. Whatever it was, it had to be something big. All roads thus far had led us here.

But still, what I couldn't understand was why not a single one bothered to come our way. They had to be here. The question was, where?

At the final door on the right, the handle turned beneath my grip. Just as I was about to open it, I stopped myself, and whispered to Sofi, "Hey, come over here. Need you to back me up."

Sofi tested her last handle, found it also to be locked and scurried across the hallway to me.

I put my finger to my lips and counted off silently. On three, I opened the door.

In stark contrast to the hallway, this room was painted all in a cherry red—walls, floor, ceiling—the whole damn thing. A woman in a leather corset, biker hat and black stiletto heels turned to face us at the door opened. In her right hand, she held a riding crop, which she tapped in her left palm. She grinned at the two of us, revealing a set of fangs, then returned to what she was doing. Against the far wall, three naked men were bound and gagged, their wrists shackled and bound above their heads to sparkling chrome rings set into the wall. As one of them spied the two of us standing in the doorway behind his oncoming mistress, his eyes widened, bulging like a bullfrog's throat.

"This is not what we came here for." Sofi shut the door and gave me a gentle shove. "Though from your pants, I think perhaps you may want to stop back here on our way out."

Aside from the weird vampire sex BDSM room, every door in the hallway was locked. All that remained was the set of double doors at the end, where we now found ourselves. I ran my hand through my hair and took a deep breath. Sofi shifted the bag on her shoulder and blinked a few times as if to clear her eyes. We opened the doors, and finally found what we'd been searching for.

CHAPTER TWENTY-EIGHT

We found ourselves in an immensely cavernous space, lit from high above by rows and rows of dead-white fluorescent tubes. I was immediately reminded of a Costco, though instead of never-ending shelves of bulk food, discounted electronics, and questionably fashionable clothing, this space held only one variety of goods—hundreds of glowing, liquid-filled pods. Each about four feet in circumference and about six feet high, the electric blue liquid inside bubbled as the room pulsed with electricity. A shiny metal ring circled the bottom and top of each pod, like tubular lava lamps. Only instead of melted and flowing colorful wax, these containers held something far more disturbing.

People.

As she realized what we'd come across, Sofi's eyes widened, and her breath stopped—though only for a moment. Within seconds, her reaction shifted from one of terrified horror to one of desperate desire, and she darted forward to the closest container, cupping her hands between her eyes and the glass to get a better view of the prisoner inside.

I didn't need to move any closer. From where I stood, things were clear enough. Dozens or even hundreds of humans held in some sort of stasis. Possibly chemically-induced. Or maybe something worse still. It didn't matter, though, because there wasn't a damn thing I could do about it. Not with Vampire Dave staring us down from the other end of the room.

He sat quietly in a single metal folding chair, the type you'd usually find a cafeteria, and stared at us. As Sofi ran from one canister to the next, banging on the glass and shouting "Cami, Cami, where are you?" he lifted his right hand to his mouth, inhaled from his vape pen and began to laugh.

"My, my… you two *are* rather resourceful." A puff of smoke blew from his mouth, and he raised from his seat. "I must admit, I did not expect to see you again. Especially you, Mr. Bones. Not after your high-dive into the sidewalk." He stepped forward, each footstep echoing in the once again silent room.

"Where is my sister?" Sofi raised her stake high above her head and rushed in his direction. A scream tore from her lips as she closed the distance between her and the undead thing she now blamed for her sister's disappearance.

Vampire Dave, aka "Deathbringer," took another drag from his vape pen and sighed as Sofi thrust the stake at his chest. With lightning-fast reflexes, he gripped her wrist and wrenched it upward. A cracking like dry twigs sounded, followed by a scream of immense pain. Sofi dropped her weapon, and Vampire Dave kicked her violently to the floor.

"Tisk, tisk," he warned with this thick German accent as he shook his finger at her. "You cannot come into my work and cause such … problems. And here I thought the French had manners."

As he scolded her, I took a step forward, hopeful she'd at least caused a distraction through her impatience. But before my foot touched the floor, his attention was on me.

"As I was saying, Mr. Bones. You are surprising. At first, I was shocked to find no splattered remains on the pavement. It was quite a mystery. She, on the other hand, I knew where she had gone. After all, she used something of mine to get there." He pointed a pale, slender finger at the canvas bag by Sofi's side. "I believe you even were kind enough to bring it back to me."

My heart sank. Not once had I thought to tell her to leave the amulet behind. So stupid. On both our parts. I should have known better. But here we were, delivering what the bastard wanted. No wonder he let us in. We were better than UPS.

"Be a good girl and kick it my way, frauline," he said. "Or do I have to come and take it from you?"

Sofi pulled herself back to her feet, careful not to put any pressure on her broken wrist and kicked the bag in his direction. He stooped down, sorted through our armory, and plucked the amulet from the sack.

"You *did*, come prepared!" He laughed and raised his vape to his mouth again. Only this time when he inhaled, he frowned. "Empty…" he muttered.

"Where did you take my sister?" Tears streamed down Sofi's cheeks as she spoke, but she did not whimper.

"Why, she is right here!" His arms outstretched, Vampire Dave twirled like the star of a musical. "And so is your Nancy.

And the farmer's daughter. And all of the other girls my dearly departed Donal procured for me."

My eyes darted from pod to pod. He was right. These weren't some random collection. These were all girls—all about the same age—and all with similar features. "What are you doing with these girls?" I asked.

Vampire Dave unscrewed a little cap from the end of his vape pen and walked to the closest pod. Kneeling on the floor, he pressed a few buttons on a touchscreen mounted in the bottom metal ring, and a small hole opened next to it. "Oh, it's very wonderful. These girls, they are so very wonderful. The answer to all my problems."

"What? They hold the key to the vampire cure?" I craned my neck for a better view of what he was up to. "Let me guess: A cure. Something in their blood that will let you hit the beach. Get a nice tan."

Still on his knees, Vampire Dave unscrewed the cartridge from his vape pen and attached it to the hole in the tank. "A cure? Why would we want a cure? You can have your daylight. The night is much more fun." He laughed, pushed another button on the canister's control board, and the machine let out a small hiss. "I've found something much, much better. Something that will give me the one thing even vampires need."

"Love?" Sofi asked. "These girls will never love you."

He plucked the vape cartridge from the canister, reattached it to its battery, and took a deep puff. "Vampires do not need *love*." He coughed as he chuckled. "But we do need money. And this right here…" He waved his vaporizer at us and blew out a cloud of dark smoke. "This will make me rich."

Whatever this guy was up to, it sure as hell wasn't anything noble. The guy was nuts. And that was enough for me to know if I didn't do something about it now, a hell of a lot more people would get hurt. I steeled my nerves, tightened my grip on the stake, and rushed forward.

Before I knew what was happening, the vampire disappeared from my view in a blur of motion, only to reappear behind Sofi. He wrapped one arm around her waist and pulled her close, his mouth mere inches from her neck. Tears again began to pour down her cheeks, leaving new trails in her mascara, as she stared at me, frozen.

"Come any closer, and I will turn her," the vampire hissed. "Try to escape, and my friends will devour you."

A wave a of fear rushed through my body, and I tensed up, fearing an attack from behind. I glanced over my shoulder and saw nothing.

"Oh, they are there." The vampire's eyes roared red as if on fire, and his neck twitched. "In the hallway. Waiting for you." He twitched again, scratched at his neck, and took another puff from his vape. Sofi's face turned a sickly shade of green, and she coughed as the cloud of smoke enveloped them.

"What the hell is that?" she asked. "Are you vaping… blood?"

"Oh yes, but not just any blood. The blood of your sister!" The vampire laughed again and blew a cloud of smoke into Sofi's face. "She is special, your sister. She and the rest of my little crop here. Something in the genes, and how they interact with the vampire change and the anticoagulants. A perfect mix that not only stays liquid and can be vaporized, but also enhances the powers of the vampire!"

"You made vape juice out of humans?" I tried not to gag. "How did you even find the right ones?"

"Finding is simple. Taking is the hard part. All these people, searching for their history. They send their DNA to a faceless corporation to find their "ancestry." What do you think happens to all that data? I have all the information to find those with the genetic marker available at the click of a few keys."

"So, you find the girls, the ones with these genes, and send some lackey to snatch them from their bedrooms while they sleep?"

"That is one way to put it. Though I like to consider it a harvest."

"A harvest? Like you're picking goddamn pumpkins for a Halloween party?" If he didn't have Sofi in his grasp, I would have thrown a stake at him.

"And think what I could do with you, Mr. Bones. Imagine what powers lie dormant in *your* blood. You must give me a taste!"

"Fat fucking chance, asshole." I made to lunge at him, then stopped again when he lowered his teeth back to Sofi's neck, the fangs making deep impressions on her soft skin.

Vampire Dave sighed. "You leave me no choice then," he said, his thick and muddled against Sofi's neck. His eyes rolled back, showing nothing but whites, and a tiny *snikt* sounded from his mouth as the fangs opened to inject their venom, ensuring Sofi would turn into a vampire. Then, with a dreadful grin, he sunk his teeth into Sofi's throat.

I couldn't save her. Not anymore. I knew that as well as I knew a vampire's always an asshole. But I could save the girls. Stop them from being farmed in this dickhead's dumbass plan to be some kind of vampire drug overlord. Send him back to square one. Hell, maybe even cause a big enough distraction that I *could* save Sofi. Grab her and get her out of here and find someone who could mix up vampire antivenom. It was the only choice that made any sense.

I spun to the left and flung the stake in my hand forward, into the glass of the nearest pod, shattering it instantly. Pools of viscous blue liquid poured from the chamber and the body suspended inside flopped onto the floor like a dead fish. Vampire Dave shrieked, and dragged Sofi's limp body farther to the back of the room, his eyes frantic. I made a dash forward, scooped up the bag of stakes, and began to fire them one at a time into the pods until all that remained was a mess of shattered glass, wet floor, and dead women. Satisfied I'd taken them all out, I then turned to Vampire Dave, but he and Sofi were gone. I raced to the door at the opposite side of the room, the one they'd surely escaped from, and found it locked. I pounded on it until my fists were sore, screaming through the metal until my throat burned.

Behind me, the sound of crackling glass announced I was not alone.

CHAPTER TWENTY-NINE

I should have expected it. After all, the asshole had warned me. But I had been too preoccupied with saving Sofi even to consider saving myself. Now, however, with the room behind me crawling with vampires streaming through the door we'd entered through, I was outnumbered.

To make matters worse, the girls in the glass pods—the ones I'd "destroyed"—well, they weren't destroyed either. One by one they clambered up from the ground, naked and dripping blue goo as they regained their footing and awareness and focused their eyes solely on me. One of them I recognized as Nancy. Another, a mirror image of Sofi. The others? One of them was probably the vampire farmer's daughter. But it didn't matter. They'd all been turned. Between them and the several dozen other, fully-clothed and fully-coherent vampires who'd already entered the room, there was no way in hell I could fight them all.

Closer they came, snarling and snapping like wild dogs. I sniffed the air, and my stomach dropped when I realized what I'd done. Somehow when I busted open those pods, I'd also let out the aerosolized blood. The entire room stank of it, and all these vampires were breathing it in like a cloud of nitrous oxide.

Cami was the first to strike. As I stood there, dumbfounded by the pure hell I'd unleashed by breaking those pods, she sucked in the vaporized blood drug and her face contorted into a look of pure animalistic hatred. Beneath the raging eyes and bared fangs, I recognized a bit of Sofi. And I'm sure that if I had known her earlier—had been able to save her in time—she'd have been just as much a wonderful person as I'd discovered Sofi to be.

In a blaze of movement, she rushed at me, almost as if she were floating across the floor. I dove left, barely avoiding impact, and caught my pants on a shard of broken glass from one of the shattered pods. Blood began to pour freely from the open wound on my knee, and the room full of recently-released vampires sniffed the air in unison, converging their focus on one single thing: a fresh meal called Phoenix.

I stumbled to my feet and returned my eyes to Cami. She'd moved faster than any vampire I'd ever seen before, and I feared her next move would be unavoidable. Her wild eyes flickered in the red fog of the room, darting frenetically this way and that. Finally, they locked onto mine, and as her lips turned up in a horrible grin, Nancy attacked me from the left.

She hit me with the force of a semi-truck and would have sent me flying across the room and into a wall if she hadn't wrapped her arms around me as she attacked. We tumbled to the ground and shards of glass tore through my clothes as we rolled, dotting my body with pricks and cuts like I'd become a human pincushion. As we came to a stop against the base of one of the broken pods, her lips peeled back, and she began to snap her virgin fangs at my neck. I reached out with my right hand and shoved it against her jaw as I searched for an exit.

Vampires surrounded me. Dozens of them. Possibly hundreds. All of them wild and feral from the vapor they breathed and all with a hunger unlike I'd ever seen. At that moment, I accepted my fate. No amount of skills or training could take out a drugged-out army like this. With one hand pressed firmly against Nancy's snapping jaws, I focused my energy inward and counted down from ten.

Then I did what I always hated to do. What hurt like hell and tore me apart, but as they say, desperate times. Time slowed as I counted, and the cacophony of screams, alarms, and screeching vampires faded. An inner heat began to swell in my solar plexus until it could no longer be contained.

At zero, I exploded into a massive ball of flames, torching myself, Cami, Nancy, and every single last one of those fuckers, into a cloud of dirty ash.

NOW

CHAPTER THIRTY

My name is Phoenix. Phoenix Bones. And I hunt monsters.

Thing is, my name wasn't supposed to be Phoenix. It was supposed to Charles.

That's what Mom and Dad called me up until the day I was born. Up until the day I died.

But as I said, I didn't stay dead. Every time I die, I don't stay dead. Instead, I come back. I rise. They could have called me Lazarus, I suppose. But although we were in Mississippi, my parents weren't all that religious. So, they didn't want to call it a miracle. Instead, it was something *magical.*

So, in their minds, when I rose up, I rose up like a Phoenix.

This whole spontaneous combustion thing? Just a coincidence. Don't ask me where it came from. I discovered it by accident, through a series of events I'm too embarrassed to talk about. But how it works? I gave up trying to figure that out a long time ago.

All I know is when I die, I come back. And if I focus all my energy, I can set myself on fire. Then, when it's all over, I rise from the ashes. Problem is, it wears me the fuck out and hurts like hell.

But that's what I did that night deep in the earth beneath a Bulgarian cemetery. I'd run out of options.

I don't know how long I was out, but when I finally came to and clawed my way out of the ash heap, I was naked as a newborn baby, and every last one of the vampires in the room were gone. I kicked around the ash a bit, found my car keys, and backtracked through the facility the way we came until I eventually found the elevator, the hallway, and the entrance back into the crypt.

That's when I found the straggler. The vampire I offed in the beginning of this story. The one little fucker who took advantage of how weak I was after my pyrotechnics display and almost managed to sink his stanky-ass teeth into me.

Yeah, I killed him. But to tell you the truth, I don't know why I bothered. This whole thing is just a pile of shit now. And I guess I won. Kind of. But I don't feel like a winner.

Nancy's dead.

Cami's dead.

The farmer's daughter is dead.

A dozen other girls? Dead.

"Deathbringer," aka Vampire Dave is still "alive."

And Sofi's a vampire.

So, did I win? Or did I lose?

Who the fuck knows.

I'm going to down what's left of those painkillers, kill myself, and go home.

CHAPTER THIRTY-ONE

In the three weeks since I overdosed and took the Eitherway Express back home, I must have been called out to old lady Jackson's house at least a half dozen times. This makes tonight feel like a bad case of déjà vu. Back into the attic which, while no longer the convection oven it had been those few weeks back before the whole vampire debacle, still manages to drive a hefty layer of sweat into my clothes and off my brow.

"This is the last time I'm doing this," I tell her as I ascend the pull-down staircase into her attic. "You call me out here again, and I'm just gonna drop off a net on your front porch." I reach the top of the steps and lean over the side, she's looking back at me with that helpless old lady expression on her face. "Seriously, Ms. Jackson. Call someone to patch up those holes."

The raccoon's back again. Same one as always. After about the third visit back here I tagged her, just to be sure. And wouldn't you know it, that tag is there dangling from her ear. It's not something I'm supposed to do, but I needed to find out if she had one raccoon hell-bent on making her home in Jackson's attic, or if there was some queue for raccoons as they waited to move in the second the previous tenant was evicted.

Now that I know the raccoon is the same one as before I at least have options. Could put a bullet in its head. Or tie it up in a sack and toss it in a river. But I'm too damn nice. Can't hurt a living thing, unless it's a monster.

Just the thought of offing monsters brings back a mix of emotions. I miss it—the thrill of the hunt. The rush of adrenaline as some evil sonofabitch blows up into a mush of guts as I stab him in his undead heart. And then I remember Sofi, though I try my best not to think of her. Every time I do, all I see are visions of her pale and sweat-soaked face, her eyes wide black saucers and her breath wet and heavy, all while she turns. I regret not taking her and Vampire Dave out when I had the chance. Once those fangs were in … I knew better than to think I could save someone once that happened. And my stupid pride, or chivalry, or just plain chicken-shitted-ness, got the better of me.

God only knows what she's going through. God only knows what kind of shit Vampire Dave's up to now.

I stare into the raccoon's eyes, and she stares back at me. This is useless.

Back down the stairs, I climb, emptyhanded. Old Lady Jackson's asking me questions. I don't hear them. All I hear is the droning echo of that asshole vampire's laugh, and the constant reminder I'm nothing but a goddamn failure.

CHAPTER THIRTY-TWO

Three hours and a half bottle of Jameson later, my new cellphone comes to life with a screeching ring.

"Phoenix here. Who's this?" I ask as I strain the water from my freshly-boiled macaroni and send it down the kitchen sink drain.

"You damn well know who this is," comes a gruff reply.

Shit. I probably should have recognized the number, but with caller ID I've kind of gotten used to the phone telling me who was on the other line. I still haven't gotten around to syncing my contacts down to this new one though.

"Asher! Nice to hear from you, man," I lie. But when the boss calls, sometimes you have to lie. "What's going on? Heard things are getting crazy downtown with the election coming up."

"Cut the shit, Bones. I just got off the phone with that Jackson lady. She tells me you refused to do your job."

"Oh, come on, Asher. I've told you about her." A little bit of milk spills on the counter as I pour it into the pan to make the cheese sauce. Before I wipe it up, Ripley hops onto the counter and licks the milk spot clean. "In fact, I believe I suggested you send someone out from housing to check out her place. See if it's fit to live in. It's like she's running a house for wayward raccoons."

A pause on the other end of the line, then a low, extended sigh. "Phoenix. When you were out sick those few weeks recently, did I make a fuss? No. I understand. I'm an understanding guy."

I scoop a few spoons full of my fresh gourmet dinner into my Styrofoam bowl and take a seat at my table. The smell, while normally something that makes my mouth water, does nothing for me. I feel sick to my stomach.

"But this? Outright refusing to do your job? Camel's back is broken, buddy. And you were the one who tossed that final straw up there." Another pause. "You're fired."

I don't bother to argue. Instead, I hang up the phone, dump my dinner into the trash, and dive back into my bottle of whiskey.

I collapse onto the couch. How long I'm out? Who the hell knows.

The police scanner crackles to life, and a little bit of life crackles through me. Not enough to shock me back to sobriety, but enough to perk my ears.

"Attention all units. We have reports of a strange individual at 1428 North Genesee Avenue," the voice announces through the speaker. "Previous residence of the Langenkamp family. Can someone give it a look?"

I hadn't been out to the Langenkamp house since the night I burned it to the ground. Thought about swinging by a few times but knew it wouldn't accomplish much other than to drive me deeper into my depression. So far, I'd been doing well enough on my own in that department, though I did keep the idea in the back of my mind for any future self-flagellation. Now that the call came through, however, I did have reason to go back there. The past few weeks were dead as a doornail as far as anything "mysterious" on the scanner. But a call out to the Langenkamp's? Even if the only description was "a strange individual" *any* individual hanging around the burned-out remains of a missing girl's house—and that's what she still was, as far as the police were concerned … I never reported her death and doubted they'd believe me if I did—is reason enough for me to grab my keys and go for a drive.

After all the Jameson and without a single bit of food since lunch, driving is the last thing I should be doing. Still, here I am. Spotify playlist all queued up, windows down, and the band Phoenix blasting from the speakers into the cool October night air. Winding through the wooded forests of rural Mississippi, worried that at any moment a deer or coyote'll jump out in front of my truck. It's hard enough to stop for them when you're sober. Shape I'm in now? No way in hell I'd be able to stop in time. I check my seat belt. Yep, all buckled up.

The forest begins to thin, and the milky glow of streetlights up ahead announce the town I'm about to enter. Just some random Hicksville in rural Mississippi. Not a place I'd ever been before, and probably not one I'll ever come back to. Gas station. Gas station. Church, church, church. They whiz by, and I glance at my dash. 11:17. Feels like I've been driving for hours.

Google tells me to take a left. I take a left. Then in a half-mile, take a right. Then another right. Before she can tell me I've arrived at my destination, I tap the little X and shut her down. I already know I've arrived. The pile of charred timber at the end of the driveway is enough to tell me that.

Cute little neighborhood, the Langenkamp's used to call home. Much less the Hicksville I first imagined it would be. Or, at least, not trailer trash. Houses run up and down Genesee, staggered far enough apart to give each family some space, but close enough together to call the place a neighborhood. Outdoor floodlights illuminate the front yard of the house to the right. The house on the left is dark. The closest streetlight is right here, at the entrance to the Langenkamp's driveway. It pitches an accusatory radiance over the chaos I left behind last time I visited.

I can only assume the police have already been here. They may not always be the speediest group of people, at least not when there's no immediate danger, but the call came through at least an hour ago. Either they've already been here, or they decided to skip it.

My truck door creaks open, and my boots land on the washed aggregate driveway. I try to stand, but everything spins, and I catch myself on the driver's seat. I'm fine. Just need a few seconds. Must be car sickness.

A few seconds pass, and I give it another go. See? I'm good. The smell of dew and wet charcoal fills the air, and I stumble up the drive and down the stone walk to the place Nancy's front door used to be. I reach out my hand, pretend to knock, and that's when I burst into tears. They stream down my cheeks as I remember Nancy the last time I'd seen her. A rabid mess. Nothing more than a naked animal turned livestock, hell-bent on destroying anyone who dared set her free.

That pain in my gut comes back and stabs at me like it thinks I'm some kind of vampire, and that's where my heart lives. Puke spurts from my mouth into the ashes and the chunky brown liquid puddles into a misshapen doormat. No one's home.

There's nothing here.

Nothing left.

CHAPTER THIRTY-THREE

By the time I wake up, the day's already half over. My stomach hurts again, and I take a few of the pills I brought back with me on my Eitherspace voyage home from Bulgaria. Only about a half dozen left. Not sure what I'll do when I run out, but I guess I'll cross that bridge when I come to it.

Another stab of pain. I take a shit and realize I'm hungry. There's a Captain D's about fifteen minutes' drive from my place, and a plate of catfish sounds damn tasty. Toss in a few hushpuppies. Nice and salty. Just what the doctor ordered.

The line at Captain D's is longer than I expected for a Thursday afternoon. Must be a lot people grabbing late lunches today for some reason. The stabbing pain in my stomach is mostly gone, but it's been replaced by an empty ache as I dream of deep-fried fish, tartar sauce, and a big old cup of orange Fanta. My cell phone rings as I pull up to the speaker to place my order. I tap "ignore" and send whoever's calling to voice mail.

Driving back, I realize I probably shouldn't have gotten this to go. By the time I pull into my driveway, the catfish'll be cold, and it gets all soggy when I reheat it in the microwave. I'm not about to eat it while I drive, though. Not so talented at multitasking and I need to be able to give it a good dip in the sauce before each bite. The hushpuppies, on the other hand, they're perfect for snacking on while behind the wheel, and I pop one in my mouth. The phone rings again, and as I chew, I glance at the screen to see who's calling.

I don't recognize the number. But the ID says the call's coming from France.

Is it Sofi? Did she somehow find my number? I don't remember giving it to her, but there's a lot about that whole escapade I don't quite remember any more. Should I answer? Do vampires call up old friends? It's probably night there now, so maybe she just woke up. My heart flutters when I think of her waking up with a yawn and a stretch then, before even getting out of her coffin, giving her old pal Phoenix a ring-a-ding-ding.

I swallow the hushpuppy and wash it down with slurp of Fanta. "Hello. This is Phoenix." My voice is cool and calm. Like I have better things to do.

"Mr. Bones!" It's a woman on the other line. A French woman, from the sounds of it. Not my Sofi, but still a voice I recognize. "I have been trying to reach you. I hope I have not caught you at a bad time?"

"No… just out grabbing a bite to eat." I hesitate. "Who's this?"

The woman on the other end laughs, and I realize who it is before she tells me. "It is I, your friend Rousseau! Please do not tell me you have forgotten."

I try to think of an answer. Not someone I expected to ever hear from again, and I don't know what to say.

"I have heard about the events in Bulgaria," she continues, before I can reply. "And what happened to our dear Sofi. It is a pity, no?"

"I'd rather not talk about it if that's alright with you." My tires crunch gravel as I pull to the side of the road. Like I said, bad multitasker. "Can you tell me why you're calling?"

"Straight to the point. I like it!"

I put the truck in park and crack open a packet of tartar sauce. Might as well take advantage of the unwelcome interruption. The fish is still hot enough to burn the tips of my fingers so I give it a little more time to cool.

"I am hoping you can help me. Or help us, rather. I know your mission did not end how you would have liked. But the mission does not have to be over."

"Seems pretty over to me."

"It is just a, how you say, hiatus. A break. Time to recharge. And we need you recharged."

"It's not a break. I'm done. El finito." I dip my catfish filet in the tartar sauce and take a bite. Pretty sure that if heaven had a taste, this is what it would be like. Pity this phone call's ruining my bliss. "And who's this *we* you keep talking about. Is your mousy little buddy there with you?"

Another burst of laughter from the other end. "No, Mr. Bones. I am afraid that when we first met, I did not get the chance to explain to you the extent of who I am and who I work for. Our conversation was cut a bit… short."

Now she has my attention. I set what's left of my first catfish filet back in its cardboard box and stop chewing. "Go on…" I say.

"I am part of a group. A much larger group. Of people like me... and like you. People who know the truth of things that go bump in the night and dare to do something about them."

"You're telling me there are more monster hunters out there? You're telling me you're a monster hunter?"

"Yes... and no. I am more a *researcher* than a hunter. My colleagues, they fill other more... administrative... roles. As for other monster hunters? In reality, there are very few left."

"How few?"

"Well, we know of one."

What the hell is this nonsense? I'm now "the last of the monster hunters?" How do they have a group of people in charge of hunting down monsters if there hasn't been anyone to do the hunting? Why do they need me...?

Oh shit, I get it.

"The answer is no," I reply. "I'm a lone wolf, and I hunt in a pack of one. Last thing I need is to get caught up in some bureaucratic bullshit red tape of assignments, approvals, briefings, and debriefings. I've seen enough Mission Impossible movies to know not to trust any agency."

"Very well, Mr. Bones. But if you should change your mind, you have my number."

And she hangs up. Simple as that and she's gone. Have to say, I expected her to put up a bit more of a fight. But, this way she's able to check off the box on her to-do list and tell her boss she did her work for the day. Maybe earn a promotion come review time.

My fish is getting cold.

CHAPTER THIRTY-FOUR

The unwelcome interruption aside, my lunch did a respectable job satiating me, and after I got back home, I managed to fall back asleep, like a fat happy cat. Ripley must have smelled the fish on my lips because she crawled up on me and kept shoving her face into mine like she was trying to eat an odor through brute force. I scratched her behind her ears, she settled in, and we both were out.

Sometime around seven, I woke up again. The stabbing pain had returned, and I downed a few more pills, and now I'm well into the second half of that bottle of Jameson. I've got the Virgin Suicides soundtrack cranked up at full blast while I lie in the dark on my couch, staring at the ceiling.

Two pills left. I counted them. What I'm going to do once these are gone is anyone's guess. Should probably go see a doctor, but for obvious reasons, I tend to avoid them. Lots of questions. Still, something's wrong, and it's not getting any better. Maybe they'll issue me a prescription, but down here in Mississippi they're pretty strict on that stuff. Might have to find an alternate source.

The song changes, and in the silence between tracks, I hear a knock at the door. Remembering the last time I answered the door in the middle of the night, I'm hesitant to answer. The knocking turns to pounding—loud enough now that it's winning a battle against the drone of "Cemetery Party" pumping from my speakers. I pick up my phone, turn on the selfie camera, and the face on the screen looks like shit. I haven't showered since Jackson's attic, haven't shaved since Paris and am decked out in nothing but a pair of day-old boxers and a sweat-stained, previously-white-but-now-yellow, t-shirt. As I pull on my terrycloth robe, I take another swig from the bottle, and pad over barefoot to see who's making all the damn racket. See if I can kick them the hell off my porch.

My door used to have a peephole. But some punk thought it'd be fun to stick gum in it a few years back and I never bothered to clear it out. Front window's off too far to the left to ever get a clear view of who's on the porch, but I scan the yard anyway. No sign of a car, let alone a person. But the knocking continues.

"I'm coming, I'm coming." The words slur as they spill from my lips. "Who's there? Tell me or I'll shoot a hole through the door and blast your guts across my lawn."

The knocking stops, but no one answers. I peel back the curtains again for a final look and still see nothing but my overgrown lawn and my rustbucket of a truck dully reflecting moonlight from the parts where the paint's still good.

Another quick drink, swing open the door, and who do I find?

Sofi "I Thought I'd Lost You Forever" LeRoux, staring me right in the face. Fangs curled over the bottom lips of her giant-ass grin. In her hands, she's holding something big and round and hairy.

She tosses it my way. I dodge, let it fall to my floor, and it rolls to the side of my sofa.

"There's been a change in management," Sofi says, as two dead eyes in Vampire Dave's severed head glare at me from my living room floor. "Mind if I come in?"

CHAPTER THIRTY-FIVE

I sure as shit do mind if she comes in. And she knows she can't. Not unless I either invite her in or I have something of hers. Sure, she could argue I have her heart. But we know that's a lie and it's probably the other way around. Dave's head? Doesn't count. No way the rules would allow a vampire to toss something of theirs into someone's house and be all "Oh whoopsie, I dropped my thing. Guess I'll be coming in to get it." That'd be way too easy a workaround.

"What do you want?" I have about a thousand questions, and any other day I'd probably be thrilled to see her. Well, if she wasn't a vampire. But she is. But now I'm thinking any time I see her from here on out I'm in for a shitty interaction.

"Please? Let me in, Phoenix. It is cold out here, and I promise not to… bite." Her lips curl up into a wide grin, exposing more of her freshly-grown fangs.

"I have to say, Sofi, you looked smokin' before, but this vampire phase, it really works for you. Not too late to become a model, you know." It's true too. She used to catch my attention before, but now? So unfortunate she's a vampire.

No Phoenix, you cannot let her in.

"Fine then, I will talk to you from here. But you should know you are not being very polite." She juts out her lower lip in a false pout, catching it on her fangs and draws two thin streaks of blood. "As you see, I have taken care of Vampire Dave," she says, all businesslike. "It turns out he was not any nicer once you got to know him."

"And what does that have to do with me? Should I say thank you? Too little, too late, Sof." I move to shut the door, but she stops me.

"He had a good thing going, Phoenix. Inspired, but without focus. I know it is hard to understand since you are not a… well, you know." Her pale cheeks somehow manage to blush a slight shade of pink. "Anyway, I need you. I have gone over the numbers, and Crimson Bliss has the potential to be huge. Bigger than he ever imagined."

"Is that what you're calling that bloody vape juice now? Crimson Bliss? Catchy name, but sorry." My fingers grip the door, ready to slam it shut in her stupid, beautiful face. "Answer is still no."

"Dis oui. S'te plaît !" Now she's batting her eyelashes at me, stepping seductively forward. Like a sexy undead French minx. "We could be together. Forever, if you'd like. And the sex? Oh, Phoenix, you can never imagine the pleasure of vampire lovemaking."

My stomach is in knots. Do I embrace her like they would in a classic film? Do I politely invite her in so we can discuss this further? Do I tear off my shirt and pants and lunge onto her like in one of those "romance" books? Or do I grab the stake from the shelf at the side of the door and slam it through her cold, conniving heart?

Sofi senses my indecision, and the seductress is gone, replaced by a face etched in madness and hate. "I am doing this with, or without you, Phoenix. With you, with your *powers*, will be much cleaner. In and out, harvesting the wild crops as cleanly as we can. Without you? There will be rivers of blood left in our wake." She pauses to reach her hand into her bag and pulls out the amulet. "I will not trust this to anyone. Deathbringer was foolish to let it into the hands of a mortal. But we vampires still cannot use it to enter a home in which we are not welcome. So, we will take this to the streets."

"All over a stupid drug? Come on, Sofi. I know you. You're smarter than this."

"Not just a drug, a path to fortune." Her hand slides into the front pocket of her jeans and pulls out Vampire Dave's vaporizer. She takes a drag and blows a coppery black cloud at my face. A flash of red rushes through her eyes, and she steps forward again. We're standing face-to-face, yet she cannot touch me, not unless I break the barrier between my house and the outside world. Her breath stinks of death. "I'm expanding operations, Phoenix. The vampire market, it is too small. The humans, there is nothing like this for them. Just a taste of vampire power is better than any drug they can imagine. But to do it, I will need more raw material."

"So, I join you, help you harvest all the humans you can identify that are compatible with your program, and my reward is vampire sex?"

"Yes, with me. Or anyone you choose. I will not be jealous."

My left hand goes for the stake, but before I can slam it through her breast and straight into her inhuman heart, she's already ten feet away.

"I will not forget this, Phoenix." She sinks her fangs into her wrist, drawing a trickle of blood. "Think it over. Next time I will not be so polite." She presses the amulet against the wound and disappears.

My heart is pounding, threatening to tear through my chest like the baby Xenomorph in Alien. I can't think straight, thoughts and emotions running rampant through my brain. Before I realize it, one hand is on the door to my bedroom closet—the other gripping the burned-up handle of my Colt. Her trail should still be bright. I can track her. Find where the hell she's been hiding and put a stop to this madness.

But what will I do when I find her? For once, I stop to think and realize rushing into battle is a pretty shitty plan. I release the doorknob and collapse onto my bed. My head cracks against something solid, and I find my new phone where my pillow should be.

I unlock it, go into my call history, and tap *dial*. On the second ring, the other end answers.

"I'm in," I say. "Tell me what to do next."

"Very well, Mr. Bones. Pack your things and rest," Rousseau replies. "Your flight leaves tomorrow."

"Where am I going?" I ask, dragging my suitcase out from under my bed.

"Germany. Munich, to be precise."

"What do I do when I arrive? Will you be there?"

"I am sorry, but no. I will remain in Paris. But someone will be there to greet you." Her voice is calm and reserved, though I detect a hint of disappointment beneath it. "And oh yes, before I forget. Please bring your gun."

"Already packed," I reply as I toss my charred gun into my suitcase. And for the first time in weeks, I crack a smile.

CHAPTER THIRTY-SIX

Deutschland. Another place I've never been before, though at least this time I've decided to prepare myself. Since I no *sprechen sie Deutsch* and I don't want to be stuck in the same kind of situation where I didn't *parlez-vous the Francais* and I sure as shit didn't *govorya bŭlgarski*, I downloaded one of those language apps before losing Wi-Fi. Turns out the plane has Wi-Fi available though, and my free ticket courtesy Rousseau & Company included access. Hell, I even got to sit First Class. Have to say, although it's slower than Eitherspace, travel this way sure is a lot less painful.

Ripley's a resourceful cat, and she did just fine fending for herself during my last extended trip overseas. But since it's getting a little chillier at night, and I didn't want to deal with another mass grave of rodent carcasses on my front porch, I decided it would be best to drop her off at Mom's. Of course, Mom wanted to know where I was going, and when I'd be home, but I mentioned something about business, and it might be a while. I didn't want to worry her more than necessary—especially since there's a high probability I might not make it back.

My flight took off at about four, and from what it says on my itinerary, I should be in Munich sometime around noon tomorrow. What I'll find there once I land, I have no idea. All I do know is my fingers are itching to stake some vampires, and if I'm lucky, take out a few other creepy-crawlies while I'm at it.

Actually, I take that back. I do know one more thing.

Stirb, du elendes drecksstück! means, "Die, you miserable piece of trash!" in German.

You really do learn something new every day.

CHAPTER THIRTY-SEVEN

Getting my gun through customs was a pain in the ass. For some reason, the Germans don't like it when you bring firearms into their country. Even with the proper documentation and licensing and all that nonsense that Rousseau (or whoever her secretary is) took care of for me ahead of time, they still had questions. *Why are you bringing a gun? Do you plan to hurt someone? Why is it burned like this? Who the hell uses a six-shooter in the 21st Century?* Etcetera, etcetera.

By the time I made it through and got hold of my luggage, the clock on my phone (now with a fancy International plan) read 13:17. Fun fact: they use a twenty-four-hour clock here. I was hungry as a gator and pretty damn tired after learning the hard way that I can't sleep worth a damn on an airplane.

Luggage in hand, I texted the number Rousseau had given me and waited. After almost twenty minutes I'm about ready to call an Uber.

Then I see him, a giant of a man with broad shoulders, a prominent forehead, blonde hair down to his shoulders and a beard so thick you could hide a marmot in it. He's holding a sign that says, "Phoenix Bones," high above his head as his eyes search the terminal.

Before the whole world knows I'm here, I hustle over, tear the sign from his grip, and pray to God he doesn't punch me.

"Herr Bones!" He looks me over and frowns. "You do not resemble your Facebook photo."

"Yeah, I'm trying a new style," I answer. "Where we going? Let's get this shit over and done with."

"Not so fast. First, we prepare." The hulk of a man takes my suitcase and marches away. "I am Wolfgang, by the way. Wolfgang Von Trier."

"I'd tell you my name, but it seems you already know it," I reply, hoping to produce a laugh. He doesn't respond but instead keeps forging ahead, the crowd seeming to split before his presences like the Red Sea did for Moses. "Not much of a talker? That's fine."

He doesn't say another word until we're in the car.

"Take us to Hirschau Beer Garden," he says to the driver. The driver nods and takes off.

I watch through my window as the landscape of the airport give way to farmland and forest and cross a river. As we drive, I'm amazed at how much of the area is still farmed to this day. For such a major city, Munich isn't what I expected. Soon enough, however, we pass by a stadium, and the city begins to thicken before us. I roll down my window for a hint of the fresh air and roll it back up immediately.

"Sewage treatment plant," Wolfgang says and starts to laugh. It's a hearty laugh. Contagious. I start to laugh too, and then I'm hit with it again, that damn pain in my gut. I pop the last of my painkillers and force a smile.

"You are having pain? We will drink beers and talk. Oktoberfest in Munich washes all pains away!" He slaps me on my shoulder, and I try not to wince. *Try*, being the operative word.

A few minutes later the car pulls up to the curb at the side of a beautiful green space, flocked with people. As I step out into the cool afternoon, the sound of polka music fills the air. Wolfgang hefts my suitcase from the trunk, and the car drives off.

"Aren't we going to the hotel first?" I ask.

"Come," he says, already heading off with my bag. "We will eat and drink. We will talk. Then we work."

I followed him as he led us through the park, stopping only to take in the odd sight of a bunch of guys in wetsuits surfing in the river. A crowd of onlookers had gathered, and I searched the area for any police since the guys obviously had to be drunk to be doing something so crazy.

"You are a surfer?" Wolfgang asked.

I shook my head. "Those guys sure look like they came prepared though."

"People love to surf Eisbach. I think they are crazy, but hey, sometimes crazy is good."

I keep watching as one of the surfers holds the wave for about twenty seconds, zooming from one bank to the other, back and forth. He idles at the side and another surfer, this one severely underdressed in nothing but board shorts, hops onto his board. Halfway across the river, he goes down, and a few people in the crowd laugh. Wolfgang tugs at my arm, and we continue on our way.

We pass a few more groups of people, (some of them stark-ass naked—I don't bother to ask) and our journey ends at a large beer garden tucked away in what Wolfgang tells me is called The English Garden.

"It is much larger than your Central Park," he says, unable to hide the air of pride on his face.

We take a seat at a long wooden table and Wolfgang orders two giant mugs of beer and a plate of Bavarian pretzels. Hundreds, if not thousands of other people mill around us, many of them in lederhosen. The wind smells like a brewery, and a mix of music and laughter fills the air. We eat, drink, and make small talk.

Hard to believe a dastardly nest of vampires lurks somewhere so close to a place this happy.

I take a long drink from my beer and ask, "So, what's the plan? Where are the vampires? Where's Sofi?"

Wolfgang scowls. "Quiet," he whispers. "We do not know if it is safe."

I scan the crowd. No one's paying any attention to us. They're all either focused on their beers or the busty waitresses in the tight white shirts and short skirts. I force myself to stop staring and turn back to Wolfgang. "It's the middle of the damn day. There aren't any vampires out now."

"You can never be certain." He shrugs, swallows his entire mug of beer in one long gulp, and lets out an earth-trembling burp. I can smell it from across the table. "Better to be safe than sorry."

As we drink, I try a few more times to make him talk. But nothing works.

"Relax and enjoy. This is the best time of year to be in Bavaria! You will have your fight soon enough." He orders another beer. I think this is his eighth. I'm still only halfway through my third. "Finish your drink," he says. "Then we will hire a car to take us to Alstadt."

"What's that?"

"Old town in Munich. It is where we will get ready. Gear up. Prepare for battle."

I tip my mug back, finish what's left in a single drink, and slam my glass onto the table.

"Let's get this party started," I say, and as I stand up, I fall right back down, face-first onto the concrete.

CHAPTER THIRTY-EIGHT

When I woke up, there was a finger in my butt. Now, on a normal day, that might not have been such a bad thing. Problem here was I had no idea where I was or whose finger might be prowling around. As I let out a grunt of surprise and clenched my cheeks, the finger slipped on out, and the snapping sound of rubber gloves echoed behind me.

"That woke him up," said a gruff voice with a thick German accent.

I sit upright, blinking the sleep from my eyes, and Wolfgang appears on a wobbly metal chair about two feet from my face.

"All clear in the poop chute," says a second voice. Also male, also German, but not one I recognize. I turn to face my invader and see a small, bespectacled man topped with a thinning patch of blonde hair. He's wearing a bleached lab coat, and a stethoscope dangles from his collar like a postmodern necklace. A diminutive giggle trickles up from his gullet and escapes from the crease between his constricted lips and my butt cheeks spasm. "How are you feeling today, Herr Bones?"

"Fine, I guess." I cough twice and the second one rattles around my chest like a busted-down Studebaker. Looking down, I expect to see an examination room table beneath me, its white paper stuck to my bare ass. Instead, I find a set of periwinkle flannel sheets. Across the room, floor-to-ceiling windows draped in ivory curtains. "Where am I?"

"Home base," Wolfgang replies. He leans forward and reaches out his hand to my forehead, tipping it back. His blue eyes stare into mine as if searching for something. Perhaps he's hunting for a lie I might keep hidden inside. "You were sick. Was worried about you and brought you here and called up the doctor."

"Nothing to worry about," says the doctor. "Other than the bump on your head, you appear to be tippity-top. Though I do not think your body is liking the medicine and the alcohol. Not a good mix."

At the mere mention of the pain medicine, my gut goes into a series of convulsions. Pain courses like a fiery blade through my abdomen and I buckle over.

"Oh, now this is something new." The doctor sounds almost excited at this new development. "What is this feeling?"

"Need something... for the pain," I barely manage to eke out the words, it hurts so bad.

The doctor rummages through his bag, pulls out a needle, and stabs it into my arm. "Temporary relief. Take these; they will help longer term." He gives me two very familiar-looking pills, and I swallow them down with a glass of water I find sitting on the table next to my bed.

They wait patiently for my body to relax, and once it does, I tell them the whole story. They don't seem too surprised about the whole "I can come back from the dead" thing, so I assume that's old news. But the part where I recount getting stabbed, then slowly dying, then being continually afflicted with pain where the supposed fatal wound happened? That, they're interested in. Problem is, they don't seem too keen to do much about it. At least not now.

"This is very interesting, Herr Bones," says the doctor, who I now know is named Demetrius. "All of it is very interesting. I would very much like to investigate your insides. For now, though, we must wait for another day."

"Assuming there is another day," Wolfgang says. "I am not lying to you, Phoenix. This is a dangerous mission."

"Yes. Very dangerous," Demetrius continues. "If you live, I will further explore your condition. But for now, it is not worth the time. Also, very expensive."

I consider arguing, not so much because I need to have this fixed right now, but more on the principle of the thing. I decide against it though, because they're right. This probably is dangerous. Everything I do is dangerous. Yet, I always come back. Who's to say this would be any different. Besides, I've made it this long.

"As long as you can give me a few dozen more of those," I say, pointing to the bottle of pills on the side table, "I think I can wait."

Wolfgang and Demetrius exchange looks and Wolfgang shrugs. Demetrius sighs, digs back into his bag, and produces three more bottles.

"Do not take them all at once, unless you are wanting to be dead again."

"I'll keep that in mind," I answer. "As a backup plan."

After the doctor leaves, I climb out of bed and take a quick shower. When I finish there's a plate of scrambled eggs and sausage waiting in my room. I scarf it down and top it off with a mug of coffee and head out the door. Downstairs, the place opens to reveal a large space, extravagantly furnished in a classic German style. Wolfgang is stretched out on the leather sofa, his nose in a book. He sits up at the sound of my footsteps on the antique wooden staircase.

"You are ready?" he asks, though it's more a statement than a question. Before I can answer, he's headed across the hand-scraped hardwood to a wall covered in bookshelves. Then, like he's some kind of kraut Batman, tips out a book and a panel of bookshelves slides away, revealing a set of stairs.

I'm immediately reminded of the last time I ventured down a set of strange stairs behind a hidden door and pause momentarily.

"Come. You must get geared up," Wolfgang urges. "We have so many surprises you are going crap a stone."

"You mean shit a brick?"

"Yes, shit brick. Crap stone. Both painful. Just come."

I do as I'm told, and when I see what's hidden behind door number two, I start checking my underpants for bricks.

CHAPTER THIRTY-NINE

It's a goddamn armory down here. Walls covered in pretty much every type of gun imaginable. Machine guns, assault rifles, handguns, a half dozen bazookas ... hell, I even see a few grenade launchers. Whoever Rousseau and Wolfgang and the rest of this crew work for, they're serious. Though maybe not *too* serious, since most of this won't do shit against a vampire. Sure, might blow off a limb or two ... piss 'em off. But nothing permanent.

"You look disappointed," Wolfgang says.

I don't know what to say to him. This is a damned impressive set of firepower they've stocked up, and I don't want to let him down. "It's just that…"

"Oh, this?" He gestures to his wall of death. "This is not for vampire. This is for… different project. Not concern you. We have better, more special surprises for you."

He flicks a switch on the wall, and a set of lights flickers on across the room, illuminating a table with a gleaming array of items I can't quite make out from where I'm standing. Wolfgang turns to me and smiles. "Go ahead. I will show you. You will be like a kid in a candy store."

Damn right I am. Before I'm halfway to the treasure trove of goodies they've prepared for me, I'm just about drooling. A gleaming new crossbow shines up at me like a heavenly beacon of justice. Rows of wooden crossbow bolts and handheld stakes spread out in front of it. A few other items I don't immediately recognize but can't help but feel excited about anyway.

"You like?" Wolfgang's smile hasn't faded, and it's spread to me like a contagion. "All for vampires. Best of the best. We have a, how do you say, *benefactor* who has many resources."

"May I?" I ask as I reach for the crossbow.

"Of course! It is yours now. A gift."

I lift it from the table, measure the heft of it in my hands. It's a sturdy piece of machinery—hand-carved and well-balanced. I pop in a bolt and fire it across the room, where it sinks a healthy four inches into the stone wall.

"Mahogany. Very strong," Wolfgang picks up one of the wooden stakes from the table and gives it to me. It's different from other stakes I've used—has a strange kind of glass capsule embedded in the shaft. "These we call glow sticks. You smash this into a vampire and the glass breaks. Chemicals inside mix and magic happens. Boom! Blast of ultraviolet light from the reaction!"

"Lethal even without a direct hit to the heart?"

"Possible. Depending on where you hit. But it will burn a big hole and hurt like hell."

"Badass." I scan the table, eager to find even more toys to add to my play chest. "What else you got?"

"Those are light grenades," he says, pointing to a stack of what seem like metal hockey pucks. "Push the button on top, toss, and count to three. At three, make sure you are looking away, or you will burn your eyes out."

"Does it come with Ray-Bans?" I ask.

"I could acquire for you a welder shield." Wolfgang slides a small wooden case, about the size of a cigar box across the table to me. "And now, for the grand finale. You brought your gun?"

I nod quietly, peek into the box, and find a half dozen bullets cradled in foam inside. They're not like any bullets I've ever seen. Though they're the right caliber for my gun, these don't gleam at me with the cold, dead stare of metal. Instead, they almost seem to glow.

"We call those fraulines cherry bombs," Wolfgang says. "Cherry wood bullets with tipped with glass points containing the same concoction used in the glow stick. Difference is these shatter on impact. Burst of UV, then splinters of wood scatter through the body. Hit them in the heart, and you will see the biggest pop you ever see. Miss? Give them a brand-new hole."

"Only six?" I ask, as I gently stroke the polished cherry wood of the bullet and run my finger down the gleaming brass cartridge.

"Very difficult to make. Rousseau requests you use them… wisely."

CHAPTER FORTY

We'll hit them in daylight. When they're least prepared. Part of me feels a pang of guilt at the idea of taking Sofi out while she sleeps. But something tells me that by the time I finally met up with her, she'll be wide awake and ready to rumble.

On the drive over, my body trembles with anticipation. Wolfgang sits beside me, calm as a cucumber, while I do my best not to break out into a torrent of sweat. Never before have I worked with a team. And nothing in my past had been as planned out and focused as this operation. Sure, I had Sofi with me for a while, but she was more of a sidekick tagalong than actual backup. Wolfgang had training. I was sure of it. What kind of training, I didn't bother to ask. But the man knew how to handle a weapon and how to handle his nerves. Even though they'd called me in like I was the savior of the human race, now, as we roll into battle, I feel unprepared and under the microscope. Probably my self-doubt. Stage fright.

To take my mind off the details of the plan, which have been on an infinite loop inside my head ever since we slapped the map on the table and drew out our approach, I dig out my phone and browse the news. Unfortunately, that doesn't help much.

Locally in Munich, at least three girls have gone missing in the past week. All in their late teens or early twenties. The news says this was abnormal.

No shit.

Police are urging women to only travel in groups and to lock their doors at night. False hopes of safety. If you read deep enough into the articles, you'll see none of this will do a damn bit of good. Each of these girls has been taken from her home, with doors locked and no signs of forced entry.

I search the global news stories, and the pattern continues. Young women up and missing from their homes. A few disappearances from the streets, out after the bars close, etc. Too, but those are harder to pin on Sofi and her crew since they could be any old maniac snatching up girls. The ones from the locked houses? Those were courtesy of *my* maniac.

And she had been such a sweet girl.

Though it hasn't been announced publicly, Sofi's now in charge of Cloud Nein. At least that's what Wolfgang says he's heard from his sources. I've heard of hostile takeovers but killing the CEO and taking his head is a bit extreme, even for vampires. In the midst of such an upheaval, Sofi's sure to be onsite. Or, at least that's what we're hoping. Where she's taking the girls now that the Bulgarian headquarters is charcoal is anyone's guess, but she's running the show from here.

In and out. As many casualties as it takes. No more, no less.

Take out Sofi, get the amulet, and shut this hellish operation down.

The car pulls up to the curb outside a short glass-walled office building. Not quite a skyscraper, but still a few dozen stories tall. Recently built. Hip-looking neighborhood. Wolfgang tells me this is the heart of Munich's burgeoning tech scene.

I open my door and step out onto the pavement. My fancy new dress shoes clack on the concrete. I tried to argue against it earlier, and I still feel like a bit of a clown. But one glimpse of my reflection in the car window, and I must admit I look damn good. Much better than back at the hideout before Wolfgang gave me a makeover.

"You look like shit, Phoenix," Wolfgang had said. "Where we are going, you must look crisp. Clean. We are not your Silicon Valley with the hoodies and Zuckerburgs."

I looked at in the mirror and the face looking back reminded me I still hadn't shaved since before that first trip to Paris all those weeks ago. Sure, I burned it all off when I torched myself, but it all grows back as soon as my body rebuilds itself Like in The Wolf Man when Lon Chaney goes from clean cut to mangy hairball in minutes flat. I don't know how my body does it, but somehow it keeps track of about how hairy I'd been before I burned all that hair off and resets itself to as close an approximation as it can make. And since I hadn't shaved in months, much less gotten a haircut, I did have a bit of that crazy mountain man hobo look going on.

"We clean you up. Fitted for suit. Something nice. Clean and classic. Like James Bond."

"How the hell am I supposed to fight in a suit?" I asked.

"I do it all the time. And so does Bond. And John Wick. Even Kingsman. You figure it out."

So, after a much-needed shower, they measured me and gave me a nice trim. As for what they did with the clothes I came in with? I'm not positive, but I think I caught Wolfgang dousing them with gasoline.

Now, as I stand on the street outside one of Munich's hottest tech startups, the reflection in the car window dons a sharp charcoal fitted suit, has a chin is as smooth as a baby's ass and his hair is cleaner cut than it's been since his mom made him go to a salon before high school graduation. I even got the aviator Ray-Bans I asked for.

I'm one dapper sonofabitch. Pity I'll be covered in blood soon.

"We go to 12th floor." Wolfgang closes his door, and the car drives off. "Is Cloud Nein."

"Sounds like some kind of club." I adjust my collar and pick up my briefcase. "Let's party."

"It is not a club." Wolfgang ignores my kickass line and heads toward the entrance. "It is a business. Very fancy. Lots of…" he rubs his fingers together in the international sign for money.

"What is they do here again?"

"Tech startup. Pharmaceutical. Like your Theranos but with actual product."

"Yeah, the vape stuff." I step through a set of revolving doors into a modern, yet stylishly appointed lobby. No security. Kind of surprising, but I'm not about to complain.

"Yes, the vape. Crimson Bliss. But much more. Mood therapy. Vape is just the quick moneymaker. They will find much more to do with this new discovery."

The elevator doors close and Wolfgang taps the button for floor twelve. I hum "The Girl from Ipanema" again, and don't manage to produce a laugh from Wolfgang either. He takes his sidearm from its holster, checks the ammo, and puts it back. My own gun hangs inside my sport coat, hidden from view, but accessible should I need it. But we both know the first round's on Wolfgang.

Our ascent slows, and the elevator comes to a halt. A ding rings out, and the doors open into an open space filled with low cubicles. The brushed metal sign hanging on the raw wood wall behind the receptionist desk announces in lowercase letters we've arrived at Cloud Nein.

Wolfgang draws his gun and starts firing.

The first shot doesn't hit anyone. It's just a warning. An announcement.

We. Are. Here.

Back when we discussed the plan, there had been some talk of covert action. But we all knew there was no way to sneak in here. We had to come in guns blazing. During work hours the place would be full of regular employees, and they'd freak out. Enough distraction to give the real bad guys a harder time picking us off. Might have meant a few innocent casualties along the way, but when you're working in the tech scene … are you really that innocent?

Screams ring out, and a few dozen heads drop immediately from view. A guy in a security uniform races our way, waving his piece and shouting something in German. Wolfgang answers with a bullet between the eyes. Blood and brains spray out. This one's human.

I suddenly realize the place is wall-to-wall windows. No way in hell vampires would be able to survive in here. But then an alarm goes off, and the lights turn red, and steel shutters begin to close down over every window. I swing my briefcase onto the receptionist's desk where it lands with a dull clunk, pop open the latches, and load up. All the while shots are ringing out from around me. People are screaming, and alarms are wailing. I pray Wolfgang's showing some restraint and only killing bad guys.

"Everyone, out of the building," Wolfgang shouts. "If you do not leave, I will shoot. Do you understand?"

The firing stops, and a crowd of people rushes by, all headed toward the elevator like cattle through an open gate. It fills in seconds, but still more people try to cram themselves in. The smart ones take the stairs.

Another shot rings out, followed by the heavy thud of a body hitting the floor. I take up my crossbow in my right hand the briefcase in my left and forge ahead.

The entire floor is dark now, aside from the red glow of the emergency lights. It's like we're inside a photographic darkroom. Up ahead I see Wolfgang, popping from row to row among the cubicles. I step over a body, careful not to slip in the bloody puddle where his head used to be.

"All is clear. For now." Despite the action, Wolfgang's voice is calm and steady. I don't think he's broken a sweat. "You go on, I will cover this entrance."

So far, everything has gone according to plan. I'm up next.

Now let's find out how well I can follow directions.

CHAPTER FORTY-ONE

I enter the second room, the glow of emergency lights casting a hellish crimson gloom across a central area filled with a maze of low-rise cubicles. Glass-walled offices line the two sides of the room, and far ahead, I can just make out the dull reflection of lights against a wall of one-way privacy glass. If our map is right, and so far, it has been, Sofi's office is on the other side of that wall.

I wonder if she can see me.

The room appears empty, but I'm a keen believer in the saying that looks can be deceiving. I wish I had the forethought to ask for a replacement pair of night-vision goggles, but you know what they say about wishes. At least by now, my eyes have mostly adjusted to the dark. Still, I'm at a huge disadvantage against any vamps that might be lurking in the shadows here. I scan the room and breathe a sigh of relief as the alarms die down.

In my version of the plan, this is the part where I would have put on my fancy new headphones, cranked up the volume, and started listening to "Connected" by Stereo MCs. I've always thought that would be a kickass tune for a monster-killing track. But when I brought the idea up to Wolfgang, he quickly shut it down, arguing that I needed to be able to hear my surroundings … something about *being one with my environment*. I disagreed. Said the headphones I want have this fancy new ambient sound technology so I'd be able to hear everything around me, even with the sound on, but he didn't buy into my argument. I'm pretty sure he was being cheap, but now that I'm in this situation, I can see his point. When you can't see worth a damn, you've got to rely on your other senses, and although vampires stink, I ain't no bloodhound. So, sound it is. One with the environment. I'm silent, like a ninja.

A badass ninja with a vampire-killing crossbow and a whole lot of other toys, ready to bring the pain.

I take a step forward, my shoes silent on the carpet.

Another step.

I look left. I look right.

I pause and hold my breath, listening. All I hear are the echoes of muffled screams from the room Wolfgang cleared.

I crouch down low. As low as I can get without cramping my legs. But these damn modern open-office-concept cubicles don't give me much of a place to hide. A blessing and a curse, I suppose. No place to hide for me means no place to hide for *them*.

Something crashes to the floor off to my right. I swing my crossbow over and stare down the sights. Nothing there. At least nothing I can see.

I consider ignoring it. Move forward. Get to the door. Get to Sofi and put an end to all this bullshit.

Another sound to my left—this one more a whoosh than a crash. A few sheets of paper flutter in the air like something fast rushed by and caught them in its wake.

Left? Right? Or just make a run for it?

A light crackling sound from somewhere ahead of me, but I can't see a thing. I can smell it, though. That burnt copper stink. One of those bastards in here having a puff of the old Crimson Bliss.

I take a step in the direction of the nearest office—the closest place I can imagine the bastard hiding.

Then another step.

Before my foot hits the ground, he's rushing at me, out of the murky shadows like a fleshy bullet — the red of the lights catching in his eyes, reflecting against his huge black pupils. I fire my crossbow and catch him in the right shoulder. It knocks him back but doesn't slow him down. No time to reload. He's less than a yard away from me, and the stink of his breath almost makes me gag, but I manage to pull a glow stick from my inside pocket and slam it into his chest as he closes the final gap between us.

Direct hit. He bursts into flames, staggers back, and blows up in a mess of chunky gore.

I spin on my heel and search the room to make sure no one's coming from behind and load another bolt into the crossbow. Other than the steady drip-drip-drip of blood from what's left of vampire number one, the room is silent. I step past what's left of the body and take the left side. Figure if anything else is coming, it's coming from the right. Might as well get as much distance between me and it as I can.

As I pass the entrance to each office, I poke my head in and do a quick scan. Aside from some laptops and way too many inspirational posters, they're empty.

Not much farther. Just two more offices on my left and I'll hit the far wall. The wall with the door to Sofi's office.

Is she watching?

Is she laughing?

Movement to my right. On the far side of the room, past the cubicles. Must have been hiding in the office. Another vampire crouches down against the wall, and his beady eyes are catching the light like tiny fireballs. A second one's here somewhere too. Can't see him, but I can hear him—his raspy breath giving away his presence. The problem is, I don't know where that one's hiding.

I can't worry about him right now. I need to focus on what I can see. I duck down low, out of sight, and line up my crossbow in the approximate direction I saw the vampire. When I pop up from cover, he's still there, and before he can move, I fire. The bolt lodges itself in his right eye socket, and I quickly load up another. As he's reeling, I fire again. Straight into the heart. Slam. Bang. Boom. Explosion.

Number two's down, but number three takes advantage of the distraction and rushes me from the rear of the room, near where I entered. His body slams into me, knocking us both to the ground, and all I hear are snarls and snapping jaws. The air smells like someone ate a used diaper, shat it out, then ate that shit, and then shat it out its mouth.

We roll around a bit, and it's all I can do to keep him from ripping my throat out. Then, when he's on top of me, I do the biggest donkey kick I can. His ribs crack from the blow, and he's off. I scramble to my feet and grab another glow stick. We're staring each other down like two wrestlers, ready for a first takedown, then he bolts to his left, down the hallway and up to the glass privacy wall. He raps on the glass three times, and the doors swing open. In come another half dozen vampires. I make a mental count of my ammo.

They're coming at me slowly, like a wave of infantrymen. Only instead of bayonets, these are bearing fangs. I take a step back. Then another. And another, until I'm backed up against the wall right next to the door I came in through.

I slip my hand into my front coat pocket and wrap it around a metal puck. My index finger finds the button on top, and I press it down until it goes click. I toss it into the center of the room and shield my eyes. Even with my eyelids closed, the flash burns at my retinas. A second later, I open my eyes and am met with a half dozen flaming vampires staggering around the office. As they burn up, they fall to the ground and crumble into clouds of dust.

I scan the room. Stacks of paper and the odd office chair burn, but nothing moves. Pretty sure that was the last of them. Within seconds I'm at the other end of the room, my hand on the warm metal of the door handle to Sofi's office.

I take a deep breath and turn the knob.

CHAPTER FORTY-TWO

Other than the expected furniture, Sofi's office is empty. On the wall to the right of the door, there's a switch marked "shutters." I hit it and the shutters open. Bright, blinding sunlight streams into the room. If there were any vampires in here before, they're gone now.

Where the fuck is she?

I search through her desk and find nothing other than some contracts waiting for a signature. Her computer's locked with a password. Nothing inside the desk other than a few pens and a stapler.

Then I see it, almost hidden, it's been built into the wall so well—another door.

I gently open it and find a staircase leading up to the 13th floor.

CHAPTER FORTY-THREE

When I reach the top of the stairs, I find another door, and it's unlocked. I step through and find myself in a luxurious penthouse apartment. Metal shutters cover the windows, but the place is lit up with candles like someone's ready for a dinner party.

I find myself in a living room with a big-screen TV and a pretty badass sound system. I recognize the song pumping from the speakers. It's *Love Like a Sunset* by Phoenix.

I pass through a dining room and a stark white modern kitchen. Opal granite countertops sparkle under the recessed lighting. Not a thing is out of place.

This is so unlike Sofi.

"Anyone here?" I call out. "Sofi? It's me, Phoenix."

I don't expect anyone to answer, but like always, Sofi surprises me.

"In the bedroom," she calls out in a nonchalant voice. Like she's my wife, and she just needs a few more minutes to put on her makeup before we head out for our weekly Friday dinner date at The Red Lobster.

I follow the sound of her voice. Down a short hallway, past a darkened bathroom, and push open the door at the end of the hall.

Sofi's lying there on her king-sized, four-poster bed wearing a white baby doll dress and the amulet. The lights are low, and she's puffing away on her vaporizer. The smoke is a blackened hue of crimson in the candlelight.

"I assume you are not here to take me up on my offer?" she asks through the cloud of smoke.

I don't know what to say. I hadn't prepared for this. In all our planning, this just ended with a big battle. No time for talk. Just passion, action, and death. And now that I'm here, I'm stuck. A thousand words want to pour from my lips.

Stop it.

You're better than this.

Is this what Cami would want?

There's still time to do the right thing.

I love you.

"You're too late, Phoenix. You cannot save them." She pats the bed, inviting me to join her. "Just like it was too late for Cami. And Nancy." She takes another puff. "Just like you are too late to save me."

She's right. I was too late. She's right, and she knows it. Just like like she knows how much that guilt burns me up inside.

But am I too late for her? The truth rips at my heart as I take in the contours of her face, once smooth and delicate, now sharp and wicked under the influence of her vampire condition.

Once upon a time, I dreamed of kissing that girl.

But now I can't decide whether I want to cry or just shoot her stupid, twisted vampire heart. My hand moves for my gun. She notices the movement, and in a flash, she's out of bed and inches from my face.

"But it's not too late for you to join me," she says. The gentle sweetness of her breath is gone, replaced by the hot stench of vampire halitosis and Crimson Bliss vapor. "Or, I could just make you." Her lips curl back and reveal her pointed fangs.

As I stare into her dead eyes, I remember how they glimmered that day on the bridge at our fairytale castle. I remember how we almost kissed. My hand wraps around the grip of my gun, and my finger finds the trigger. I slowly raise it until the barrel is pressed firmly against her left breast. My other hand goes for the amulet.

"Phoenix, Phoenix, Phoenix." She starts to laugh. "You and I both know you can't kill a vampire with a bullet."

"No, not a bullet," I say, as I close my eyes, lean forward and press my lips to hers. "But this is a cherry bomb, baby."

I pull the trigger, and she explodes into the biggest mess of blood and guts I've ever seen.

CHAPTER FORTY-FOUR

Fifteen minutes. That's about how long we figured we'd have until the police arrived. Wolfgang's long gone and there's no way in hell I'm fighting my way out of this mess.

I go to Sofi's closet, pull the door shut, and slip the amulet into my pocket.

Then, in the pitch-black dark, I pop a cherry bomb in my brain.

CHAPTER FORTY-FIVE

Three weeks since Munich and not a word from Rousseau or Wolfgang. Not even an appointment follow-up reminder from Doctor Dmitri. Ripley's home and from the way she's been living on my lap, I'm pretty sure she's happy I'm out of a job.

Three days after I popped back home from that cherry bomb ticket to the Eitherspace Express, I checked my bank account. The house is paid for, so I don't have to pay a mortgage. But the macaroni and cheese was gone, and the milk had gone bad. Plus, Ripley was in bad need of some tuna.

My final paycheck should have shown up in my account, so I'd have enough to get by for at least another week or two. But, being the responsible adult I am, I thought it best to wrap my head around my finances so I could budget appropriately.

It turns out there was an extra twenty thousand bucks in there. I guess being a monster hunter pays alright.

I tried calling Rousseau. Part to thank her, and part to ask her for a job. But the line had been disconnected.

I went back to listening to the scanner. Praying something would come across that felt somehow *not right*. But monster attacks in Mississippi aren't all that common. And they don't pay the bills.

The pains in my gut are still here, and I ran out of the pills from my German doctor friend a week ago. Tried fighting through it, thinking I could manage the hurt. Tried switching to ibuprofen but it didn't help a bit. The only solution I've found is to randomly break into houses through Eitherspace and search their medicine cabinets. So far, I've only hit pay dirt once, and that score only resulted in enough to last a few days. I could try going to a doctor, see if he can get me something … but my insurance expired the second Asher fired me.

I pick up my phone and scroll through my call history. As I'm about to hit dial on my ex-boss's number and beg him to give me my job back, the phone rings.

Unknown Caller from Cairo.

"Hello?" I answer.

"Oh, excellent, you're there. I thought I might have lost your number."

My heart skips a beat as I recognize Rousseau's voice. "Nope, still here. What's up?"

"First I wanted to say thank you for your work in Munich. You did excellent work." Rousseau's voice is hurried, breathless. "But I have to ask you something, and I need an answer quickly."

"Anything. What can I help you with?"

"Well… I… we… we were wondering. What do you know about werewolves?"

Phoenix Bones returns in…

EVERY BULLET

HAS A

SILVER LINING

Available NOW at Amazon!

Made in United States
North Haven, CT
09 June 2023

37538972R00171